Praise for Jo

'I read this story with ever-increasing interest. The dynamics and tension felt reminiscent of my thriller films from the 70s and 80s, which have been appreciated by many American directors such as Quentin Tarantino. It would make a great film for lovers of the genre. Ottimo intrigo! Enjoy the read, everyone!'
Sergio Martino on *Five Deaths for Seven Songbirds*

'Intricately plotted in the classic giallo style, with plot twists and murders galore. John Everson has written a thriller that is sure to appeal to devotees of lurid Italian mystery thrillers.'
Troy Howarth, author of *So Deadly, So Perverse: 50 Years of Italian Giallo Films*, on *Five Deaths for Seven Songbirds*

'Passionate, overwhelming, a classic thriller with a rock rhythm.'
Ernesto Gastaldi, screenwriter of *So Sweet... So Perverse*, on *Five Deaths for Seven Songbirds*

'Excellent novel, excellent nod to a genre that needs to be remembered and love the kills as it brings me back to the novels I used to read as a teenager, such as those by Richard Laymon.'
The Literary License Podcast on *Five Deaths for Seven Songbirds*

'A rousingly good murder mystery that had me guessing all the way to the climactic ending, John Everson has nailed this one to the wall.'
Don Gillette, former Bram Stoker Award juror, on *Five Deaths for Seven Songbirds*

'*Five Deaths for Seven Songbird*s is a wonderfully perverse and gloriously gruesome mystery/thriller. In other words, it's a solid entry in the giallo genre to which it is also a love letter. Aside from all those movie references and homages, John Everson has crafted an entertaining read with plenty of mystery and mood to spare.'
Considering Stories

'John Everson has written a pitch-perfect tribute to the genre of Giallo films. With the black-gloved killer, the wild kills, the red herrings, and a title and cover that tells me it is a Giallo without even reading the first page, I cannot think of a better modern take on this subgenre than *Five Deaths for Seven Songbirds*.'
GhostVilleHero.net

'*Voodoo Heart* offers a solid blend of supernatural horror and hard-boiled detective fiction, and should appeal to horror devotees as well as mystery buffs.'
Booklist

'John Everson has created one of my top ten books of all time. *The House by the Cemetery* is a cauldron filled with devilry and witchery – all my favorite things.'
Cedar Hollow Books

JOHN EVERSON

THE BLOODSTAINED DOLL

This is a **FLAME TREE PRESS** book

Text copyright © 2024 John Everson

All rights reserved. No part of this publication may be reproduced, stored in a retrieval system, or transmitted in any form or by any means, electronic, mechanical, photocopying, recording or otherwise, without the prior written permission of the publisher.

FLAME TREE PRESS
6 Melbray Mews, London, SW6 3NS, UK
flametreepress.com

US sales, distribution and warehouse:
Simon & Schuster
simonandschuster.biz

UK distribution and warehouse:
Hachette UK Distribution
hukdcustomerservice@hachette.co.uk

Publisher's Note: This is a work of fiction. Names, characters, places, and incidents are a product of the author's imagination. Locales and public names are sometimes used for atmospheric purposes. Any resemblance to actual people, living or dead, or to businesses, companies, events, institutions, or locales is completely coincidental.

Thanks to the Flame Tree Press team.
The cover is created by Flame Tree Studio, with elements courtesy of Shutterstock.com and: aleksander hunta, Chatchawal Kittirojana, nathanmcc, Palii Oleg, PanicAttack.
The font families used are Avenir and Bembo.

Flame Tree Press is an imprint of Flame Tree Publishing Ltd
flametreepublishing.com

A copy of the CIP data for this book is available from the British Library and the Library of Congress.

HB ISBN: 978-1-78758-888-2
PB ISBN: 978-1-78758-887-5
ebook ISBN: 978-1-78758-889-9

Printed and bound in Great Britain by Clays Ltd, Elcograf S.p.A.

JOHN EVERSON

THE BLOODSTAINED DOLL

FLAME TREE PRESS
London & New York

For my fellow gialloholics

PROLOGUE

Berger Mansion, near Hildegard, May 3, 2001, 10:59 p.m.

"Doctor, I think it's time."

The thin man looked up, intense blue eyes colored with unease. His expression was not that of a man about to bring a new life into the world. His nod was weary. Strangely sad.

"How fast?" he asked.

"Three to five minutes apart," the woman said. She didn't look like a nurse. She wore jeans and a black t-shirt, with a silver chain decorated with small silver bones around her neck. The doctor didn't seem to care. He took a last sip of his sherry and rose from the old wooden chair. It creaked, just like him.

"Let's take a look." His bravado was audibly false.

The woman smiled and raised a finger. "Follow me."

The hallways were long and echoed with every step. Old wood. Old house. Old family.

The doctor shook his head silently and his eyes followed the slender waist that walked just ahead. On another day, he'd have thirsted for that waist, but tonight...his mind was on other things. Somber things. Life-and-death things.

The walls on either side of him were hung with the memories of generations gone by; black-and-white photographic portraits of people trying very hard to look perfect for the camera. But they didn't look perfect; they looked false and old. The doctor paid little attention; his mind was elsewhere as they walked down the long hallway and then stopped at a wooden door.

The screams assaulted him as soon as the door opened. It was amazing how soundproofed the room was; the hallway had suggested none of the anguish within.

The woman on the bed writhed in pain. They had covered her in white sheets that were now spotted with blood. A big man with dark eyes paced nervously near the bed. His face instantly looked relieved when the doctor walked in.

"How are we doing?" the doctor asked.

The answer was a scream of pain and a tense contraction from the woman on the bed.

The doctor pressed his hand to her forehead.

"It's okay," he said softly. "It's all going to be okay."

The problem was, he didn't believe it.

Nevertheless, the doctor bent to the bed and tested the girl's temperature and blood pressure, before moving his hands farther down.

She moaned at his touch, but he didn't react. His eyes only focused on the round, taut mound of her belly.

It was thick and bulging. Ready to pop.

He moved his hand over the soft, pale skin. Anyone watching would have seen the wrinkles in his eyelids crease.

"I think it's time," he said, and moved to take a position between her legs. With a quick and practiced motion, he slipped two blue rubber gloves up his hands and arms, and then reached forward.

That's when the screaming really began.

* * *

Fifteen minutes later, when the worst was over, the doctor stood up, with a squalling, bloody human child in his hands.

The cord was severed, and the baby's cries pierced the air and ears of the room. It was a painful but positive sound. Life-affirming.

At least, until the doctor turned around.

He began to move toward the door with the squirming, crying infant cushioned in his arms.

"Doctor, wait!" the girl on the bed called. Her forehead was wet with sweat, dark locks of hair plastered to her skin. Her face was flushed, but her eyes were bright. Intense.

"Can I hold my baby? Is it a girl or a boy?"

The doctor turned halfway, met her eyes for a moment, and shook his head slowly. The close-cut silver of his hair cut the air like a knife.

"Your father gave me strict orders about this," he said. And then he opened the door and motioned to someone outside. Seconds later, two hands lifted the crying infant from his arms. The child disappeared from view.

"You know what to do," the doctor said.

When the door closed, he turned to face the crying girl on the bed.

"Shhh," he intoned. "It's all over now."

But he was wrong.

CHAPTER ONE

Outside of Munich, June 9, 2024, 2:03 p.m.

The road moved like a snake, winding through the grassy fields near the highway and then shooting like a dart into a dense copse of trees. The sun had all but disappeared. The forest hugged the road tight.

Allyson's cheek bounced against the window as the pavement changed from Teflon-smooth to rugged.

You are officially off the beaten path.

It felt like her entire life was now off the beaten path. Last month, she'd been ditching classes with her friend Megan during their final year at the Elms Academy and hanging out at Pop Brixton to catch bands and people-watch at night. And then one day, she was pulled from class by one of the school secretaries and escorted to the principal's office, where, in one of the most horrible sixty seconds ever, her life changed forever.

Allyson had thought she was about to be in trouble because someone had reported her for ducking out of the building during school the day before. But instead, after a halting, uncertain start, the principal blurted out that her mom had been hit by a car on her way to work and….

"It was over quick," the woman said. "She didn't suffer."

Maybe not, but Allyson's suffering had just begun.

The next few days had been like waking up in a strange world. She had no close relatives in London so she stayed with Megan's family while her mother's funeral arrangements were made. And then, once the tears had slowed and her mom was laid to rest, she'd packed her things and boarded the train to Germany. Her mom's brother, Otto, lived there. He'd been away on business and couldn't come to the funeral, but he had agreed to take her in.

And so she was here, riding in the backseat of a long, black car behind a man named Kurt, who apparently worked for her uncle. He'd met her at the train station, loaded all her suitcases into the trunk with a series of unhappy grunts, and then opened the door for her. The only words he'd really said in the half hour she'd been with him were "*Guten Tag*" and "I will drive you."

The silence in the cab while staring at his thick, bald head was unnerving.

Then again, Allyson didn't have much to say. The longer she sat in the car, the lower her heart sank. They had driven through what looked like a quaint little German town called Hildegard with lots of shops and people bustling about on the old sidewalks.

Maybe it would be fun to live here?

Instead, the car left the town farther and farther behind and now, it had been at least five minutes since she'd seen another house or car.

Maybe her uncle had had a change of heart and didn't want her to stay with him. Maybe Kurt was really just driving her to the middle of nowhere to leave her there on the side of an untraveled road in the forest, surrounded by her small mountain of suitcases.

Did they have bears in Germany?

But then, without warning, the tree cover cleared, and the car drove between two brick pillars that supported an intricate wrought-iron arch with the family name woven in the center. Allyson saw their destination.

Her eyes widened.

Uncle Otto lived in a castle! Well, a mansion at least. The building was sprawling, with twin gables on the third story that bordered either side of the ornate stone arch entry below. The lower brick was covered in deep green ivy. The grounds were impeccable, with topiary gardens and winding stone pathways that led around the house. There were trees too, huge ancient oaks that gave parts of the mansion shade. Begonias bloomed in large wooden pots near the front door and purple irises decked out the garden nearby.

The car pulled up in front of two monstrous stone pots overflowing with color. Her driver exited the car without a word. A moment later, her door abruptly yanked open and a thick voice said, "*Willkommen zuhause.*"

She knew enough German to know 'welcome home'.

So far, she didn't feel very welcome.

Allyson slid her feet out of the cab and onto the pavement. Meanwhile, Kurt walked around and popped the trunk. By the time she was standing outside the car he was well laden with three suitcases and a bag strap around his shoulder.

When she caught his eye, he gave an abrupt nod and turned to walk up the path toward the large arched entryway ahead. With a shrug, she followed.

Allyson's eyes widened once more as she stepped inside. The ceiling stretched high and round in a white stone arch. Wooden window frames punched through a perfect white 'sky' and let in the rich ambient light that strayed through the thick trees outside.

The walls around them were paneled in a deep, rich, dark wood and two couches flanked a broad fireplace. To the left, a series of lofty windows looked out on the gardens.

"So, you have arrived at last," a gruff voice said. "Come in, come in."

Allyson looked to her right to see a small but intense-looking German woman standing there with a finger raised, beckoning her. The woman's eyes gleamed a cool blue and her dark hair was pulled in a bun so tight that it could have been carved from wood. Allyson realized she was not as old as the severe apparel suggested. There were no wrinkles around her eyes and her complexion was soft and youthful; she just looked officious and stern.

"*Guten Tag,*" the woman said, extending a long, thin hand. "I trust you had a good journey. My name is Ingrid. I keep things in order here for your uncle. He will be here to meet you at dinner, but in the meantime, Kurt can show you your room and you can get settled. If you need anything, please use the housephone and I will answer. Otherwise, please come downstairs at six to meet the family for dinner."

And with that, Kurt moved ahead and motioned for her to follow. Allyson walked a few steps across the granite floor. When they reached the winding stairwell leading up, she glanced back. The room behind was empty. She felt a shiver at the back of her neck. That woman gave her the creeps. And apparently moved like a ghost.

She shook it off and followed Kurt up the wide, winding stairs. When they reached the second level, he moved quickly along the balcony, which looked down over the foyer and turned left at a hallway with a series of closed wooden doors. Allyson didn't know anything about architecture, but she could tell that this place was old. Classic. The varnish on the doorframes was rich and deep as honey and the cornerpieces ornately carved in delicate curved patterns. Nobody took the time to do that kind of work anymore.

"This will be your room," Kurt said, and turned a bronze knob, decorated in a twisted pattern of leaves, to open the door.

Allyson gasped. The room beyond was magnificent. Tall, narrow windows were flanked in rich burgundy drapes with golden rope ties. A four-poster bed dominated the space, with the mattress high above the floor. The floors were a deep rich hardwood, covered in long, intricately patterned rugs. To the right stood a wide bureau and a sitting table for makeup, with an oval mirror set to the side.

It was like a fairy-tale castle room.

"I will leave you to settle in," Kurt said with a gruff rasp. "There is a lavatory two rooms down the hall if you need to freshen up."

With an abrupt turn on his heel, the man was gone, leaving Allyson alone.

Before she began to unpack her stack of suitcases, Allyson explored. There were empty drawers in the bed frame below the mattress and a door to the left of the bed that led to a walk-in wardrobe, complete with wooden hangers. She had plenty of space to store her clothes, that was for sure. The closet was as big as her entire bedroom had been back in London.

"Oh my God, Megan would die if she saw this," Allyson whispered. The thought only made her feel depressed. Megan would never see this. None of her friends would. She'd probably never see any of them again. She was stuck here in a beautiful room a million kilometers from everyone she'd ever cared for, with no way to get back to them.

The thought brought tears to her eyes. She shook them away, grabbed the large brown case and threw it on the bed. Refusing to let the feeling overtake her, she began to unpack, hanging all of her blouses and skirts in the ridiculously large 'closet' and shoving underwear and socks and shorts in the drawers beneath the bed.

She stuffed the contents of a box of makeup in the vanity next to the dresser and dumped a pile of buttons and plushies and photo albums in a wide drawer in the bureau. But as she stacked all of the photo frames from home into the drawer, she stopped at one.

The picture in the plain black plastic frame showed a woman with a cascade of brown curls and earnest brown eyes. She looked deep in concentration, her gaze staring down at a guitar in her hands. Presumably the photo was captured as she strummed.

It was Allyson's mum, Esther.

She pulled that one from the pile of photos of her and her friends and set it on the dresser. They might both have left London behind, but Allyson would always keep her memory close.

Angrily wiping a tear from her face, she turned back to the job of emptying her suitcases.

CHAPTER TWO

Berger Mansion, June 9, 6:03 p.m.

"Ah, well there you are," a deep bass voice announced as soon as she stepped into the high-ceilinged dining room. The voice emanated from a corpulent man with a broad welcoming grin who waved a hand in the air to gesture her closer. "You must be my niece, eh?"

Instantly, Allyson felt ill at ease. She had set her alarm so that she would be down to dinner at six and didn't think she was late. She resisted looking at her phone to check. It had taken her a couple minutes to navigate from her room, down the stairs and across the main foyer to where she could tell, from the sounds, the rest of the family was. She knew she couldn't be more than a minute or two late.

"I am Allyson," she agreed, not knowing what else to say.

"Well, Allyson, we are happy to have you with us. Please sit. Wherever you like."

She stifled the urge to run to a chair. In front of her was a long, ornate dining table, surrounded by several faces staring back at her. At the far end sat her uncle Otto, beaming with thick lips and awkward eyes. Next to him, a woman with rich, black flowing hair sipped from a wineglass as her dark eyes bored into Allyson's face. Across from her, a young man toyed idly with a fork. He looked close to her age, maybe a couple years older, but had an air of easy superiority. Without any reason, she felt an instant dislike of him.

"Do you remember Martin?" Uncle Otto said, pointing at the boy she'd just decided she didn't like. "He's your cousin, but I don't think you've seen each other since you were probably five or six years old. Your mother didn't come to Germany these past few years."

"No," Allyson said. "We couldn't afford to travel. We couldn't afford much, really." In her head, she tried to remember the last time she had been here. There were vague memories, like clouds really. Nothing was clear.

"Yes, well, that was your mother's choice," her uncle said with a faint smile.

A secret grin, it seemed. She wondered what he was thinking. After a few seconds, he pointed again at a seat. "Well, you are here now," he said. "And we are happy to have you again after all these years."

She nodded demurely and took an empty seat next to the attractive woman with long black hair. The woman continued to focus a measuring gaze on her as she raised her wineglass once again.

"Here's to you," she said, holding it high. "Welcome to our fucked-up little family."

"Ella," her uncle chastised. "Don't make us look bad before she's even had the chance to break bread."

The woman smiled, and lifted a plate of buns and offered it to Allyson. "Here," she said. "Chop one of these in half so we are allowed to talk, eh?"

Otto shook his head and audibly sighed. "Allyson, allow me to introduce Ella Viktoria. She is my secretary, but as you can tell from her tongue she is also like family. You will find her here at the table on most nights."

"Don't let him make you think I'm just here for a free meal," Ella said. "He wants me here. In fact, if I'm not at the house, he calls me to ask where I've gone. It's really easier to simply come home from work with him and cut out the awkward questions part."

Just then, a graying woman in long white slacks and a brightly flowered blouse entered the room from the winding stairs just beyond. Her hair was a mass of tight curls and her eyes were surrounded by creases. She looked old. And vaguely suspicious when she noticed Allyson.

"Aunt Ida," Otto announced. "Please meet my niece, Angela."

"Allyson," Ella corrected.

"As I said," he continued smoothly. "Let us enjoy the dinner Ingrid has prepared for us."

As Aunt Ida eased into a seat across from Allyson, Ingrid appeared with a platter piled high with fragrantly steaming slices of meat. "Pork roast and potatoes," she announced. As soon as she set it on the table, she disappeared for a moment, only to come back with a serving bowl.

Moments later, the platter was circulating. A delicious aroma pervaded the room; the rich scents of rosemary and caraway mingling with the steam of the succulent pork and buttery potatoes. Allyson's stomach rumbled of its own accord as she waited for the food to be passed her way. She hadn't realized how hungry she was, but the journey had definitely left her wanting.

As she dug into her plate, Allyson tried to focus on the conversations going on around her. Ella was asking Otto questions about a business account while Martin looked aloof and poked disdainfully at his food. Aunt Ida pronounced the day "a ruin" thanks to the heat as Ingrid and Kurt pulled up chairs and joined the family at the table. Apparently, the servants were part of the dinner here, once their duties were accomplished, which seemed a trifle odd to Allyson. But good, too, she supposed. They didn't contribute to the conversation, but they looked engaged.

Allyson felt one hundred percent like the odd girl out.

"I always heard that the food in England sucks," Martin said from across the table. "Is that true? What do you think now that you've had Ingrid's cooking to compare?"

Allyson looked up, a little baffled. *Who would ask such a thing?*

"Food in England is great," she countered. "We have crisps and bangers and all sorts of things. Germany isn't a food mecca or anything."

Martin laughed. "Have you ever had pork like Ingrid makes?" he asked. "I'm betting not. You all eat chewy lamb across the Channel, don't you?"

Allyson frowned. *Why was this guy ranking on her?*

"Have you ever had a good fish and chips?" she asked. "There's really nothing better on a late night."

"Oh," he said, exaggerating the O. "So, you're a *late*-night girl, are you? Do tell!"

The table conversation suddenly quieted, and Allyson looked up, chagrined. Everyone seemed to be staring at her, including old Aunt Ida.

"I…um…. No…" she fumbled. "I liked to go out at night sometimes."

"Martin, are you baiting your cousin?" Otto asked. "It's not becoming."

The entire table grew still at that. Allyson didn't know what to say, so…she said nothing. Instead, she shoveled another couple bits of pork and potatoes into her mouth as she gauged the reaction around her.

"It's okay," she said after another bite. "Fish and chips isn't as good as this pork."

"See," Martin said. "I was right. Food sucks in England."

"I didn't say that," Allyson said. "It doesn't."

"Martin!" Otto said.

Allyson said nothing. That only made the silence drag out longer.

"I am very sorry about your mother," Otto said. "I just want you to know. I loved my sister very much."

That did not lift the silence one iota. Everyone paused…and then returned to eating without a word.

Allyson considered a response, looked up and saw the very intently focused eyes around the table all considering their plates… and continued eating.

Okay then.

She felt like she should say something…but also had nothing to say.

Awkward.

The moment was interrupted by the sky. As the silence grew uncomfortable, the roof suddenly shook, aggressively, with the vibration of thunder. The anger of a building storm outside overcame the inside quiet.

"Looks like you brought the nice weather from London with you," Martin said. "Thanks for that."

Allyson glared at him. "It was perfectly sunny when I left," she said.

Ella looked amused, and poured herself another glass of wine. The sky outside rumbled again. Inside, the room was filled with the quiet clinks of silverware on china.

Eventually, the uneasiness evened out and everyone just focused on eating. Which was good. Whatever taunts Martin may have had, Ingrid's cooking was great. Allyson finished everything she'd loaded onto her plate.

She stopped paying attention to the conversations around her. She had no context to know what they were about.

Toward the end of dinner, much to her chagrin, her uncle brought the focus back to her. "I just want to say that we are happy Allyson has joined us here today. We have a lot of things going on and I know we're all busy but...I think it's great to share all of our things with a new member of the family."

Martin met her eyes with a lascivious grin. "All of our *things*." He held an eyebrow raised for several seconds.

Great.

Her cousin was a perv.

"By the way," he said. "My room is just a couple doors down from yours. If you need anything."

Even better. The perv slept right nearby.

It just went from crap to worse.

CHAPTER THREE

Berger Mansion, June 9, 6:52 p.m.

Dinner was painful, but the aftermath was worse. After dessert, Otto asked if she had seen the whole mansion yet, and when she admitted that she hadn't, he gave Ingrid the task of showing her around.

The housekeeper and cook clearly had no interest in giving a tour. "Wait for me in the foyer," Ingrid instructed as the dinner broke up. "I have other things to take care of and then I will take care of you."

That last comment sounded more threatening than inviting, but Allyson followed Martin and the others out of the dining room and sat on a dark leather couch in the area off the foyer to wait. Otto was deep in a conversation with Ella, and Martin flashed her a sideways smirk but didn't slow. He took the stairwell quickly, easily passing up Ida, presumably headed back to his room.

Allyson checked her cell phone but social media was ambivalent to her. Nobody, not even Megan, had messaged or tagged her in the past few hours.

Out of sight, out of mind.

The thought only made her miss home even more. But home was lost to her now. There was no home to go back to. She was cast adrift. Lost in Germany.

"All right, let us get this done, then, shall we?" a harried voice said from behind her. Allyson shifted in her seat to see Ingrid hustling toward her, legs moving stiffly but with clear purpose.

"Well, don't just sit there. I've still got a kitchen to clean."

"That's okay," Allyson said. "We don't need to do this right now. Maybe tomorrow...."

Ingrid shook her head. "Master said tonight, tonight it shall be. But let's not drag it out, hmmm?"

Allyson took the hint and hopped up from the sofa.

"You've seen the dining room," Ingrid said. Then she pointed down a hall. "This wing is the master's quarters and offices." She led them past the stairwell and down a hallway with rich wooden planks covered in places with thickly woven Oriental rugs.

"This is the master's den. He might invite you here to sit after dinner at some point, but it is a room only open by his invitation."

She opened the dark wooden door and gestured at the interior. "Back when my mother was the housekeeper, I remember your cousin Catherine used to love to sit in this room in the wintertime, when the fire was warm. She was such a delicate creature, all curled up there beneath an afghan, reading some silly romance novel at night."

Ingrid paused for a second, as if lost in a memory. Allyson got a glimpse of bookcases and leather chairs and an unlit fireplace before the door abruptly shut again.

"Come along, then," Ingrid urged and moved down the hall.

She opened a door on the left and stepped inside. Allyson followed and was instantly hit with the smell of age. Musty paper and old leather. The walls held the answer why. Every space not interrupted by the door or the window looking out on the gardens outside was filled with shelves of books. Old books. She could tell by the faded bindings. There were no cheap paperbacks here; this was a classic library.

"If you are interested in reading, there are many things available here. But you must take great care and read them here in this room. Your uncle does not allow books to leave the library. Too many of them are very old and valuable."

"It looks like it," Allyson agreed. "Maybe I will spend some quiet evenings here." In her head she added, *and fall asleep*. The contents of the room did not look like scintillating reading, though she had no doubt there were some important things shelved there. And then it occurred to her – they'd probably mostly be in German anyway. She knew enough to have a reasonable conversation, but not enough to sit and read books of it.

Ingrid led them to the end of the hall and turned left. There she opened a pair of glass doors, which led outside to a stone patio surrounded by lush bushes and flowers. The center was dominated by a round glass table with metal chairs. There were also some reclining chairs on the sides.

"There are occasions where the family breakfasts out here," Ingrid said. "So now you know where to come if you don't find anyone in the dining room."

She led them back inside and down another hall with a storage room and her uncle's home office. She pointed to that door and said, "I suggest you do not disturb him when he is in here. He's very busy and doesn't enjoy interruptions."

There was a door at the end of the hallway beyond her uncle's office, which had a large bronze deadbolt. "We don't use that section of the mansion anymore," Ingrid said. "The family used to be much larger, but these days, there is no reason to heat and cool so much empty space. So."

With that she led them back to the main foyer and up the stairs. The second floor was all sleeping rooms, with her uncle's suite being the farthest one from Allyson's room. Like on the floor below, a locked door blocked the entry to the closed wing.

They ascended another winding stairwell to the third floor. It was just a single hallway with five doors, four on one side and one at the end of the hall.

"There is only one room up here you may want to use," Ingrid said, and opened the first door on their left. It was a long, wide space, with a fireplace on the right side and a sofa set at an angle to allow someone to enjoy the full effect of the fire when lit. The opposite wall was covered in white shelves, with several boxes that looked to be board games. There were chess pieces set up for play on a small table with two chairs, and a billiard table nearby. Clearly this was the family's 'game room'.

"You may choose to find some amusement here and this is the only way to access the rooftop garden, which is a nice place to sit in the mornings or at sunset." She gestured at two tall, narrow white doors with multiple panes of glass and then moved to open them, revealing a balcony outside that apparently wrapped around the side of the house. There were several chairs with outdoor cushions on them set along the balcony rail that stretched to the right. Long wooden planters hung off the rail, with a plethora of blooming pink and purple and yellow and blue flowers.

"Your cousin Martin is up here a lot," she said.

Allyson took that as a warning.

"If you bring any food up here, please do not leave it out on the balcony. It draws animals and then they ruin the flowers," Ingrid added, and then closed the doors and led them back inside and out to the hall. When she turned and began to descend the stairs, Allyson pointed to the rooms they had not visited.

"What's down there?" she asked.

Ingrid frowned. "Nothing for you," she said. "Some places in this house are off-limits and those are rooms your uncle would not have anyone enter. There are old things stored in those rooms and the door at the end of the hall leads to the attic. Stay out of there. The floors are old and could be dangerous. Nobody goes in there, it is old and dirty. You're welcome to go in the room I showed you, but stay out of the other rooms up here."

★ ★ ★

Back on the first floor, Ingrid led her to another sitting room near the dining room and then showed her the kitchen, which was huge. The dark granite counters seemed to stretch on and on and the refrigerator looked big enough for a restaurant. There were two different doors behind which Allyson assumed were pantries. It was overwhelming. Ingrid must have seen her amazement.

"We used to feed a lot more people in this mansion," Ingrid said. "So, the kitchen needed to be large. When your cousin was still here and my mother was alive, this was a very different place...." Her voice trailed off in memory of, presumably, happier times. And then she abruptly turned to face Allyson.

"If you need a late-night snack or drink, feel free to come in here and get it. The drinking glasses are in that cabinet." She pointed to a white door over the counter near the dishwasher. "Otherwise, please just ask me and I'll get whatever you need. I'd prefer it if the family leaves the kitchen in my care, do you understand?"

Don't mess with my shit. Got it.

She nodded.

"That's the tour, then," Ingrid said, showing a row of white teeth that reminded Allyson of a shark's grin. "We've closed off over half of the mansion these days, but there are plenty of places for you to spend time while you're with us."

Allyson smiled, and then considered Ingrid's words. *While you're with us.* Did that mean she wasn't intended to be here long?

Her concern was interrupted by a loud thundercrack outside.

"It may be time to retire," Ingrid said. "The storm is getting worse and you don't want to be lost if the lights should go out."

Allyson's brows knitted. "Does the power go out here a lot?"

Ingrid shrugged. "We're far out from town. The service is not as good as being in a big city like London. You'll have to get used to that. There are a lot of things you'll have to get used to here."

That sounded enigmatic, but Ingrid did not elaborate. Instead, she turned away and began to fuss with dishes and dinnerware. "Good night," she said, without meeting Allyson's eyes.

Allyson took that as her cue to leave.

Tour given. Get the hell out.

"Thanks for showing me everything," she said, and began to walk away.

"It's a shame you never knew your cousin Catherine," Ingrid said from behind. "She was the light of this house for so many years."

Allyson wasn't sure what to say to that...so she said nothing. Instead, she walked through the foyer as the sky outside crashed and cried.

Nature mimicked her own emotions. She wanted to scream and cry at the same time. Why was she here? Why *wasn't* her mom here?

As she headed back up the stairs, she realized that it had begun to look a bit frightening outside. The sky was black as midnight, water cascading wildly down the tall windows with a blurry anger. It looked as if they were in the center of a hurricane, erratic light flashing and green branches of bushes and trees whipping back and forth, threatening the house in the storm just outside.

The second floor was weirdly silent after the frenzy evident on the first floor; there were no external windows here. Allyson walked quickly to her room, anxious to close the door behind her and shut the rest of this house out. Shut all of Germany out. Despite the gorgeous mansion around her, she wanted to be home in her tiny flat. She would have given anything to be there now with her mom to coddle her and say, "Don't worry about the storm, it will pass."

The storm in her heart definitely didn't feel like it would pass.

Ever.

Never mind the squall outside.

As she pushed open the door to her room, a wave of relief washed over her chest.

For a moment.

Until she saw what was waiting for her on her bed.

"Well, hello there," Martin said. "Thanks again for bringing London's crappy weather with you. Really appreciate that. Now that you're back from Ingrid's little tour, how would you like to know how things really work around here?"

CHAPTER FOUR

Berger Mansion, June 9, 7:26 p.m.

"What are you doing in my room?" Allyson demanded.

Martin pushed himself up on one elbow, grinning lazily. "You know, it's not really *your* room, but at least now you can say there was someone waiting for you in your bed. Girls like to brag about things like that, don't they?"

"Maybe *here* they do," Allyson spat. "But where I come from, we have better manners."

"Ah, you mean you're all stuck-up prigs?" He cocked his head and his chin bobbed. "Yeah, I've heard that about Londoners."

Allyson wanted to scream. Why was this guy *on* her?

"What is the matter with you?" she asked.

Martin grinned and hopped off the mattress. "I just thought I'd make sure you felt welcome," he said. "I know my dad can be a little bit of a dick sometimes. And Ingrid? She's got a perpetual stick up her ass. I thought you'd be happy to see a friendly face but, no worries, I can take a hint."

He brushed past her on the way to the door. When his shoulder bumped hers roughly, she did not believe for a moment that it was an accident.

"Wait," she said, as he opened the door to leave. "I didn't mean to—"

She never got the chance to finish that thought.

Outside the window, there was a blinding flash of light, followed by a crash that sounded as loud as a military bomb exploding. The windows of her room shook with a deep, rumbling bass echo. The vibration made her worry they might shatter. Allyson literally felt the floor move beneath her.

"What the hell was that?" Martin said. All of the tease went out of his face and he rushed past her to look out one of her bedroom windows into the yard.

"Holy shit," he said. "When you bring the weather with you, you really *bring* the weather!"

She ignored the comment and instead tried to look past his shoulder. The window was awash with pelting rain that seemed to be coming sideways from a fire hose. Everything was dark and blurry until a bolt of lightning split the sky. And then she saw exactly what he meant.

In the back of the yard, a huge old tree lay splintered and broken across the grass. Its roots had ripped clean out of the ground; she could see the yellow of freshly cracked wood jutting like ragged teeth from the ground.

Then the thunder came and the night went black again. But the image of that mammoth tree fallen so near did not leave her mind as quickly.

"That could have killed us if it had fallen just a little more in this direction," Martin whispered. "Would have taken out this entire wing."

"That's frightening," Allyson said softly. How would that have been to have had the roof above her, a roof she had barely even seen before, suddenly smash down on her head in a deadly slap of timbers and plaster?

The lightning flashed again, and this time, Allyson saw a little more than before. In the midst of the new hills of fresh soil that had wrenched up with the roots to leave a mammoth pit in the ground, as if from a grenade strike, there was a wooden box.

An oblong box. Broader on top than the bottom. It was small, but....

It looked like a tiny casket.

"Did you see what's lying there?" she asked.

"Yeah. I wonder if my father has seen it yet," Martin said. "C'mon."

He abruptly turned and strode out of the room. Allyson followed.

★ ★ ★

The foyer was alive with voices. Everyone was there, and Otto was bent and peering through the storm out the side window, craning his neck to see the backyard.

"If it had fallen the other direction, we could have all been killed," Ida said, shaking her head. Ella patted her shoulder and looked faintly nauseous.

"That tree has been here since long before this house," Kurt said. "It would have been a bit of justice."

"Whose side are you on?" Ella said, slapping him on the shoulder. "Thank God for small miracles."

"This one, maybe not so small," Ida said.

"We'll have to wait until the storm slows to see if anything else is damaged. Part of it could have hit the back wing."

"It didn't look like it from upstairs," Martin said from their spot halfway down the stairs. "But we did see something interesting."

Otto looked up, curious.

"There was something by the roots. Something that was unearthed when the tree pulled out of the ground. It looked like…a casket."

"Casket?" Otto exclaimed. His brow creased before he let out a low, dismissing laugh. "That's ridiculous."

Martin shrugged. "Maybe, but there's some kind of old six-sided wooden box sitting out there."

"I guess we'll just have to wait until the storm breaks to find out what sort of buried treasure Mother Nature has unearthed," Ida said.

With that, she walked over to a sofa and eased her body down. She crossed her arms across her chest as if she was not going to say or do another thing until the storm passed.

"I don't know that it's worth waiting up for," Otto said, giving Ida an amused smile. "This storm could rage for hours."

Ida shrugged. "I've got all night."

"Well, I for one am not sitting here all night," Otto said. "If the storm subsides soon, I'll go out and take a look but...if not, I'm going to bed and will see you all in the morning."

With that, Otto walked up the stairs, presumably headed toward his room.

Ella followed without a word.

And it was only a few seconds before Kurt and Ingrid also disappeared down the hall toward the kitchen.

Even Ida opted not to wait. The old woman pushed herself up on her cane and began to walk up the stairs. As she passed Allyson she nodded and said, "We'll be back, eh?"

All at once, Martin and Allyson found themselves standing alone on the stairwell, as the storm continued to crash and boom outside.

"Well then," Martin said. "Can I take you back to your room?"

"I think I can find my own way, thanks!" Allyson said. With that, she began to walk back upstairs. Martin followed her all the way to her door.

"Do you need me to tuck you in?" he offered.

Allyson rolled her eyes. "You're quite the welcome wagon, aren't you?"

"Is that a yes?"

"No."

Allyson turned the knob and carefully slipped inside while holding the door so that Martin couldn't follow. "See you in the morning, cuz," she said, and pressed the door closed despite his hand on the other side.

"And a welcoming good night to you too!" Martin said from the other side of the door.

Allyson shook her head. Then she kicked off her sandals and threw herself back on the bed. This had been the longest day ever. She closed her eyes and took a deep breath.

This was going to work. This *had* to work. She had no other place to go. All of the events of the past couple weeks replayed in her head and that horrible moment when they told her that her mother was dead repeated itself like a skipping record. Everything led her here like a toboggan slide. No escape.

Allyson knew she needed to get up and get ready for bed but instead, she lost herself in memories and began to doze.

★ ★ ★

She was awoken by a pounding on her bedroom door. It took a second to remember where she was, but then the voice reminded her.

"Allyson, are you awake?"

"Huh?" she answered, and pushed herself up on an elbow, frowning and trying to clear her head of spiderwebs. Before she did, Martin was suddenly through the door and standing by her bed.

"I didn't say you could come in," she complained.

"The storm is over and everyone is still awake so we're going to check out the tree," he said, ignoring her. "Do you want to come with us? I didn't want to leave you out."

"Um, sure, okay."

She pushed herself off the bed, slipped on her sandals and followed Martin out into the hall.

She also made a mental note to make sure she locked her bedroom door moving forward.

The rest of the family was already downstairs. Ida looked perplexed, and Kurt and Ingrid seemed to be exchanging their own silent conversation with dark expressions. Otto looked up from pulling on his shoes and grinned. "So, you both are joining the expedition, eh? I can't say that I've ever heard of an entire family going out in the middle of the night to look at a tree but…the Berger clan has never been completely normal."

He straightened up, turned on a large flashlight, and opened the front door. "Let's see what nature has wrought."

It was cool outside, the air rich with the scent of fresh rain. They followed the stone path around the side of the house and stopped at the edge of the patio. They all stared as one.

It looked like a bomb had gone off. The mammoth tree had not gone down easily. The ground facing the patio was a fresh wound with huge splinters of root and trunk sticking up crazily in multiple spots. The bulk of the tree had fallen away from the house, which was lucky for the Berger Mansion. The trunk was mammoth; the branches were as thick as the core of most hundred-year-old trees.

But it wasn't really the tree that the family seemed concerned with. All eyes were fastened on the casket. It lay on its side in the midst of an explosion of black dirt.

"It really is a casket, isn't it?" Ella said.

Otto didn't say anything. He left her side, walked across the wet grass and stepped over broken tree limbs until he stood next to the wooden box.

"It looks like it has been broken open," he said, lifting some splintered planks from the top lid. "Probably from the force of the tree uprooting."

"It didn't look that way when we saw it from upstairs," Allyson said.

Kurt and Ingrid both looked at her with expressions that suggested that she had just called the pope a satanist.

"Things look different from up high," Otto said, dismissing her. Martin glanced at her but said nothing. Which…annoyed her. He'd seen the same thing she had. The top of the casket had not been shattered when they'd seen it from the window.

Otto tossed the broken boards to the side and pried off a couple more, until the casket was completely open to the night air. Then he shone his flash into the opening. After a second, he shook his head.

"There's nothing in there," he said. His voice sounded concerned and surprised at the same time.

Kurt stepped forward and bent down next to his boss's arm. "Are you sure?"

Otto nodded. "If there was something in here, it must have rotted away."

"Bones don't rot," Kurt said.

"No, I suppose not," Otto said. "Nevertheless, this box is empty."

Ingrid walked around the area of the box, staring intently at the ground. "Perhaps the bones fell out with the force of the casket coming to the surface and breaking."

"It wasn't broken," Allyson said quietly. Nobody acknowledged her.

A distant peal of thunder broke the midnight sky and Ella reached out to take Otto's arm in her hands. "We should go back inside," she said, gesturing behind them. "Clearly none of the branches has fallen to damage the house, and the sky could open up again at any time."

Otto nodded, but continued to stare at the broken wooden casket. He followed Kurt's footsteps around the perimeter of the box with the flash. But nothing caught the light besides broken wood and mud. If anything had been expelled from the box, it had landed a long way away.

"Kurt, can you call an arborist in the morning and have them come out to take the tree away?"

"Yes, sir," the gardener answered, stepping back from the muddy hill to the grass.

"It's a shame," Otto said. "That tree was really from another time."

"Indeed," Kurt agreed. "Another time entirely."

With that, Otto and Kurt began to walk back to the house, followed by Ella, Ingrid and Ida, who hobbled along with a cane. They all spoke in low voices and Allyson couldn't tell what they said. She reached out to grab Martin's arm, holding him back for a second from returning with the others.

"Hey," she said. "When we saw the casket from my bedroom, the top lid wasn't broken, right? You saw it too."

Martin pulled his arm away and shrugged. "I don't know," he said. "Maybe. I can't really remember."

Allyson opened her mouth to call him a name, but bit it back. Still, it echoed in her head.

Liar.

CHAPTER FIVE

Berger Mansion, June 10, 11:05 a.m.

Allyson woke to the sound of a loud, distant buzzing. She sat up and stretched, wondering what the noise was at first. It sounded like it was coming from somewhere outside. And then she realized exactly what it had to be.

Chainsaws.

She slipped out of bed and walked to her window to look out. There was a flurry of activity in the yard below. A crew was working on breaking down the giant fallen tree. Two men attacked it with chainsaws while three others were picking up each log carved out of the trunk and carrying them to a truck parked at the edge of the gardens.

"That was fast," she murmured. But then she looked at her phone. *Shit.* It was eleven in the morning. She'd missed breakfast, and somehow she bet that was going to get her a Berger demerit. She pulled open her new drawers to search for a fresh t-shirt and underwear.

Which reminded her, despite the tour, she had no idea where the bathroom was on this floor. She'd used one downstairs last night.

She bundled up her clothes and bathroom things and headed to the hall to figure it out. Allyson found herself walking softly past Martin's room, afraid that he'd come out to torture her rather than help. Luckily, his door didn't stir and she found the bath at the end of the hall. It was tiled in white, pink and black and she felt like she'd really arrived in the lap of luxury when she locked the door and turned on the burnished copper showerhead. The wide spray of water was hot and luxurious and the fluffy towels made her feel like she was in a spa. She leaned her head back and enjoyed the warmth of the water flowing through her hair and down her chest and legs. She could stay in here for hours.

All of that good feeling was shattered once she dried herself with the ridiculously thick towel, and then dressed and opened the door.

Martin was leaning against the wall outside.

"Figures," he said when she met his eyes. "There are other people here who need to use the bath, you know. I suppose now that there's another girl in the house, I'll never get in there."

"I'm sorry," she said. "Was I in there that long? I didn't realize...."

He grinned. "I'm just pulling your leg. I just got here. I was outside checking out the demolition crew."

"Those saws are loud," she said.

"Not loud enough to wake you up, apparently."

"Have they been here long?"

"Couple hours," he said. "One of the crew said that coffin had to have been in the ground for at least twenty years."

"Did Uncle Otto live here then?"

Martin nodded. "This place has been in the family for generations. But none of the women who lived here twenty years ago are still around, so it's going to be hard to figure out who buried a baby under the old oak tree. My dad said he doesn't know anything about it. Nobody else left to ask."

"You think there was a baby buried in it for sure?"

Martin gave her a look that said, *What, are you an idiot?*

"That's what they make those little caskets for. I can't imagine someone buried an empty one."

"But there were no bones inside."

"Yeah, odd, isn't it? I even walked around out there in the daylight a bit, figuring maybe I'd spot a rib cage or a tibia or something. Nothing out there that looks at all like bones. Just mud and sticks."

"Weird."

"Welcome to Berger Mansion!"

Martin laughed and walked into the bathroom, shutting the door behind him. Allyson took her things back to her room and headed down the stairs. She hoped Ingrid still had some coffee. And something to eat. Her stomach was rumbling.

There were voices coming from the foyer. Masculine tones. She paused halfway down the stairs. A police officer was standing just inside the door, talking to Otto. The man wore a traditional blue police uniform and was tall and thin to the point of gangly, with a long neck and a nose that looked sharp and beakish.

"…the tree crew *had* to report it," the officer explained. "Anytime human remains are unearthed outside a cemetery…."

"But there were no remains," Otto corrected.

The cop nodded. "That makes it a little unusual, to be sure. But it definitely was a child's coffin, so I had to come by to check it out. Do you have any idea who could have buried it?"

Otto shook his head. "It's clearly been in the ground for a very long time. I'd guess it was one of the help at the time trying to hide a pregnancy. Maybe she miscarried or had an abortion. But I don't remember any scandals like that here. Whoever buried it must have been very secretive about the whole thing. At this point though, I'm nearly the only one still here who lived here that long ago."

The cop nodded and wrote something on a small pad of paper. "Understood," he said. "Sorry to bother you, but we had to take a statement. Have a nice day."

As Otto shut the door, Allyson continued to descend the stairs. Her uncle turned as she reached the main floor, a troubled look on his face. When he saw her, his eyes lit.

"There you are," he said. "Good morning! Not exactly the first night in a new home that one would expect, eh? Trust me, things are almost never this exciting around here. Come into the kitchen with me and we'll find you some breakfast."

He took her by the shoulder before she could refuse and walked her straight through the dining room and into the kitchen. He had just put his hand on the refrigerator when Ingrid's head popped around the corner from a back room.

"Ah, our sleepyhead is here. I'll fix her something, sir, don't worry."

Ingrid shooed Otto out of the room and back to his office. Once he was gone, her expression changed from helpful to irritated.

"Breakfast is at eight a.m. in the dining room," she said. "Please make a note of it and set your alarm. This is not a house of slugabeds and I can't be fixing meals all day long."

"Yes, ma'am."

Allyson suddenly didn't feel hungry at all.

CHAPTER SIX

Berger Mansion, June 10, 11:40 a.m.

Otto Berger heard the phone ringing in his office and quickened his step to get inside to answer it. When he picked up the receiver, he thought he'd just missed the caller at first. Silence answered his initial "*Guten Tag*."

"Hello?" he said again. This time, there was an answer. Though the voice seemed muffled and distorted.

"Mr. Berger."

"Yes, how can I help you?"

"You can help me by delivering 250,000 euros to a drop point of my choosing by tomorrow night at seven p.m."

The voice was hard as steel. At first, Otto thought it a very good gag.

He laughed. "Very funny, who is this?"

"This is no laughing matter, Mr. Berger. If you want the bones and what they mean to remain buried, you will deliver the money I requested in unmarked bills. And you will not speak of this call to anyone. I have the skeleton from your closet, Mr. Berger."

Otto's face grew ashen. This was actually for real. "I can't get that much cash in twenty-four hours," he said. "I will need to convert some things. I'll need at least three days."

"Are you stalling for time, Mr. Berger? I know that you have a great deal of wealth, and I ask for a very small amount in the scheme of your things."

"No, I will get you the money. But you need to give me enough time. I don't keep that much just sitting in a bank account. I will need to liquidate some things."

"All right, then. Seven o'clock on Thursday night. You have three days to get the money. I will call you on this line one hour before we are to meet to tell you the location. Make sure you answer the phone or I will share your secret with the authorities. I think they would be very interested to know what was in that wooden box, don't you?"

"Possibly."

"Oh, most assuredly, Mr. Berger. Get me the money. And do not involve anyone else or the money will not buy my silence."

"I understand."

"Good. Then, until we speak again, may you have good health."

The line went dead.

Otto held the phone for a minute, staring at the receiver in disbelief. Then he set it back in its cradle and logged in to his computer, heading straight to the website for managing his stock portfolios.

Someone had gotten to that casket before he had. Someone closely connected to the family circle. It had only been a couple hours from the time the tree had been uprooted until the end of the storm.

Who had gotten to the box before him?

CHAPTER SEVEN

The Tankard, Hildegard, June 10, 9:40 p.m.

Some nights, you just needed to have a stiff drink.

And then five more. After the events of the past couple days, Kurt was very much of the mind that it was time for a stiff drink. First a new girl in the house to worry about, then the ground coughing up a reminder of something that he very much wanted to forget. Something he had managed to mostly forget.

But now he couldn't stop seeing that child's coffin.

"Another U-Boot for you?" Ellen, the bartender, asked. "Looks like this one is sunk!" She rattled the shot glass in the bottom of his beer mug around and then dropped it in the sink to be washed.

"Sure," he said. The room was feeling pleasantly warm at this point, after he'd downed several U-Boots.

"Hope you don't have to work any heavy machinery tomorrow," Ellen said, and pushed a fresh beer mug with a sunken vodka shot across the bar at him. "You can only sink so many of these before they sink you."

He laughed and waved a hand at her. "I'll be fine. Don't you worry."

She shrugged. "It's not *my* morning after. You drinking to forget something? 'Cuz, I think you're gonna."

Kurt grinned. A little lopsidedly. "Yeah," he said. "A lot of things really."

Ellen leaned her elbows on the bar. "What's the stick that broke the camel's back?"

Kurt laughed.

"A stick indeed. Last night a giant tree came down out at the Berger Mansion. Ripped the roots right out of the ground. Looked like a meteor had hit. And a child's coffin came up out of the mud with it. Only problem is, when Mr. Berger opened it, the bones were missing."

Ellen made a face. "Maybe an animal got them," she said. "Or maybe there never were any. Sometimes people bury an empty casket just as a memorial for a miscarriage, you know?"

Kurt shook his head. "No miscarriage there. I don't think Mr. Berger wanted to see that casket pop out of the ground after so many years. It's an election year for the Bundestag, you know."

"Oooh," Ellen's eyes widened. "There's some scandal here, then?"

Before he could answer, someone at the other end of the bar called for service. And then a large group of boisterous young men came in and filled all the seats at the bar. By the time she was finished setting them up with mugs and shots of stuff that would no doubt make them even louder before long, Kurt finished his last drink. He realized it was his last when he slipped off the stool to walk to the restroom and almost kissed the floor. His legs felt like rubber. Time to head home.

He called for the check, and Ellen rang him out.

"I never heard the rest of the story," she complained.

"Another time," he said, with a bit of a slur. "I need to call it a night."

She aimed her finger at him like a gun and pressed her thumb down. "Another one sunk."

★   ★   ★

As Kurt headed toward the door, a man in a dark jacket, who had been sitting with his back to the bar, got up from his table and left behind the glass of water he'd been nursing. The man had been listening to every word and now he followed the gardener outside.

"Come with me," he said and grabbed Kurt firmly by the arm. When the gardener opened his mouth to protest, a glimmer of silver flashed through the night air. It stopped just centimeters from Kurt's nose.

"Step over here and do not make another sound until I tell you to."

The man led Kurt around the stone corner of the building and into a small alley beyond. All at once, he stopped walking and pushed Kurt against the wall. A knife appeared at Kurt's throat.

"Where are the bones?"

"I don't know."

"Bullshit. You took them away yourself, didn't you?"

"No, I would never—"

"Then if you didn't take them, who did you tell about the casket that night? Who did you call?"

"I swear to you, I didn't take them, and I didn't tell no one. You've got to believe me."

The man nodded. "I figured that's what you'd say."

"I swear it's true."

The man pursed his lips in thought, as Kurt's eyes pleaded.

"I am telling you, you have to believe me," Kurt said, his voice raising in panic.

The man put a palm over Kurt's mouth, silencing him. With a quick swipe of his other arm, he slashed the knife blade across the drunken man's throat. When Kurt opened his mouth to scream, the killer pressed his hand down hard, holding the noise in. He didn't hold in the blood, which bubbled rich and red from the new opening in Kurt's throat.

"You should have buried her deeper," the man said.

Kurt's body shook and slapped against the unyielding stone wall. His eyes bulged wide and unbelieving, begging for release. Asking for salvation from this unexpected savagery. The cold eyes of the killer stared right back at him and silently told him his answer.

The answer was 'No'.

When the dying man's convulsions stopped, the killer at last released his hold on Kurt's mouth and allowed the body to slump to the ground. Then he reached into his jacket pocket to pull out a ceramic doll.

It had broken beyond repair in their struggle, just like the man lying in the alley.

The killer dropped the pieces on Kurt's chest, and bent to carefully wipe his knife and hand clean on the tail of the dead man's shirt.

Then he rose and calmly walked back to the street.

CHAPTER EIGHT

Berger Mansion, June 11, 8:05 a.m.

"Has anyone seen Kurt this morning?" Otto asked, interrupting the clinks of silverware at the breakfast table.

Allyson looked up from her plate of eggs and sausage and shook her head. She'd made damn sure that she was at the table before eight this morning. She was happy someone else was late this time.

Martin and Ella also shook their heads.

"He probably can't lift his head off the pillow," Ingrid said with a cruel grin. "He went into town last night."

Otto looked up with an amused expression. "So, you're telling me that there's not going to be very much gardening done today."

Ingrid raised a knowing eyebrow. "That'd be my guess. Some of us don't have the luxury of deciding not to do their jobs in the morning. I am not holding breakfast for him. He made his bed, so I guess he'll just have to starve in it."

Yikes, Allyson thought. The housekeeper did not exactly exude warm and cuddly.

Ingrid stood and picked up the platter of thick white sausages and walked around the table to stand next to Martin. "Would you like some more of these? It would be sinful to waste them."

Martin put his arm out, but hesitated. "Kurt might still come down," he said, clearly ready to take more.

She shrugged. "We must all pay for the impact of our actions."

That seemed to convince Martin, who rolled two more sausages onto his plate. Ingrid put a hand on his shoulder and squeezed.

Martin looked up at her with a secret smile, and forked a large bite of meat into his mouth. He made a show of enjoying it.

"What's on everybody's schedule today?" Otto asked, looking around the table.

Old Aunt Ida cackled. "After my ballet recital, I'll be running a 5K to benefit the homeless, and then after a few laps around the pool I'll be having dinner with Christoph Waltz. He's got some inside dirt about the next James Bond movie he promised to share."

"Very funny, Ida," Otto said. "So, you'll be reading outside on the terrace all afternoon?"

She rolled her eyes. "How did you know?"

"Lucky guess," Otto said. Then he looked directly at Allyson. "Did you have any plans for today?"

"Who, me?" she answered, surprised at his sudden focus. "Um, no, I hadn't really thought of any."

Otto nodded. "Well, this would be a good day, perhaps, to visit the town. If you have anything you need, there are shops there. And you might consider if there are places there where you would like to work. I'm happy to support you as long as you need, but you'll want some of your own money for things, hmmm?"

Welcome to your new home, now go get a job?

"I could do that," she said. "I would need a ride into town, though."

Ida coughed, a strange wheezing hack that sounded high-pitched and exaggerated, as if she was trying to clear a hairball from her throat. Nobody at the table moved.

Allyson began to get up. "Do you need help?" she asked. "A slap on the back?"

The old woman laughed at the offer in the midst of hacking. And waved Allyson to sit back down.

"She does that," Martin said. He sounded bored. "You always know where Ida is. Just follow the sounds of choking geese."

Ida shot him a glare and took a gulp of orange juice, which, after a couple swallows, helped quiet her throat irritation.

Otto ignored it all and looked at Martin. "Perhaps you could take your cousin into town and give her the tour?" he suggested.

Martin shrugged. "That wasn't on my list for today."

"Perhaps you could put it there."

"Alllll right," he complained.

"Your cousin is part of our family now," Otto said. "And I expect you to treat her that way."

"Are you *sure* you want me to do that?" Martin asked pointedly. He was rewarded with a glare that could have pierced stone.

Martin looked away from his father to address Allyson. "What time would you like to go into town?" His voice dripped with false helpfulness.

Before she could answer, an electronic bell chimed through the house.

Ingrid rose from the table immediately, setting her napkin down next to the plate. "Someone is at the door," she said. "Were we expecting anyone?"

Martin and Otto both shook their heads.

Ella frowned. "No appointments are scheduled."

The housekeeper hurried out of the room and a moment later they could hear voices at the door.

Ingrid returned to the dining room with a flustered look on her face. "Mr. Berger, there are two gentlemen here to see you. I think you'd better come, sir."

Otto's brow creased, but he slowly put down his utensils and pushed back from the table.

Allyson wondered how often people arrived at the door to this mansion. They seemed so far removed from the town. She sipped some orange juice and noticed that everyone at the table had stopped eating, apparently waiting for her uncle to return.

It didn't take long.

Otto stepped back into the dining room, but he wasn't alone. Two police officers followed, one of them the same one who'd been here just yesterday, after the tree fell. The narrow point of his nose was too prominent to forget.

"I have some horrible news," Otto said, addressing the whole table. "Kurt didn't skip breakfast because he's still asleep upstairs," he said, looking at the police for a moment before continuing. "These gentlemen have come to tell us that Kurt has been…murdered."

Ingrid's eyes bugged out. "What? No. No."

Ella said nothing, but her mouth hung slack as if she were struggling to comprehend the words. Ida shook her head over and over, trying to will it that the words weren't true.

"How did it happen?" Martin asked quietly.

The familiar tall and thin officer answered. "His throat was cut in the alley behind the Tankard bar in Hildegard."

"Oh my God," Ingrid said. "But why? Who would do this?"

"That's what we're going to try to find out," the officer said. "He wasn't robbed. His wallet still had money and credit cards in it. And it wasn't from a bar fight. The bartender on duty that night said he hadn't been talking to anyone but her. She saw him walk out alone."

"This is horrible," Ida murmured. "Another tragedy on this house. How many more…."

"Ida," Uncle Otto said. She silenced herself.

"We're going to need to take statements from all of you and hopefully learn something that will lead us to the killer. All we know is that it happened last night, apparently just before midnight. And we found this."

The policeman held up a broken piece of porcelain that was molded in the shape of the lower half of a man. It looked very detailed, with seam marks on the jeans, thick black shoes and a belt buckle that protruded slightly from the broken waist.

"Whoever killed him left this behind. Did Kurt collect dolls?"

CHAPTER NINE

Berger Mansion, June 11, 9:25 a.m.

Allyson let herself out the front door of the mansion and walked down the steps to follow the stone path. Her interview with the police had been very short; she'd known Kurt all of forty-eight hours, so there was really not much that she could say. Otto was now in his office talking with one of the cops; Ella had gone with the other one and was speaking in hushed tones on the far side of the entry foyer. Allyson had passed them on her way outside.

How could so much bad stuff happen all at once? First her mom, then the horrible storm and now the gardener. It felt as if a dark cloud was following her. What horrible thing was going to happen next? The thought gave her a chill.

Don't ask such things.

Allyson followed the path around the house and onto the patio out back, where there were some lounge chairs with plastic outdoor cushions. When she stepped onto the grass, something snapped beneath her feet.

A stick that had been partially hidden in the tall grass. A long one.

She bent down to pick it up and then idly moved it along the ground like a divining rod as she continued to walk. She headed toward the remains of the fallen tree. The ground where the roots had ripped up was now a mound of mulched wood. The arborists had chopped up the trunk and carted it away and then chipped up all the smaller branches to fill the gaping hole where the tree had once been. All around the epicenter were sticks and bark and leaf fragments. And honestly, they were everywhere, not just around the fallen-tree area. The storm had not simply ravaged the old oak; the entire yard still bore evidence of the heavy winds. The grass on one side of the yard where the slope angled down was still matted from where groundwater had formed a small river to drain away from the house and down the hill.

But if you looked away from the grass and up at the sky, you'd never have known there had been a dangerous storm thirty-six hours before. The sky was a vibrant blue, with just a scattering of high fluffy clouds, and the tall treeline at the bottom of the hill swayed in a light breeze. A variety of cheerful birdcalls echoed throughout the yard and there was a steady flutter of wings as they ranged from tree to tree. On the ground, squirrels ran to and fro, intent on business humans could only wonder at. Despite the pall of death, it was a beautiful day.

A branch snapped behind her. Allyson spun around.

Martin stood there, looking her over.

"So, did you kill Kurt?" he asked matter-of-factly. "What did he do to you?"

Allyson's jaw dropped. "Are you serious?" she gasped. "Why would you even say such a thing?"

Martin shrugged. "Seems like death is following you around. First your mom. Then a baby casket pops up out of nowhere. Now our gardener is murdered. Why'd you have to bring your dark little cloud to our door?"

"Get stuffed," she said. "I had nothing to do with any of that. Asshole."

The corner of Martin's mouth tilted in a gesture of irritatingly silent humor. She realized that he'd just baited her, set the hook and won the prize. Clearly her cousin liked to push people's buttons. She refused to give him any more satisfaction. Without another word, she turned on her heel and walked away, heading down the hill.

When she reached the bottom, she followed the path the water runoff had taken and risked a glance back at the place where the enormous tree had once anchored the top of the hill.

Martin had not followed. The yard was empty.

"Where does he get off?" she mumbled to herself. She'd run into bullies and assholes before, but Martin seemed to have it in for her for no apparent reason. What had she ever done to him?

There was a metal archway near a copse of trees to her right and Allyson headed in that direction to see what it was. It stood over three meters tall and half as wide, and the name NEUMANN was spelled out in the metal threads of the archway. A reminder that this mansion had belonged to her mother's father before it passed to Otto Berger. Beneath it, a wood mulch path threaded its way through the trees. It was like the kind of entryway you saw in fairy-tale picture books. With a shrug, Allyson set out to find where it led.

She had the answer quickly when a row of oblong carved stones came into view around the second turn in the path.

The family cemetery.

There was a clearing dotted with a couple dozen oval and square burial stones. And in the back, a large stone crypt guarded by a beautiful angel statue. The small stone 'house' was faced with a faded wooden door and a stone cross on the peak of its roof.

"Well then," Allyson said.

Death seemed to be following her everywhere indeed.

She knelt at one of the first stones to read the faded dates carved into the limestone. And raised an eyebrow. She wasn't one hundred percent sure, but it looked like whoever Gertrude Neumann had been, she'd died in 1554.

The Neumanns had been here a long, long time apparently.

She stood and walked over to the mausoleum and noted the area above the door was carved with the family name. Presumably the oldest patriarchs were buried inside.

The stones grew more and more recent, and she almost stopped when she reached dates in the nineteen hundreds.

But then she found the stone for her aunt, Otto's late wife, and knelt beside it for a moment. The weather had not dulled the writing or muted the color of the stone as it had for most of the other grave markers.

ELLEN NEUMANN BERGER
Born 20 April, 1968
Died 11 November, 2006
Loving wife and mother was carved beneath her death date.

Then a slightly newer stone nearby caught her eye and she moved over to view it.

CATHERINE BERGER
Born 3 June, 1992
Died 9 December, 2008
A daughter like no other, the inscription read.

Her cousin. Somehow, she hadn't realized that the girl had been that much older than her. Allyson had been just two years old when the girl had died. She supposed it made sense, though; she knew Aunt Ellen was a lot older than her mom and had only the faintest memories of ever seeing her. Her mom had never been close to her family, and they had only come to Germany a couple times that she remembered when she was younger.

She straightened up then. It suddenly felt morbid to be kneeling in a private cemetery looking at the graves of people she never really knew when a man who she had (briefly) known had just died. Poor Kurt. Hopefully he hadn't suffered long. And hopefully whoever did it would be caught quickly. And punished. Before he hurt someone else.

Something snapped nearby. Probably just a squirrel in the trees. But…suddenly she didn't feel like being alone in a cemetery. Allyson looked around but didn't see anyone.

Still, her pace was extra fast as she hastened back down the path toward the hill to return to the mansion.

It felt like a bad idea to be alone today.

CHAPTER TEN

Sweet Dreams Motel, Hildegard, June 11, 10:55 p.m.

Lita finished the last touch of eyeliner and leaned back to admire the result. There were lines on her face that no amount of makeup was going to cover, and her hair seemed to look more like wire than silk of late. Her body offered plenty of other warning signs that she was well past her prime to be selling it on the street, but as long as she left her black hose on, at least her spider veins were hidden. Still, she thought she was doing okay for fifty-three. The guys never complained, that was for sure. Of course, her clientele had largely grown older with her, so they didn't have a lot of room to talk. On the rare instances that she was picked up by a guy under forty, they usually wanted to call her 'mommy'. A little weird, but it came with the territory. Their money spent just the same.

She looked at her watch and suddenly felt anxious. He said he'd be here at eleven. She looked around the hotel room and there was nothing else she could get ready. Her street clothes were stuffed in her duffel bag, and a purple candle burned on the nightstand, filling the room with the scent of lavender. A midnight-purple silk robe was sashed over her best lingerie; she didn't suppose she'd be wearing the robe for long once he arrived.

But she did wonder why he was suddenly so insistent on meeting up with her. It had been years since he'd paid for a spot in her bed. And then out of the blue, he needed to have her tonight, no matter what. He'd even told her to cancel any other 'plans' she had tonight and he'd reimburse her for the loss, as well as pay his own way. As it happened, she was free. She'd thought about gouging him for a little extra but quickly dismissed that. She might be a whore, but she wasn't *that* kind of whore.

For whatever reason, he was anxious for her, indeed. Not that she minded. It felt good to be wanted so much. She ran one hand down the silk over her hip and smiled. She might have a few wrinkles and sags, but she still had thighs to die for. If you didn't look too closely.

A knock on the door interrupted her moment of self-love. Lita took a deep breath, leaned in to stare at her makeup in the stand-up mirror once more, dabbed a finger at the edge of her lipstick and then, satisfied, walked barefoot across the stained carpet to open the door.

"Long time no see," she said when she saw the tall figure standing just outside. "Come in, come in."

He shut the door behind him and a second later, she heard the click of the lock.

"I can't offer you a full bar, but I did bring a bottle to keep us warm." She pointed to a green bottle with a yellow label and red letters that read J&B. "Can I pour you a glass?"

"Sure," he said. He sat down on the edge of the bed, which squeaked with the sound of rusting springs.

"I'm afraid the hotel only has plastic cups," she said, handing him one half full of amber liquid. "And I'm not sure I'd trust the icemaker down the hall."

He shook his head. "Neat is just fine." He took a sip of his drink, while obviously looking her over.

She took a long sip herself and when she set the cup back down on the nightstand there were thick red lip prints on the edge. Then she stood up and undid the sash of the robe. She took her time with it, exaggerating the striptease.

"It's been a long time since I let you look at this," she said, as the silk slid lazily down her right shoulder, exposing the black straps of her bra beneath. She'd worn the one with sheer silk revealing the lower curves of her breasts, while the upper part was accentuated with a spiderweb lace that obscured her nipples. The panties were similar, with a spiderweb band that wrapped but still revealed her hips, while a dark silk V obscured the ultimate goal of her johns.

"You look as good as ever," he pronounced after another sip of his whiskey.

She let the robe fall completely to the ground and lifted one leg over his lap before settling down to rest her thighs on his knees.

"Have you missed me?" she breathed, her eyes suddenly wide pools of sensual promise.

"Sometimes," he admitted.

She leaned in and planted a kiss on his lips, leaving her lipstick mark in another place.

"Only sometimes?" she said, leaning back with a pout. "It was always good between us, you know."

He nodded. "It was. But…people wouldn't have understood. My wife back then wouldn't have been happy if she'd finally gotten wise."

"Excuses, excuses," she said, and then took the cup from his hand and placed it next to hers on the nightstand. She began to unbutton his blue-striped shirt. She pulled the tail out of his pants and ran her palms up the hairy slope of his pecs before bending down to put her teeth on one of his nipples.

He shivered at her attention and began to stroke the wavy fall of her dark hair. Wiry or not, it easily wrapped around his hand.

Lita smiled. He was letting go. She'd worried at how stiff he seemed when he first walked in. She stopped kissing his chest and instead used her hands to push him back down on the bed. And then she set about unbuckling his belt.

"I hope things down here are still what they were," she whispered, as she shimmied and slid his trousers to the ground. When she pressed her face to the white briefs beneath, a broader smile crossed her lips.

"Oh, I can feel that they are," she said. She made a show of licking her lips in anticipation.

"You haven't changed a bit," he said.

"Are you disappointed?" she asked, as she teased the waistband of his midrise briefs down to reveal an erection that was clearly desperate for her attention. She didn't waste a moment in giving it.

"No, not at all," he said. "I never thought I'd feel your mouth on me like this again."

"This is just the beginning," she promised, and then slid her lips slowly down him in a way that brought out a satisfied moan that the adjoining room probably heard.

Lita's heart and thighs warmed at that sound. She still had the touch, even with him.

★ ★ ★

Later, he lay still, breathing in long, heaving gasps. The sheets beneath them felt disgusting when she moved – so cold and wet with the sweat of their passion. She ran her fingers over the hairy pelt of his chest once more.

"I've missed you," she said. "It used to be so good with you."

He nodded. "I know. But things change."

"Why are you here now? I hate to ask, but I'd like to know."

"I've been thinking a lot about those times," he said. "Back when we didn't have to meet in seedy motels to be together."

She smiled. "There were so many rooms in the Berger Mansion," she said. "And we christened them all."

"It seemed that way."

"Maybe we could revisit some of them again, if you're interested," she suggested. "That one room in the empty wing with the old fireplace and the huge four-poster bed was amazing."

He looked as if he was considering it, but then his face grew serious. "Do you remember when Catherine was pregnant?"

"Oh my God, how could I not? The scandal that could have caused if anyone had ever known what really happened."

"I thought you might have forgotten," he said. "It was so long ago."

"How could I forget how that child was gotten on her?" Lita asked. "I may be a prostitute, but that was obscene. Unforgiveable.

I love being with you, but you know I never approved of that…or of what was done to the baby." She made a face and shivered, her breasts shaking against his arm. "I can't believe it all stayed buried."

"Well, it came unburied this week," he said.

"What do you mean?"

"The casket that child was buried in came up out of the earth this week during that big storm. The tree next to the gravesite was uprooted."

"Wow," she said. "That's embarrassing."

"It could be, if the bones were found."

"What do you mean?"

"There were no bones in the casket. I thought you might know something about that."

Lita made a disgusted face. "Is that why you're here?"

"There aren't many people who know what happened that night, and you're one of them," he said. "So…."

"I can't believe you would think I would know anything."

"Maybe you had the child reburied in a regular grave afterward, I don't know."

"I would never have done anything of the sort." Lita sat up, angry now. He'd not really come to fuck her, but just to pump her for information. To see how much she remembered. She reached out and took a deep sip of the J&B. It went down with a pleasant burn.

"If anyone had ever asked, I would have been happy to have told them about that poor baby. And about poor Catherine. It's a crime what you all did to her. And you should be punished for it."

"That didn't stop you from taking me back to your bed," he observed.

"Your purse is worth just as much as anyone else's." Her voice was harsh; she suddenly felt used in a way she rarely did after a night with a customer. She sold herself, sure, but she liked to be used on her own terms.

"Would you really still tell the police about Catherine? After all this time?"

"If they came to me, I'm not going to lie. But they never will at this point. Though maybe I should call them up and tell them what used to be in that sad little casket."

He rummaged for a second with his pants on the floor, and then came back up with his hands hidden in a pair of black leather gloves. He held her robe balled in one fist.

"I'm afraid I am going to need to make sure that doesn't happen."

Before she could react, he shoved her back on the bed and stuffed the robe in her mouth. Lita tried to scream, but all that did was give him the room to push the robe in deeper, until she began choking. She brought both fists up and tried to beat his head, but with one strong arm he grabbed one in midair and pushed it down to the bed. He pinned it with his thigh, and then quickly grabbed and forced the other arm down the same way. He was straddling her chest, crushing her with his weight to the bed. Once her arms were pinned, he took the robe sash and slipped it under her head and cinched it tight, tying a knot over her mouth to hold the gag in.

Then he looked down at her with a look that sent pure terror down Lita's belly and spine. This wasn't a bondage game. He wasn't playing.

He was going to kill her.

Her eyes bugged out, pleading silently for him to stop.

"I'm sorry that this is going to take a little time," he said. "But we need it to look like one of your johns got just a little too exuberant. I'm afraid you know too much. And we can't afford any loose ends right now."

With that, he encircled her neck with those soft black gloves and began to squeeze. The gloves didn't seem so soft then.

Lita struggled, kicking at the bed, and trying to roll him off. But he was much bigger than her and knew exactly how to use his weight to keep her trapped. The bed creaked and slammed the wall, but she couldn't break free. She tried again and again to make a scream that would penetrate her robe, but all that did was make her lose air. If anybody heard the noise of the bed, they would just assume that a couple was having the usual fun next door. She had chosen this hotel for a reason.

"Shhh," he encouraged. "It will go faster if you just let it."

Her eyes really bulged at that, and she tried to pound his ass with her knee. But then it got harder to lift her leg. Her vision was full of red and her chest burned as if she'd swallowed acid. Her lungs were melting.

When she finally admitted that she was not going to get free, she quit struggling, and just stared into his eyes with one last plea. Tears streamed from the corners of her eyes.

And then the light in her gaze went out, and those seductive pools were somehow empty of promise in an instant.

He held his hands on her throat for another minute, but then finally sat back and took a deep breath. A trace of moisture wet the corner of his own eyes, and he brushed it away with the back of his gloves. Then he slipped one off and pressed the back of his finger to her neck, searching for any hint of a pulse.

There was none.

He slipped the glove back on, stood up and retrieved his pants. After dressing, he reached into his pants pocket and pulled out a well-glossed ceramic. A glass doll. The body appeared to be of a sexy woman, one bare leg crooked with the black ruffle of a garter visible around one thigh.

He gripped it between his hands until something snapped. And then he dropped the broken pieces on the broken body.

"Some dolls are best buried," he whispered.

He picked up his cup to remove any evidence of his fingerprints and began to walk away. Then he hesitated, turned and went back for the remaining J&B before exiting the room.

CHAPTER ELEVEN

Berger Mansion, June 12, 12:42 a.m.

Allyson was hungry.

And couldn't sleep.

She'd been tossing and turning in the large bed for an hour. Sometimes she felt like the mattress was smothering her; it allowed her to sink in deep, and with the super-stuffed pillows they'd given her, it was like she was floating in cushions. But tonight, instead of soothing her into a heavy slumber, everything just felt...close. And she was warm. She brushed a lock of hair off her forehead and felt a damp spot where it had been.

"Enough," she declared and rolled out of bed. She walked to the window and stared out onto the gardens – and the expansive mound of wood chips – below. The moon lent an eerie glow to everything it touched, but where the trees added their shadows, the darkness was impenetrable. Anything, or anybody, could have been standing down there just a hundred yards away, staring right back at the house.

At her.

The thought gave her a chill and she backed away from the window. She shook her head. *Stupid.* She needed a glass of milk. Or something.

Allyson opened the wardrobe and pulled out her old baby blue terrycloth robe. They'd said she could grab a snack in the kitchen on her own if she ever felt the need, and this felt like a night of need. She just hoped she wouldn't run into Ingrid.

She let herself out of the room and closed the door extra slow, making sure nothing creaked or clicked too loud. Then she padded barefoot down the hall, taking long, slow steps to avoid noisy floorboards.

The house was still and dark, but enough moonlight shone through the front windows that she could see her way safely down the stairs. The dining room was a different story – pitch black and she couldn't find the light switch. There was a faint light beyond the far doorway. She used the backs of the chairs as her guide until she reached the kitchen. The nightlight she'd seen burned in an outlet near the sink. It was dim but showed enough that here she could see the regular light switch. She flipped one of the three switches and a bank of lights beneath the cabinets illuminated.

Perfect. Just enough to see by without a blinding torch.

Allyson opened the fridge door and pondered. There were several containers of food, but she didn't feel like exploring the leftovers. She considered a block of cheese – a couple slices would make a good snack – but then she decided just to pour a glass of milk.

She set the milk container on the counter and began to open the cabinets one by one, searching for a glass. The first cabinet held an array of china, and the next one, a potpourri of bowls. The third door paid off. There were several shelves with a wide selection of drinkware. She reached up to take a tall, clear glass and nearly dropped it when a voice right behind her suddenly spoke.

"Looking for something?"

Allyson almost jumped a meter in the air.

She turned quickly, feeling 'caught red-handed'. Her uncle stood on the other side of the kitchen island. He looked as if he had just come in from a business meeting; he was dressed in dark slacks and a button-down blue-and-white pinstriped shirt. Which was weird, since it was long after midnight.

"I…uh…just wanted a glass of milk," she stammered.

He smiled. "Best thing you can drink before bed. Tells the stomach that you've been cared for by the mother and now it's safe to sleep."

She nodded, still feeling 'caught'.

"I hope you aren't having problems sleeping here," he asked. "I know that you've been through a lot and this is a new house and all. But I don't want you to feel uneasy here. This is your home now."

She forced a smile. "I really appreciate you taking me in," she said. "It's all different, but I know I will get used to it. The house and my room and everything are wonderful."

He looked satisfied with that. "Sleep well," he said. "Do let Ingrid or me know if you need anything at all."

And with that, he turned and walked back through the dining room.

Weird, Allyson thought, slowly sipping her glass of milk. *Why was he out so late?*

When she was done, she rinsed the glass out and left it in the sink. She hesitated then, because she really didn't want Ingrid questioning who had been in the kitchen, but...she wasn't sure what else to do with it and she didn't see a towel to dry it off with so she could put it away clean.

Shrugging, she flipped off the lights and left, slowing her gait as she returned to the dark shadows of the house. There was a light on in the hallway on the first floor and she paused at the entrance, wondering who was up. She walked a few steps down and realized the light was coming from her uncle's office. Of course. She'd assumed he'd gone straight upstairs to bed, but now she could hear the faint rumble of his voice.

Did he have someone in there?

She moved a couple steps closer, eavesdropping in spite of herself.

"...She is an unanticipated wrinkle, a wild card, I know. But I will take care of her. Tomorrow, I must have the funds. Make sure that they are delivered or I will be very displeased. You do not want that, do you? Good night."

The plastic click of a phone being slapped down hard on the receiver punctuated his last words, and the creak of an office chair told her that Uncle Otto was standing up. She couldn't have him find her standing out here. Allyson turned and darted back to the foyer and the main stairs. She wanted to be near her room before her uncle stepped into the hall.

She didn't quite make it. The echo of a wooden door closing with a degree of impatient force reached her ears just before she hit the second-to-last stair. She didn't allow herself to slow, but instead hit the upper hall and turned right.

When she pulled the bedroom door shut behind her, she leaned her back against it and gave a huge sigh of relief.

The words of her uncle still echoed in her head. *"She is an unanticipated wrinkle, a wild card, I know. But I will take care of her."*

Who did he mean? Was he talking about her? She was certainly an unanticipated addition to his life. And if so…what was he going to do to 'take care of her'?

Somehow, she didn't think the milk was going to help at all now.

CHAPTER TWELVE

Berger Mansion, June 12, 8:22 a.m.

Ingrid kept staring at her. Every time Allyson looked up from her plate of golden-brown pancakes and sausage, she found the housekeeper's eyes on her. Was the woman mad because she left a glass in the sink last night? Ingrid hadn't said anything about it, but Allyson felt like somehow Ingrid knew that *she* was the one who had been in the kitchen. Which...shouldn't be a crime or anything. She'd been told to take what she wanted. But she still felt like somehow Ingrid disapproved. Maybe that wasn't it at all, but the staring was creeping her out.

"...what do you think?" she heard Otto say.

Allyson looked away from Ingrid and found that the rest of the table was staring at her. She realized that Otto must have said something to her.

"I'm-I'm sorry," she stammered. "What?"

His face creased in surprise. He probably wasn't used to not being heard.

"I said, I'm going to Munich this afternoon, and I'd like you to come with me."

"I thought *I* was going with you," Ella complained. Her brow knitted in confusion. Maybe suspicion.

"Not this time," Otto said.

His secretary set her fork down and swallowed. But didn't say another word.

Allyson's stomach rose to her throat. Otto's words from last night played in her head unbidden: "I will take care of her."

"I...um...." She tried to figure out how to make an excuse that she was too busy when she clearly had absolutely nothing to do.

"Excellent," he said, not even waiting for her to finish a response. "I have an election campaign dinner tonight and it will do you good to get out and see something outside these walls. I will have Ingrid find you an appropriate dress. Pack something for overnight. We'll be staying over."

"But.... What I was going to—" Allyson began, but Ingrid cut her off.

"I will have something brought up by lunchtime," the housekeeper promised. "We will make sure that she looks presentable for the event. We can't have your niece looking like a girl from the back country."

What the hell did she mean by that?

Was she saying Allyson didn't know how to dress well? It was true that her mom hadn't been able to afford fancy clothes but....

"Then it's settled," Otto said. "Please be ready to leave by two p.m. I have a couple of appointments I need to attend to before the dinner tonight, so we'll check into our hotel early."

"I don't know if..." Allyson began to say, but Otto had already moved on to other concerns. He had turned to Ella, and while his voice was too low to hear from across the table, his hands were in motion, underlining whatever point he made with staccato chops through the air. Meanwhile, Ingrid was bent over to hear something that Martin was whispering, and Ida chewed in silence, staring across the room as if ignoring everybody.

Nobody cared if Allyson had anything more to say about it. Except Allyson. Who desperately did not want to go. What if Otto was taking her to Munich...but not bringing her home?

The rich, silky taste of the pancakes turned to chalk in her mouth and she pushed her plate away. She couldn't eat anymore. She needed to think of a way to get out of this trip. But how? Claim she was sick?

"This will be wonderful," Otto said, looking directly at her again. "I know some of my opponents make me out to be a cold, friendless man who will not serve the heart of the people. But having you there at my side, well...my beautiful niece will melt the eyes of the opposition, I have no doubts. This is perfect, I believe."

He stood up suddenly and Ella followed. "I'll see you in the foyer at two," he said. "Bring your overnight clothes and an outfit for tomorrow, but you won't need much. We'll come straight home in the morning after breakfast. This will be fun, I'm sure."

With that he excused himself and stepped away from the table. Ella grinned thinly and followed him out the door without a word.

Allyson didn't like her. There was something about her uncle's secretary that just seemed...cold. She worked for him and yet...she was here at every meal. At his every beck and call. What did Ella do for him at night after everyone went to bed?

And then she mentally slapped herself. That was unfair. She barely knew the woman, and she was just doing her job. Trying to make sure an important man had all of his affairs properly tended to. She kept him organized, certainly.

And what else? that evil voice whispered in the back of her head.

Allyson pushed her plate back and drank the rest of her coffee. Her stomach wasn't going to accept another bite now.

"Excuse me," she said, and rose from the table.

"You don't have to start packing right away, you know," Martin said. "Keep in mind the car only has one trunk."

She glared at him and turned away. But not before she saw the slight tremor of humor in Ingrid's lower lip. The housekeeper stood at Martin's side, hands on her hips, and watched Allyson go.

To hell with them all, Allyson thought, and hurried through the foyer and up the stairs to her room. When she reached it, she slammed the door shut behind her and then threw herself on the bed. She squeezed her eyes shut tight, as if doing so could hide her from the world.

And she desperately wanted to hide from the world. If she could, she would have erased almost everything that had happened in the past month.

She couldn't, and that's why tears leaked out slowly from the sides of her eyes as she balled her fists and, still holding her eyelids closed tight, wished for a different reality.

* * *

Allyson was still lying in bed when the knock woke her. She jumped at the sound and blinked away the fuzziness of fading dreams. She rolled over and saw that the clock read 11:43. Had she really fallen asleep for two hours?

Shaking her head, she staggered across the room and opened the door.

Ingrid stood on the other side; a black dress hung over her arm.

The housekeeper raised an eyebrow at Allyson's drowsiness, and then thrust the dress into her hands. "Try it on," she said. "I think you'll find it fits well. I'll wait out here."

"No, that's fine, you don't have to wait," Allyson said.

"I'll wait," Ingrid said. "I want to see for myself."

Oh, good lord. I am not in the mood for dress-up.

But she didn't have a lot of choice, did she?

Allyson laid the new dress on the bed and stripped off her t-shirt and jeans; then she pulled the dress over her head. It slid down her thin frame, tugging until it fully passed her bra; it clung in just the right places and felt cool and sleek. It only covered the very top of her calves and a deep V left much of her back exposed.

She slid her hands down her sides and smiled at the coolness of the material. It felt good. Light.

"Well?" a voice said from the other side of the door.

Allyson grinned and walked back to open it. "I think it's great," she said.

Ingrid looked her up and down. "It will do."

Allyson squirmed inside. That was it? "It will do?"

"This is an important dinner for your uncle," Ingrid said. "Make sure you are on your best behavior. Please let me know if you need anything else before you leave."

And with that, Ingrid turned and marched away.

What a bitch.

Allyson slid the dress back over her head and then folded it carefully on the bed. She supposed she should just pack now and get it over with. Presumably they would stop at the hotel before doing anything, so she pulled her jeans back on. Might as well be comfortable for the drive.

Then she grabbed her smallest bag, an overnight tote, and began to drop in deodorant, hairspray, underwear, a blouse and a t-shirt (would the morning be formal?) and other things. Once she was packed for a 'night in the city', she sat down on the bed and stared at the bag.

The words of last night came back to haunt her once again.

She had an overnight bag.

But would she survive overnight?

CHAPTER THIRTEEN

Berger Mansion, June 12, 2:14 p.m.

Ida watched the black sedan pull away from the front of the house while she stood on the balcony outside the game room.

Good riddance.

She relished the days that pompous fool went off on trips and left her with the house to herself. Not that she could do much with it these days. It sucked to get old. But even five years ago, she had been able to move around the grounds, tend her gardens and sometimes even manage to find a way into town.

Otto had effectively kept her a prisoner here at the mansion since Ellen had died. Her brother Helmut had foolishly left his entire estate to his daughters. But Esther had left her inheritance on hold when she refused to return from England, and once Ellen was gone, all of Helmut's wealth became Otto's by matrimonial right. She had asked him to cut her a share, since the estate and the business was built by *her* family, not his, but Otto, the fat prick, had simply grinned and shook his head.

"You're welcome to live here to the end of your days," he'd said. "I know that Helmut would have wanted that."

She'd brought up the idea several times since, suggesting that it was time she moved into her own place, perhaps a nice little apartment in Hildegard. With just a fraction of the money the mansion was worth, she could have been free of Otto and had a weekly allowance that would surely have kept her happy until she died. How many years did she really have left?

"Who would take care of you when you become infirm?" Otto had said and dismissed her by returning to the paperwork on his desk.

Unfortunately, she had reached that point now. Dr. Testi held a full file of documentation on her various ailments. If nothing else, she could take some vindication in the fact that her health care was now costing Otto.

Bastard.

The taillights of the car flashed red as it reached the edge of the property and turned out onto the road beyond. She pitied the poor English girl in the backseat. No doubt Martin would torture her the whole trip. Her grand-nephew showed some of the heart that her niece had had, but he also displayed some of Otto's worst traits. He could be cruel.

And relentless.

Oh, Allyson, what purgatory have you found yourself in? And will you escape it unbroken?

That thought stuck in her mind. She sat on the terrace and tried to return to her book, but every sentence somehow led her back to thinking about Allyson. The poor girl had just experienced one of the worst traumas in life. And now she was stranded here; just like Ida, the girl had food, water and lodging…but all at her uncle's whim.

But…as the granddaughter of Helmut, the daughter of Esther, wasn't Allyson an heir to Berger Mansion? The *Neumann* Mansion?

A smile lit the corner of the old woman's face. Perhaps there was another way to invoke some justice on Otto's greed.

Ida walked inside and lifted the old black phone from the receiver and dialed zero. She didn't know the number she was trying to reach off the top of her head, but the operator would be able to connect her.

"Hello, Wilhelm," she said once she got past his secretary. "It's Ida."

A flutish but still hearty voice replied, "How are you doing, old girl? It's been years."

"Well, there's not much to talk about when you're just the girl trapped forever in an ivory tower."

He laughed. "I'm pretty sure that Berger Mansion does not have an ivory tower. Is Otto treating you well?"

"As well as can be expected. But I'm not calling about me. I'd like to ask your help on behalf of Esther's child."

"Do tell."

"She is living here with us, since Esther's death."

He made a grunt of affirmation. "Yes, I heard."

"Under the terms of Helmut's will, that would make her eligible for her mother's portion of the estate, would it not?"

There was silence on the other end of the line.

"It would, yes?"

"Technically, I suppose she would have a case," he said. "But it has been so many years...."

"Bullshit, solicitor. I believe the terms remain in effect and Allyson Neumann should be able to exercise them, if she so chooses."

"I can check," he said.

"Then I'd like you to do that. And when you see that I'm correct, I'd like you to inform Allyson of what she is entitled to by Helmut's stipulations."

"I don't know that Otto would want me interfering here," Wilhelm said. "And I work for him now."

Ida cackled into the receiver. That quickly degenerated into a wheezing cough before she recovered.

"You served Helmut before him and your duty both by your former employer and by your oath of office is to uphold Helmut's will, is it not?"

"It is."

"Then I insist that you make Allyson Neumann aware of her birthright."

CHAPTER FOURTEEN

Munich, June 12, 6:05 p.m.

The restaurant was fabulous.

The ride to get there...was not great.

Martin had come with them, which she hadn't expected. She wasn't sure if that was a good thing, but it did mean she wasn't simply alone with her uncle. Still, she now had to weather his acerbic taunts. He'd ridden in the back of the sedan with her, and while he spent most of the ride scrolling on his phone, it still made Allyson a little uncomfortable to have him so near.

They checked into a cute hotel in the heart of old town Munich and, once settled, walked down the street a couple blocks to the site of the 'important dinner'. She couldn't help but marvel at the architecture of the buildings all around; it was like walking through a Christmas card of a classic Bavarian town, or an antique snow globe. Many of the structures had ornate carvings on their cornices and curved stone overhangs protecting the windows. The geometry of the red, tile-covered roofs was intricate, with sections cutting in and out, triangles escaping triangles. And everything was unique. There were windows and entryways on the ground floor bricked in wide tan arches instead of squares, while a building right next door might have dozens of tall, narrow rectangular windows outlined in white stone amid red brick. There were narrow turrets and wide, flat yellow stone walls that looked hundreds of years old, outside of the Starbucks sign or other branding fastened above the entries. It mostly all looked as if they were from a very different time.

Allyson still didn't really know why they were here, but she did know that Otto was trying to save his seat in Parliament, and it seemed as if this was some kind of event to thank his 'backers'.

"When we walk in," he'd cautioned, "I'll have Martin on my right, and I'd like you to take my arm on the left. Show that you're with me."

"Of course," she'd agreed, and that is how they walked in.

Strutted in, really.

The tall, stout and proud Otto, flanked by two examples of the next generation, were all decked out to impress. Martin had on a dark gray suit jacket and a silver and black tie that just seemed to cry 'money'.

They were quickly met and escorted inside to a banquet room where a crowd applauded as they walked in.

Quite the red carpet.

After they were seated at a large, round table at one end of the room, well-wishers came out of the woodwork to greet and talk with Otto. And gradually, the five empty seats at their table filled as her uncle invited people to join them.

Eventually, someone began to clink glasses and Otto stood and pulled Martin and Allyson with him, introducing them as his dearest family. Their introductions drew applause and after they sat, he moved to a podium, where he began to talk about the changes he hoped to make in his time in Parliament.

"Now is the time for dreams to be writ onto the real paper of law and to finally come true," he promised.

Allyson wasn't buying it.

Dreams are dreams because they're wishes that aren't true. And no politician has ever made it any different.

But she smiled and nodded and sat down to her plate of pork with dark gravy and rich tangy sauerkraut. She'd never eaten lunch and had aborted breakfast. So, she was starving.

After he finished speaking, a jazz trio of bass, drums and piano began to play on the side of the room and Otto returned to eat with Martin and Allyson for a short while. He didn't stay long, however, because then someone came and pulled him away, insisting he had to meet some people. Soon Otto was several tables away, smiling and shaking hands.

"Get used to being abandoned," Martin said. "We're just set pieces. We look good as his base, his ever-loving family, while he works the room."

"That sounds a bit jaded," Allyson noted.

"You haven't lived at Berger Mansion long enough. You'll understand, soon."

"I'm just happy to have a place to live," she murmured.

Martin looked up at that, and just stared at her for a minute. Then finally he said, "Listen, do you want to get out of here?"

Allyson made a face. "We can't just walk out!"

He laughed. "Sure we can. I do it all the time. We're window dressing and he's shown us off. We're free to go now."

Allyson put her napkin on the table. She had to admit, she would love to be away from this room of stuffed shirts and gray-hairs. "Are you sure he won't be mad?"

Martin shook his head. "I do it at all of these things. He knows I know my way back to the hotel."

"If you're sure...."

"C'mon. There are better places in Munich to waste a night in than here."

She got up and followed him through the vestibule and back out onto the cobblestones outside. Neither of them noticed the man who got up from his table near the door and trailed them out onto the street. When they stopped to discuss their next move, the man leaned against the entryway brick and pulled something from his pocket. A moment later, the flash of a match lit his long, drawn face for a second and then a puff of smoke lifted from his lips into the air. Nobody would question a man having a cigarette on the street. And Martin and Allyson took no notice of him.

★ ★ ★

"Where did you want to go?" Allyson asked. A little late, now that she was committed.

"There's a nice Irish pub over that way." He pointed. "But you've probably had your fill of those. How about we grab a pint at the Hofbräuhaus?"

"Is it close?" she asked. She'd heard of the place, some kind of old, famous beer garden. But she'd obviously never been.

"Right down the street," he said. "Follow me."

He led her along a winding street of gray and reddish cobblestones that was lined on its perimeter with green and gold umbrellas. It was a beautiful clear night and clusters of people were enjoying steins of beer and cups of coffee outside bars and cafés on nearly every block. The low hum of conversation was almost the only noise to break the evening air. The soft light through the windows of the buildings was all that lit many of the tables, and it caught the sides of faces and beamed through raised pints with a warm golden glow. The moon hung overhead, near full, and made for a postcard-perfect picture as it rose in the blue-black sky above an old weathered clock tower.

They turned down another street and Allyson saw their destination just ahead. An HB with a golden crown above the letters was encircled by blue. It glowed on the sign two stories up on the side of an entryway that jutted out from the main structure. She could hear the muffled sounds of both voices and music echoing through the street as they drew near.

"Sounds like a party," she said.

"Every night," Martin agreed.

They walked through a large arched entry and suddenly were in another world. An older time where barmaids dressed in blue-checked dresses with square-cut fronts edged with lace that were clearly designed to show off their bosoms. Barmaids darted back and forth in front of them to serve long, heavy wooden row tables beneath an arched ceiling covered in murals of green leaves and blue fish. The crowned HB logo decorated one yellow-hued wall, while a quartet of men wearing long white sleeves, dark shorts and long gray socks sat on a raised stage behind a wooden rail. They played classic German music on accordion, tuba, cornet and trumpet. The smell of roasting pork and the din of a thousand conversations competed with the music for attention as they wound their way past packed tables.

"There's an open biergarten in the center," Martin promised and led them to another door that emptied out onto a huge patio also filled with revelers. "The whole building wraps around it. Hopefully we can find a spot," he said.

They wound their way through the tables that spread across the large outdoor area and eventually, Martin pointed out a small table near the opposite wall from where they had entered. Two people had just stood and were about to walk away.

"Grab when you can," he announced and hurried forward, slipping into one of the two seats before anyone else could lay claim.

"Well played," she said, sliding into the opposite seat. "But I think we're a little overdressed."

Indeed, there was nobody else in the outdoor throng wearing a dinner dress or formal suit.

Martin nodded. "You are right there. This is not a place to stand on ceremony." He reached up and opened his shirt's top button, undid his tie, and then yanked it from around his neck. He rolled it up and stuck it in the inside pocket of his jacket, which he then removed and hung on the back of the chair.

"There. A little better, no?"

He still had shiny shoes and a collar, but Allyson nodded. At least he wasn't completely suited anymore.

"Now your turn," he said. "Maybe just rip the dress down the middle at your chest and show off your bra. That will look more casual."

Allyson made a face. "Sure. A girl in a ripped formal dress who looks like she was just attacked is casual?"

"It's all about your face, the way you carry yourself."

"No."

He shrugged. "Suit yourself."

Just then, one of the bosom-baring waitresses turned up at their table with two menus. "Welcome," she said. "Do you know what you want to drink, or do you need a minute with the menu?"

"We'll both have a dunkel," Martin said instantly.

Allyson shot him a look. She'd never had a dunkel and didn't know that she had any interest in trying one. He ignored her gaze.

The waitress nodded. "Would you like the liter, or the half?"

"We'll start with halves," he said.

"Will you be eating or just drinks tonight?"

"We'll think about it," Martin said.

The waitress smiled. She had a round face with freckles that made her look probably five years younger than she was. She didn't look like she could be serving alcohol.

"I'll leave the menus, then," she said. "And I'll be right back with your beer."

Allyson glared at Martin. "Why did you do that?"

"Because everyone should taste a dunkel at the Hofbräu," he said. "And if you don't like it…we'll order a Märzen or Hefe or something else next. But when you have a waitress here, you don't ask for her to come back. It might take twenty minutes before you see her again."

Allyson grudgingly had to admit there was some wisdom there. This place was jam-packed. She couldn't imagine waitressing here. She bet her feet would swell out of her shoes long before her shift ended.

"So why are we here?" she asked.

"Because the Hofbräuhaus is the crown jewel of Munich?"

"No," she said, shaking her head. "Why are *we* in Munich?"

Martin grinned. He'd known what she meant. "Because Dad needs to impress some people so he can get back into Parliament this fall. And having a family is apparently impressive to some people. I don't understand why, really. Any dipshit with a dick can pump his hips a few times and germinate a kid. That doesn't mean the dude is a decent human or an electable representative. But…the mob wants to see a candidate with a happy, attractive family. So...they get me in a suit and you in a formal dress. I guess if nothing else, you can be happy that you look good and Father didn't have to make apologies for you."

"Do you think he's going to win the election?" she asked.

Martin shrugged. "Probably? He's the incumbent and has got a good reputation. As long as he doesn't get into any weird scandals in the next couple months, it's probably smooth sailing."

"You mean like a coffin popping up in his backyard?" Allyson asked.

Martin looked amused. "Yeah, like that."

"Or his gardener getting murdered?"

Martin's smile disappeared. "Yeah, like that too."

"Do you think we should be back at the dinner?"

He shook his head. "It's all about the entrance. We made it. People saw us. He thanked us and we smiled and looked happy. We did our part. Nobody is looking for us now as he makes the rounds and shakes everybody's hands. I've been on this merry-go-round before. I know how it spins."

The waitress returned with a glass mug in each fist. "All right," she said, slipping them in front of each of them with a light clink as they hit the table. "Two dunkels. Can I get you any food?"

Martin declined and lifted his glass to hold it out in the center of the table. After a couple of seconds, Allyson did the same. He tapped her glass and said, "Drink up," before doing exactly that himself.

Allyson lifted the tall, thin glass mug with an HB label on the side and tasted the dark beer. It had an almost smoky flavor, malty and rich but also thin; it looked like it would be thick and heavy, since it was dark, but no. It went down easy and full of flavor. She was not unhappy now that Martin had ordered it for her since she would never have chosen it herself.

He set his mug down and pushed the chair back. "I need to visit, how would you say? The water closet."

"Okay."

"Don't drink my beer."

"Not with your spit on the glass," she said.

That drew a smile.

And then he was gone down the crowded hall.

Allyson lifted the dunkel to her lips and sipped a long draft. The beer was already starting to hit her head when she felt a presence standing nearby.

Close nearby. The hair on the back of her neck seemed to rise to attention.

She turned slowly. A tall man with broad shoulders and ice-blue eyes stood just behind her. He was clearly watching her.

"Hi," she said, staring directly at his face, forcing him to acknowledge his spying.

"Hello, Allyson."

How did he know her name? Her chest suddenly felt weirdly tight.

"Who are you?" she asked.

"My name is Ivan," he said. "But that's not important, and I don't have much time before Martin returns. What *is* important is this. Have they made a ceramic doll of you yet?"

She frowned. "Who?"

He shrugged. "The family. Have you sat for your doll?"

She shook her head. "I don't know what you mean."

"At some point, you may have to sit for a Berger family portrait… so that you can have a porcelain doll made in your likeness. All I can say to you is, be gone before that happens. Dolls were made to be broken. Don't let them break you. Go back to England while you can."

His eyes suddenly looked up, across the crowd. He clearly recognized someone. Without another word, he turned and threaded his way between milling people to disappear into the crowd.

A moment later, Martin reappeared.

"Why the sad look?" he said. "Did you think I abandoned you?"

Allyson made a face of disgust. "That wouldn't make me sad at all."

"Coulda fooled me. You looked utterly lost there."

She opened her mouth to say something about the man who had just been there and then...caught her tongue. Martin was one of *them*, after all. He was one of the family the strange man had just warned her about. Plus, she didn't completely trust him. He got far too much delight in taunting her.

"No, I was just thinking."

"So that's what all the smoke is from."

She rolled her eyes. "I feel awful about Kurt," she said. "And I barely knew him. It must be really hard on you."

Martin looked away for a second as if considering his response. When he turned back, he lifted his stein and took a long drink.

"Ingrid and Kurt were like parents to me," he said. "My mother has been gone since I was a child and my father is often out of town, dealing with his business and politics."

"I'm really sorry," she offered. "Were Ingrid and Kurt a couple?"

Martin's eyes widened and he snorted in his beer glass.

"Oh God, no," he said. "That would be gross!"

"Gross, why? They are...were...two consenting adults."

"He was much older than her," he said. "She's maybe more like my older sister than mother. And he used to drive her crazy. She was always correcting him."

"Sounds like every married couple ever."

He shook his head adamantly. "No, it was never like that."

She shrugged and downed the rest of her beer.

That brought a grin from her partner. "Want another dunkel, or do you want to try something else?"

"I think I'll do another one of these," she said. Before she had finished her sentence, he was flagging down another waitress.

"We'll take two liters of the dunkel," he ordered.

"Liters? Are you trying to get me wasted?"

"That always seems to work for my father," he said with a wicked grin.

"Well, it won't work with me," she said.

"You seem so sure," he said, raising an eyebrow. "I may have to test this."

Allyson rolled her eyes again and decided to change the subject. "I'm curious, do you remember anything about your mother? I have vague memories when we were kids. But I wonder if she was a lot like my mom or what. I mean, they were sisters."

Martin looked uninterested. "I don't really. Past is past. I remember she and Dad used to fight a lot. Ingrid used to hold me on her lap and cover my ears, especially when Mom started yelling about him and his Swedish maid. I didn't realize until I was a lot older that she was talking about Ingrid's mom. She was pretty, and I think Mom was jealous of how much attention Dad paid her."

"Do you think he cheated on your mom with her?"

"She would never have done that," he said. "And if she did, I don't want to know about it."

A moment later, a barmaid with a bosom that threatened to burst her buttons at any moment bent down and shoved two heavy steins of dark beer in front of them. Martin held up two five-euro notes and then made a point of inserting them in the cleft of her cleavage. The girl offered a patently false smile and curtsied before turning away and removing the bills from her breast.

"Pig," Allyson said.

"You offer the milk, I'm gonna drink it," he said.

Allyson lifted the stein, which was twice as wide and thick as the last one. "Holy shit, this is heavy," she said.

"Good exercise," he agreed, and lifted his up and down twice before guzzling a good draught.

Allyson sat back and enjoyed the cool beer slipping down her throat as the humid night air kissed her cheek. The air was still and a bit heavy, but it felt good to be outside beneath the stars on a summer night. Not that she could see many of them. There were small trees in pots set around the patio, and umbrellas remained open all around. The faint hum of insects just barely held its own above the murmur of a hundred conversations all around them.

"This is nice," she said after a while.

"You're welcome."

"So, you don't really remember much about your mom," Allyson began. "What about your sister? I hope you don't mind me asking but...what happened to her?"

Martin's face clouded for a moment, but then he shrugged. "My mom died when I was two, and my sister went when I was four. I don't really remember anything about either of them. I just know the family pictures we have and the stories that people told about them. I've basically been an only child all my life."

"I'm sorry," she said automatically. She didn't want to be sympathetic to him because he was kind of an asshole. But...she got it, too.

"I've been an only child all my life and didn't have a dad for a long time. Which meant that my mom was never home because she was always trying to make enough money for us to afford our flat. I know what it's like to grow up alone."

Martin shook his head. "I was never *alone*. I always had Ingrid. She's always taken good care of me."

So much for sympathy, Allyson thought. She said nothing, focusing instead on her beer. The buzz of happy inebriation was already creeping up on her brain. She didn't drink much at home. Couldn't afford it, to be honest. The oompah bass-drum sound of the classic German band inside the walls of the restaurant filtered out to the patio and she focused on that as she drank and looked up at the dark night sky. For a little while, she really felt good...warm and happy in a private place. The patio around them was filled with conversation and energy, and the sky above was marvelous; a perfect summer night. Martin stayed silent, and for that she was thankful. He had brought her here, but she didn't really want to hear anything more from him. She wanted to revel in her private moment – buzz, stars and beer.

It was good.

Until Martin was standing up and suggesting they leave. She came out of her haze and looked up and around, clearing her head. As she did, she realized there was someone watching her, standing at the back of the patio space near a door.

She recognized the blue eyes. They pierced the darkness of the half-lit patio like spotlights. She knew that man. And he was staring intently at her, waiting for her to realize he was there. Because as soon as she did recognize him, he held up his hands, as if he were gripping something long and narrow.

Like a doll.

And then he mimed snapping whatever was in his grip. The doll that he said would be made in her likeness?

With a nod, he met her eyes, and then turned and vanished out the door to the main building.

Her heart sank, though she didn't even know what she was afraid of, exactly.

"Want to head back to the hotel?" Martin asked.

"Yeah."

She looked for the man with blue eyes on their way out as they passed the German band and the hostess stand.

But he was nowhere to be seen.

CHAPTER FIFTEEN

Berger Mansion, June 13, 2:08 p.m.

"Allyson?"

Ingrid stepped out of the dining room and into the main foyer. Allyson had come out here after lunch and instead of going to her room, lounged on one of the soft sofas. She was tired after their drive back from Munich and didn't feel much like doing anything today.

"Yes," she answered, looking back. The housekeeper's face was typically bereft of emotion.

"You have a phone call. You can take it over there if you wish."

Ingrid pointed to a phone on an end table nearby. There were several clear buttons on the front, and one was blinking with an orange light. Her uncle must have had the extensions wired to only ring in certain rooms, because it had not rung here since she'd been sitting.

"Thanks," she said, while at the same time wondering who it could possibly be.

Ingrid gave no clue, though Allyson thought she saw a glint of curiosity in the woman's eyes. But only for a second. And then the housekeeper disappeared back into the shadows of the dining room. Allyson moved to the soft leather chair that sat next to the end table with the phone. She picked up the receiver and pushed down the blinking button.

"Hello?"

"Allyson Neumann?" a male voice asked. He sounded older, his voice high-pitched but just faintly rusted from years of late-night whiskey.

"That's me," she answered.

"My name is Wilhelm Schmitt," he said. "I'm the lawyer for the Berger family, and my understanding is you are now living under your uncle's care."

"Yes, that's correct," she said. "What can I do for you?"

"I need to see you soon to go over your mother's affairs."

"What affairs?" Allyson asked. "She didn't have a lawyer."

"No, no," the man said. "Of course not. But she was part of the Berger family, and her passing makes certain things your responsibility now. Would you be able to come to my office in Hildegard this afternoon, so that I can discuss these things with you in person?"

"Um, I guess?" she said. "I'll need to see if someone can drive me into town."

"Excellent," he said. "If four-thirty p.m. is convenient, I have an opening then at the end of the day."

He asked her for her email address and then sent her an appointment request, including the address of his office. She agreed to confirm that she could, indeed, get there at that time, and then hung up. She sat for a moment, considering. What could he possibly want? Her mother had nothing; they'd lived in a tiny flat that she could barely pay the rent on. Why would a lawyer need to be involved in her 'affairs'?

There was only one way she was going to get the answer to that question.

Allyson got up to go look for Martin. Hopefully he would agree to drive her into town.

As she stood, she heard a faint rustle in the dining room nearby. Allyson rolled her eyes. She knew what the noise meant. Ingrid had been standing on the other side of the doorway, listening. Hoping to find out what the lawyer wanted. Nosy bitch.

Whatever.

She hadn't said a thing that would have told the housekeeper what they'd been talking about. And that made her smile.

Go ahead and wonder.

She shook her head and walked up the stairs. She hadn't seen Martin since they'd gotten home from Munich; he was probably up in his room.

The hallway was silent as she walked past her room to his door. Maybe he'd gone out and she hadn't seen him?

She knocked and there was no answer. But when she knocked again, she heard something thump on the other side. He was in there.

A moment later the door opened. Martin looked sleepy and annoyed. His hair was tousled and bunched on one side. She'd woken him up.

Oops.

"What do you need?" he asked grumpily.

"A ride into town in a couple hours?"

Martin sneered. "You think I'm your chauffeur? You have a driver's license, right?"

"Sure."

"And Google Maps on your phone?"

She nodded.

"Hang on."

He disappeared for a moment and then came back with one hand extended. He offered her a set of car keys.

"Take the blue Audi," he said. "And don't fuck it up."

"Thanks," she said.

"What's the rush?" he asked. "Aren't you tired from yesterday?"

"Yeah, but I need to take care of some business."

He looked unimpressed. "Whatever. Just don't mess up my car. And I'd be back by dinner if you can or Ingrid will be annoyed."

"Sure," she said. "I will. Thanks."

He yawned and, without another word, closed the door in her face.

CHAPTER SIXTEEN

Hildegard, June 13, 4:18 p.m.

The Audi drove nice.

Allyson had never driven a car that accelerated so quickly and easily and made such little noise while doing so. Her mom had always had old, creaky third-hand cars that sometimes seemed like they wanted to be pushed to their destination versus driven there. Grumbles and rumbles and coughs.

She covered the distance to town in just ten minutes and threaded her way through the narrow city streets carefully. When she parked a couple blocks down the street and around the corner from where the lawyer's office was, she eased into the parking spot like a geriatric. The one thing she did *not* want to do was to have a fender bender or scrape Martin's tires or hubcaps on her first outing alone in Germany. She had been surprised at first that he'd even given her the keys, but then she realized...it was simply the path of least resistance. If she'd gone to her uncle, Otto probably would have told Martin to drive her...and her cousin clearly didn't want to leave his room today.

Allyson parked the car without incident and made sure to click the automatic lock as she walked away. She could not imagine explaining that the fancy-ass car got stolen while the keys were in her hands.

She walked down a cobblestone sidewalk to the address, an old three-story building with a yellow stone façade and light green shutters that bordered the handful of windows facing the street.

It was clear she had found the right place; a bronze plaque was attached to the building near the door that read *Wilhelm Schmitt, Rechtsanwalt.*

She pulled on the thick metal door handle and stepped inside. A rich burgundy carpet led from the foyer to another wooden door just a few yards down the hall. Again, the lawyer's name was emblazoned on a plaque. This time when she opened the door and stepped inside, there was a hum of voices and activity.

A heavy-set woman with silver hair looked up from behind a greeting desk. The reception area was filled with leather chairs and framed posters of jazz festivals and classical orchestra concerts. Apparently, Mr. Schmitt was a big music fan.

"Miss Neumann?" the woman asked, looking her over from behind a pair of blue-framed glasses that perched low on her nose.

"Yes," Allyson said. "How did you know?"

The woman smiled. "Last appointment of the day. And Mr. Schmitt had a picture of you in the file."

She reached into a folder on her desk and held up a photo. It showed a girl of fifteen or so with dark hair and a red United soccer t-shirt leaning in close to a woman in a similar shirt. They were clearly related and were either at or had just been to a game.

Allyson remembered the picture. Her mom had taken a selfie of the two of them just before they entered the stadium that day. They had had such a good time. It was a rare moment when her mom was actually lighthearted and really enjoying their time together, instead of being wiped and broken from too many hours at work trying to make enough to keep a roof over their heads. Seeing the picture dropped a rock on her heart. She would give anything if she could go back to those days.

The woman slipped the picture back in the folder and eased herself up from the chair with a faint groan. "I'll let him know you're here," she said, and carried the folder through a dark wooden door a few steps behind her. A moment later she reappeared and gestured for Allyson to go inside.

"He'll see you now."

* * *

Wilhelm Schmitt was a big man, in more ways than one. He stood nearly two meters tall, but he also wore a belt that had to measure over one hundred centimeters in girth. His gut looked like a weapon. A button-down light blue shirt mushroomed over that belt line when he stood from behind his mahogany desk and extended a thick hand for her to shake. His knuckles were fat with wiry black hair, but his scalp looked much less healthy, with silver and black strands struggling to hide the pale skin of his head.

"It's good to meet you at last," he said with a voice that was comically high in pitch considering his physicality.

"Please, have a seat." He directed her to a heavy, red leatherbound chair. "How are you enjoying your time in Germany? It's much different from London, no?"

She nodded. "Very different. Uncle Otto lives far from town. My mom and me…we didn't have much, but we were right in the thick of it in London. So many things going on all the time around us. It was vibrant."

Wilhelm nodded, pale lips pursed as if he wanted to say something but was holding back.

"So, how do you like your uncle's house? Surely it is different than what you're used to but…."

"It's very nice. Everyone has tried to make me feel at home."

He looked both slightly surprised and relieved. "Good. This is surely a very trying time for you."

Allyson didn't really know how to respond to that. Trying was a joke. It had been hell. But nobody else was going to understand that, not really. So why complain? She had a roof. That's all she could really ask for in the end.

When she remained silent, he shrugged faintly and began shuffling papers around on his desk.

"Well, let me get to the point. The reason I called you here, as I said on the phone, is because your mother's estate has some things that need to be tied up."

"Yes, you said that," Allyson agreed. "But I don't understand. My mother had nothing but a few pairs of clothes, a lot of old

Rolling Stones albums and a stack of overdue bills. What estate? We were poor."

"Not exactly," the lawyer said. "Your grandfather, Helmut Neumann, was a very successful industrialist, and in his will, he left his home and business investments to Esther and her sister Ellen. His one restriction was that your mother would have to return and reside in Germany in order to claim her inheritance. You were named in that will as Esther's heir. But he was adamant that his money would not leave the country, particularly to go to England. Your mother refused to do so. At the time of his death, Ellen and Otto were already married and living in the family mansion, so outside of changing the name of the estate to Berger, they simply kept on as they had before."

"How does all this relate to me?" Allyson asked.

"When Ellen died, your uncle inherited all of the estate. With the death of your mother, you inherit her portion of the estate... but again, the stipulation still applies that you must choose to live in Germany. Which you are now doing. Her portion has been held in trust for you if you choose to accept the terms. If you so choose, you can make a claim for half-ownership of the Berger family mansion."

Allyson's eyes widened. She pictured Martin's reaction when she told him that she owned half of his house. "You can't be serious."

"Oh, very," Schmitt said. "The way it is written, you could not take on ownership until you have lived in Germany for at least six months and you would have to sign a document avowing that you will continue to do so. If you left Germany to begin residence in another country within five years of inheriting, you would forfeit whatever remained of the inheritance. Your grandfather set up many safeguards that lock the money to his intent."

"He really did not like England, huh?"

"He did not like it that your mother left. But I'm sure she had her reasons."

"I know she didn't want to come back here," Allyson said. "I only remember visiting a couple times as a kid."

"Yes, your grandfather was not happy about that situation at all. But your mother was determined to live on her own."

Allyson smiled at that. "She was really independent," she said. "She hated taking any help from anyone. She always said she didn't want to owe anybody anything."

The lawyer nodded. "There is wisdom in that." He looked quizzical for a moment, and then said what was on his mind. "You will turn eighteen in November, if I'm not mistaken?"

"Yes."

"Not long after that point, you will have lived in Germany for six months," he said. "We can have another discussion at that time, if you believe it is warranted."

He reached into a folder and pulled out a sheet of paper. "This is a document just acknowledging that I've told you about the inheritance you are entitled to and its restrictions. If you could sign it for me?"

Schmitt extended his hand and offered her a fancy pen fashioned out of a rich dark wood. She took it and was surprised at its weight. It felt good between her fingers. Solid. Rich. She didn't use pens like that at home. Just flimsy plastic things.

Allyson skimmed the document, which was simply a recitation of the things he had told her about needing to live in Germany and having to give the money back if she accepted it and then left the country.

Allyson signed and dated the document after looking at her phone to see that it was June 13. She'd had no idea what the date was! The days were just blending into each other now. She had no school, no job, and no friends. There was no reason for her to know what the date was.

"Do you think you will decide to exercise your right to the inheritance?" Schmitt asked. His eyes looked flat, unemotional. Holding something back.

"I don't know. I mean…that would be weird to tell everyone that I was part owner of their house, you know?"

"There are business holdings as well," he said. "By the standards you are used to, you would be rich beyond your dreams if you liquidated it all, though, as you say, that could be difficult. You wouldn't likely sell off the family home, though you could sell your shares in the companies."

"I don't know," she said. "I would love to go back to England, honestly. Everyone I've ever known...well, my whole life is there. But I have no way of going back right now."

Schmitt nodded. "My suggestion? Get a job. Earn enough to go home as quickly as possible and then go reclaim your life as fast as you can."

He put one hand on the desk, leaned in closer to her, and spoke in a lower tone, as if he feared someone nearby was eavesdropping.

"There are reasons your mother did not want to come back here. I'm sure you could find a treasure trove of her reasons in that house, tucked in the attic or in old boxes or closets if you wanted to look. But suffice it to say, I think your mother's advice was sound. Don't owe anyone here anything. Hildegard seems to be dangerous these days and it's better to be alive than rich. Go home, Allyson."

CHAPTER SEVENTEEN

Hildegard, June 13, 4:46 p.m.

Allyson walked down the stone path from the lawyer's quaint, old-fashioned building and turned onto the sidewalk to walk to her car. The afternoon was quiet; the faint hum of cars and activity all seemed far away in the distance. Here, it felt as if there was nobody around for blocks.

It was kind of perfect. The last vestige of a summer day's heat was fading from the air and the buildings along this block all were rich in plant life, with short green hedges and vines and flowerpots exploding in color. As she walked, Allyson thought about her conversation a few minutes before. It was not exactly the news she had expected. After scraping for every pound her entire life, to find out that she could be rich in just a few months if she played a dead man's game was…disconcerting to say the least. But also disturbing was the lawyer's suggestion that she leave the money on the table and run. Strange. But it made her wonder, why would he suggest it? There had to be a reason. What things had gone on in the Berger Mansion that she should be afraid to stay there? And he was now the second person to advise her to go back to England.

The thought gave her a chill.

At the same time, she realized that there were steps clicking on the pavement behind her. There hadn't been anyone on this entire block a moment ago. She glanced over her shoulder to see who else was nearby and got another chill.

There was a man just a few yards behind her. It was his garb that made her a little frightened because…he dressed like the night. He was tall and thin and his shoes, slacks and shirt were all funeral black. His hair was dark too and he wore dark shades so she couldn't see his eyes. He gave her the creeps for no reason other than his outfit. He just looked...sinister. Without thinking, Allyson doubled her pace. The car was just another block or two down and around the corner.

The steps behind her quickened to match her own.

Allyson felt the hair on the back of her neck stand up.

The guy was not just someone else on the street. He was keeping pace!

She walked even faster, her ears attuned to the clicking echo on the pavement. She dared not look back and let him know that she knew he was pacing her. And he *was* pacing her. His steps increased again to match her own.

Now Allyson felt the pangs of panic. Why was a man in black pacing her?

She could see the corner not far ahead. Just a couple more quiet business buildings and then she'd be on the street where her car was. And where there were some restaurants and maybe...people. She broke out in a run toward the corner.

The click of the steps behind her instantly increased to match.

Holy shit. Was she about to be robbed? Raped? What the hell?

Allyson wanted to look behind her but didn't dare. She needed to focus on running now that she'd started. Because fancy shoes or not, a tall man might easily be able to outpace her. Allyson leaned forward and dashed as fast as she could toward the corner, imagining the hands behind her reaching out at any second to touch her shoulders. To grab and spin her around before throwing her violently to the pavement.

She refused to make that possibility easy. Allyson ran hard.

The clicks behind her did not fade away. If anything, he was gaining.

Shit.

Just a few more steps...

Were his hands reaching out just behind her shoulders even now?

…and she rounded the corner.

There was a group of people a few yards away and she threw herself toward them as if they were salvation itself.

"Help!" she cried and nearly plowed over a silver-haired man. He looked confused and she had to push herself to the right to avoid smacking into him. Her foot slipped where a cobblestone was missing. It caught between the stones for a second when she kept running. Instead of moving forward, Allyson's whole body suddenly hit a wall…she jerked and twisted backward.

Something white-hot stabbed her ankle, and Allyson's shoulder hit the pavement. She rolled three times down the walkway before her momentum stopped.

There were stars in the blue summer sky and Allyson took a moment before registering the hands on her shoulders and the voices saying, "Miss, miss, are you all right?"

Allyson looked up to see three concerned faces peering back at her. The man in black, thankfully, was not among them.

At that thought, her heart hammered. She rolled to her side and looked past the knees around her to see the street.

The man was nowhere to be seen.

"What's wrong, miss?"

"There was a man chasing me," she said, still looking up and down the sidewalk. "Did any of you see where he went?"

"A man?"

A kindly-looking older gentleman crouched down and put his hand on her shoulder. "There was nobody behind you, dear," he said. "You just came running around that corner like a bat out of hell and took a spill here. You almost ran us down."

"I'm sorry," she said. "But you have to believe me, there was a man chasing me. I don't know what he was going to do."

The man patted her shoulder. "Well, he's not here now. So, let's worry about you. Are you hurt? That was quite a fall."

Allyson could feel heat in her leg, right along the side of her calf where it had scraped the pavement when she went down.

"I think I'm okay," she said. "Thanks, though."

He offered his hand, and she took it and began to stand.

That's when the pain shot through her ankle like a nail through the bone.

"Oh geez!" she cried and went back down to the ground in a heap.

A younger woman with pale blonde hair and an overly wide mouth bent down next to the older man and held her by the shoulder. "That's not good," she said. "I think you're going to need some help that Franz can't give."

"Bite your tongue, missy," the older man spat back. "I can help just fine."

"Uh huh," the woman said. And with that, she tightened her grip under Allyson's arm and pulled her upright, all in a single motion.

But when Allyson tried to put pressure on the ankle, her leg instantly ceased to hold her and she began to fall. That's where the old man came in. He slid an arm around her middle and kept her from sinking back down.

"We can both help, I think," he said. And with that, he pivoted and began to move them toward a car parked along the street.

"I think you're going to need some assistance getting home," he suggested.

"No, no," she said. "It's my left foot…I just need to get into my car and I'll be fine." She pointed at the blue car parked just a couple spots down the street. "If you could help me get there, though, I'd be really grateful."

Together the three of them hobbled down the street and they held her up as she fumbled for her keys. Once the door was open and they poured her inside, the man shook his head, white eyebrows clenching and spiking.

"I don't know if it's a good idea for you to drive," he said.

"I'll only use my right foot." She grinned. "I'll be fine. But thank you so much. You saved my life."

The old man shook his head. "I just helped you up out of a hole."

"You have no idea," she said. And then she revved up the engine and waved at the man and woman. They stepped off the street and waved back.

Allyson put her good foot on the gas, pulling the car away from the curb.

The woman and the old man smiled, happy to see her able to move under her own power.

She needed to get out of here. The man in black may not have rounded the corner but he was certainly nearby. Just waiting for her to be alone again, so he could strike.

She didn't intend to stick around and give him the opportunity.

The car swerved easily onto and down the road.

★ ★ ★

A block away, from behind the ridged bark of an old oak, a man in black pants, shirt and glasses watched her go. He exuded a quiet, relentless patience.

"This time," he said quietly. "But there will be a next."

CHAPTER EIGHTEEN

Hildegard, June 13, 5:35 p.m.

"Are you still here?" Wilhelm Schmitt said after dropping a stack of papers in his secretary's inbox. "You should have left a half hour ago."

"Lots to do," she answered, peering pointedly at him and then at the papers he'd just dropped into the basket.

"Nothing that won't keep," he said. "Off with you now."

"Thank you, sir," she said, grinning and pushing back from the desk. In seconds she'd grabbed her purse and shoved the last papers into a drawer. "See you in the morning."

"Indeed," he said absently, staring at the transcript of a court hearing that she'd been in the midst of transcribing.

The faint chime of the doorbell heralded her departure, but he didn't pay attention. Instead, he was deep in thought as he read a witness account that could be extremely damaging to his client. He took the papers back to his office, intending to read the entire transcript much closer now. There was some preparation in store for him before the next hearing, clearly.

The front door chime went off again.

"Did you forget something?" he called out, still not looking up from his papers.

"No," a deep male voice answered. "But clearly you have. Your loyalty."

Wilhelm's eyes widened and he turned to confront his visitor. The man was dressed all in black and stood with arms folded in his doorway. Even his hands were black, encased in leather gloves that seemed very out of place in the season. It would not be cool enough for gloves for many weeks yet.

"You!" Wilhelm said. "What are you doing here?"

"Just collecting some unnecessary paperwork," the man said, and reached out with a gloved hand to pick up a file that sat on Schmitt's desk. A glance at the contents showed it was not the folder he was looking for. This batch of papers all had to do with a real estate transfer for someone named Franz.

"It might have been better if today's meeting had not happened," he said, dropping the folder. His voice sounded like ice. Cold and sharp.

"I *had* to meet with her," Wilhelm complained. "It's part of my duty as the executor. If I did not, I could be put on trial."

The man laughed. Low and humorless.

"Really?" he said. "Who would initiate that proceeding, if you don't mind me asking? I'd love to know."

"I was just doing my job," Wilhelm complained again.

"Indeed," the man answered. "As am I. And I'm sad to report that your conduct today does not leave me a great many options in how I am to do it."

"What do you mean?" Wilhelm's voice rose higher than usual, fear coating his words.

"You not only told the girl things she doesn't need to know, you also put her on her guard."

"I did no such thing," Wilhelm began, but the man pressed a black leather finger to his mouth. The universal symbol to be silent.

"That's not exactly true, is it?"

"I swear, I didn't...."

"Perjury, Mr. Schmitt. You're familiar with the concept. False statements. Be careful."

He walked across the room and reached behind a framed photograph of a fair-haired woman in a long evening gown. And then he held out his hand for Wilhelm to see a small, black plastic block. It had buttons on the side and a small red light glowed on top.

The man used his other hand to press the STOP button and the red light went off.

"Shall I play you the evidence proving your crime?" he asked. "It shouldn't be hard to remember what you said just an hour ago, but I can refresh your memory quite easily."

With that, he pressed a button and the warble of words sped up fast whirred by. Then he pressed PLAY and Wilhelm's voice filled the room. *"I'm sure you could find a treasure trove of her reasons in that house, tucked in the attic or in old boxes or closets if you wanted to look."*

"Indeed," the man said and pressed STOP. "What would you have her go looking for? What is to be gained by Allyson Neumann sifting through papers in the attic?"

"I just thought…she might find some of her mom's things and…."

"And what, Mr. Schmitt? Start asking questions that we both know would be very problematic if asked right now?" The man shook his head. "I know what you were doing, Mr. Schmitt. Now, where is the paperwork you had her sign?"

"That's a confidential document," Schmitt said. "I can't share that with you."

"Oh, I wasn't asking you to *share* it. Give it to me. Now."

"I'm sorry, I can't do that."

"You can, you simply choose not to. Which is unfortunate. Because I will have it with or without your assistance."

Wilhelm began to rise from his chair but the man put one hand on the lawyer's shoulder. With a firm grip and gentle pressure, he pushed the frightened man back into the chair.

"You know, Mr. Schmitt," he said, staring hard at the frightened man's eyes. "There is a lot of knowledge locked up in that skull of yours. Knowledge of so many things. So many legal cases that probably should have not been won, but were, thanks to your intellect. So many Neumann and Berger family secrets. You are a smart and dangerous man, Mr. Schmitt. You know so much. Sometimes it is much better for everyone if secrets remain secret… or are lost altogether."

The man pulled a small black revolver out of his pants pocket. "Remember when that innocent baby was buried all those years ago, Mr. Schmitt? I'm afraid we're at a similar fork in the road right now. We're going to need to bury some secrets today."

He held the gun out in front of him, the barrel aimed at the lawyer's forehead.

"No, please," Wilhelm begged. "My job is to keep confidences, I would never...."

"You already have," the man said. "You proved in your discussion with the girl that you are not to be trusted any longer. And truly, sometimes it is better if knowledge is lost. I'm so very sorry, Mr. Schmitt. I believe you were a good lawyer in your time."

The man pulled back the trigger and Wilhelm jumped out of his seat, attempted to round the desk and head to the door at a full-blown charge.

The man with the gun was ready and Wilhelm Schmitt was about one hundred pounds too heavy and thirty years too old for such a track move. The other man easily blocked him and shoved him right back into the chair.

"I don't think so, Mr. Schmitt," were the last words that he heard.

The cold barrel of the revolver pressed hard to the side of Wilhelm's head just above his earlobe and then there was a white-hot pressure through the middle of his brain. A blaze of red stars ruined his vision.

A bloom of red also appeared on the leather chair beside his head and began to trickle down into the deep, soft folds that he'd enjoyed leaning into for so many years.

And then Mr. Wilhelm Schmitt knew nothing anymore.

★ ★ ★

The gunman knelt and opened all the drawers, riffling through papers and files to look for the thing he knew was there, somewhere. And then, when he did not find it in the desk, he began to pull on drawers in the nearby file cabinets set against the wall. They were locked and did not budge.

The man cocked his head and considered...and then moved back to the dead body in the leather chair behind the desk. He slid his hands inside the man's suit jacket and into its pockets...and sighed when he came back with nothing. It didn't slow him. He pressed his fingers into the man's pants pockets and groped for something metallic, not fleshy. He needed a key.

A moment later he smiled and teased something cool and shifting from the pocket. He held his right hand in the air and an array of keys dangled from a circle of metal.

"That's the ticket," he murmured. And without pausing, he tried each key in the file cabinet locks. It only took a few attempts before he'd isolated the winner and pulled open a drawer. Then, it was just a matter of following the alphabet.

In moments he held a manila file in his hand. *Allyson Neumann*, it read.

He opened it on the desk, right in front of the sightless gaze of the man who'd filed it. He flipped it open and began to sift through the documents inside.

A moment later he grinned wolfishly and held up a piece of paper with a blue ballpoint signature amended to it. Allyson's signature – tall, looping letters and today's date. The man pulled out a cigarette lighter and clicked the flint to send a spark into the butane. A moment later, a yellow flame began to climb up the piece of paper. When it came close to the man's hand, he released it and the paper floated down into the metal trash can near the dead man's desk. It burned out quickly, leaving only ash behind.

No more document noting that Allyson had acknowledged her right to a portion of the Berger fortune. No evidence that she had ever been alerted to the possibility.

That was something. It didn't change the legalities, but it eliminated some of the technicalities.

The man pulled a porcelain doll out of his pocket. It captured the portrait of a small man, dressed in gray with a long-lipped visage that suggested, 'I have no humor.' The doll did not look happy. The man stared at the eyes of the doll for a second and then laughed.

"You always were a bit of a stiff one, weren't you?" he said to the dead man and the doll at the same time.

Then he twisted the glass doll in his hands until the audible crack of its neck shocked the room. He dropped the pieces on the suited chest of the dead man, and brushed off his hands, seemingly caring little where the jagged fragments fell.

"Sorry to have cut short your night, Mr. Schmitt."

CHAPTER NINETEEN

Hildegard, June 13, 6:01 p.m.

The phone rang. The shrill bell sound of the classic squat landline phone – with cords! – on his desk gave Otto a start, even though he'd been sitting in the leather chair waiting for it. The second ring hadn't finished before he had the receiver in his hand and moving toward his ear.

"Yes?" he answered simply.

"Mr. Berger." The smirk was evident in the man's voice, though he sounded distorted and far away. "It's so good to speak with you again. I trust you have acquired the bounty we discussed three days ago."

"I have," Otto said. "Though it wasn't easy."

"I had faith in you, Mr. Berger. After all, it's an election year. You need to keep the promises you make."

"I always keep my promises," Otto said through gritted teeth.

"Indeed?" the man said. His words dripped with audible disbelief. "Well, here's where you keep an important one. Do you know the barn on the vacant Klosbier place down the road from you a bit? I believe there was a time as a young man when you were friendly with old Karl Klosbier, maybe even used to work for him in that barn."

"Yes, yes," Otto cut him off. "I know the place."

"Good. I wanted to pick a spot that would be simple for you. I don't want this to be hard. No confusion."

"So, you will meet me there?" Otto asked.

"Oh no," the voice said with a hint of a laugh. "We won't be meeting. But at seven p.m., you will walk into Klosbier's barn. You'll find a box just inside the main door. It won't be locked. You'll leave me your payment for said box and then you will pick up and take your secrets safely home to do with them as you wish."

"I understand," Otto said.

"Of course, you will not tell anyone of this exchange," the man cautioned. "You will come alone or I promise you, you will not leave there a happy man."

"I will do exactly as you ask," Otto said. "I just want this business over."

"One hour, Mr. Berger," the voice said, and then with a click the line went dead.

Otto returned the handset to the receiver and leaned back to stare for a moment at the old black phone. His mind raced. He had kept the blackmailer's secret but…what if Otto showed up at the old barn – which was out in the middle of nowhere – and was gunned down?

Otto didn't have an answer to that one. But he also knew that if he took anyone with him, they'd be spotted. The Klosbier homestead was in the midst of rolling open fields. You could see all cars coming and going for kilometers all around. Anyone with a pair of binoculars would be able to see his car and any occupants long before he reached the abandoned house and barn. He'd have to risk it, because there was no way he could arrive with reinforcements.

He took a deep breath and decided to stick with the plan. Pay off the blackmailer, get the evidence back, and lose a big chunk of cash in the offing. But he could at least have a chance to protect himself.

Otto rose from his chair and pulled a keychain from his right front pocket. There was a small bureau on the side of the room with a locked upper drawer. The key slid in and twisted in the lock easily. The drawer opened, and Otto pulled out a small black revolver from where it rested on the velvet lining of the small drawer. He checked the chambers, and then pulled out a box of ammunition and loaded the cylinder with six rounds. He slid the gun into his pants pocket, put the box of bullets away and locked the drawer. If this was a trap, he'd do his best to draw blood besides his own.

Then he opened the upper cabinet of the bureau, reached in for the vibrant yellow label and pulled out a bottle of J&B. He poured himself two fingers and sat down at the desk to sip for a while. Liquid confidence. He shouldn't leave for another half hour at least, and he didn't feel like talking to any of the family before then. So, he'd hold his own silent vigil here, locked in his office with liquor, a gun and a bag of money.

★ ★ ★

A cloud of dust marked Otto's passage as he pulled off the narrow rural road and onto the long, winding gravel path that led to what had once been the family home of Karl Klosbier, the man who had taught him so much of what he knew about politics. The older man had lived through the first and second world wars and knew how fickle the public could be when it came to support. He'd taught Otto about how to curry favors and how to set hooks in place with allies that could not be denied even when the allies were no longer so friendly.

Klosbier had been Machiavellian in the most effective of ways; nobody ever suspected him of the strings and traps he set until it was far too late to escape them. It wasn't lost on Otto that his blackmailer was dragging him back to his teacher's house with equally well-devised strings. He was being maneuvered to pay for his 'crimes' at the place where he learned how to best get away with them.

The entry gate to Klosbier's farm hung open between its two brick pillars and Otto drove slowly through it. The sprawling farmhouse lay just ahead, a ménage of heavy cross timbers and brick. There was a one-story section on one side and a two-story classic V-roofed section in the center. But behind that, another section jutted higher, a rounded turret interrupted by a tall narrow window frame that looked poised to capture the sunset.

The house had been empty for the past five years now, with no millionaire takers interested in locating this far out from the urban center. The days of the rich gentleman farmer were of a different generation. Otto rolled slowly around and past the aging mansion of another age and soon was bouncing downhill toward the large barn beyond. The thing looked almost medieval, with a foundation of stone and heavy, rough logs forming the base. Square and diagonal segments of dusky red brick were held in place by old gray timbers. Two-story green doors dominated the middle, which was curved at the top, like castle doors. Narrow white windows interrupted the brick on either side, and smaller one-story green doors were set on the corners. Nearby, a row of hedges and roses had exploded through their fencing to obscure the walking path that once led to the grazing fields behind the barn. There had been no grazing or cultivation here in years.

Otto stopped in front of the massive entry doors and noted that the one on the right hung slightly ajar. An open invitation. What… or who…waited inside?

He looked at his watch. The time was six fifty-seven. He leaned back in his seat, staring first at the barn and then up the hill at the house. He squinted, trying to make out any figures lurking at the windows or a brush of movement from inside. But the place looked abandoned. Empty and forlorn.

Six fifty-eight.

Otto believed in punctuality. It was time to pay the piper.

He reached down on the floor of the passenger's side and pulled up the black bag by the two heavy plastic handles. It was not light; the bag was bulging with euros. Once he'd pulled it onto the seat, he opened the driver's side door and slid his body out of the car, pulling the bag after him. He stood there on the gravel path leading to the barn for a few seconds, carefully looking all around. The property rose in a gentle hill toward the house, and the copse of ancient oaks that surrounded the old home stirred just barely in the evening breeze. The sky was still blue, with a few scuds of white cloud in the sky. The faint hum of insects throbbed in the fields. It was a perfect summer evening. There was no evidence that anyone had been on the property in ages. But the hair on the back of his neck stirred when he looked at the narrow opening that led into the barn.

Someone had been here. Someone probably was still nearby. Watching him.

Six fifty-nine.

He walked toward the barn, gravel crunching audibly beneath his shoes. He was acutely aware of the metal weight in his pocket. And the sweat rolling down his ribs from his armpits. Otto had perhaps never been more afraid in his life than he was now. And he'd had plenty of chances.

He put his free hand against the rough wood of the old green door and pressed, just a little. The door swung inward easily, though a faint squeal clearly announced his intrusion. The pale light from outside elongated against the dusty ground inside. He pushed the door further and the light eventually stretched far down the main walkway through the barn. There were vacant stalls on either side. Even after years of being empty, the thick, earthy smell of old hay still assaulted his nose.

He scanned the shadows on the edge of the light, but saw nothing but the dark. Satisfied that there was not an obvious gunman waiting for him to step inside, he finally looked at the ground right in front of him. A small wooden box sat on the wood plank floor just a few yards ahead.

It was not simply a box. It was a box in the shape of a small casket. Just like the empty one that had started this whole mess. It was ominously alone in the walkway.

It was what he had come here for.

Part of him, however, stayed rooted to the ground. He was petrified of stepping all the way inside the barn. His imagination saw the barn doors swing shut behind him, and the sudden appearance of a firing squad erupting from the shadows.

But Otto hadn't gotten to where he was by allowing himself to be paralyzed by fear and what-ifs. He forced his feet forward. He dropped the bag of money on the ground and tried to lift the lid of the box.

It was nailed shut.

Otto swore. The bastard was going to make him work for it.

Did he do it here, exposed and open to attack? Or did he trust that his bag of euros had been traded for what was promised?

Otto made a quick decision and scooped up the box in both hands. Imagining the bullets erupting at any second, he turned and rushed back out the door and clumsily ran back to the car. He opened the passenger door to drop the box on the seat, and then, after scanning the dark windows of the house on the hill and looking back and forth at the slowly waving hip-high grass all around, he darted around the car and threw himself into the driver's seat. Then he hit the ignition, and the car sprang to life. Before the engine could settle into idle, he put the car in gear and stepped on the gas; gravel shot out hot from behind his tires to bounce off the walls and doors of the barn.

Seconds later, he was up the hill and beyond the house. He passed the farm's entry gate, turned onto the silent road and floored it. The car slalomed slightly on the uneven surface of the old road as it picked up speed, and he drove for a couple minutes at one hundred twenty kilometers per hour before letting the car slow down. Once he'd put a couple kilometers between him and the farm, he pulled over to the shoulder of the road.

He had to see.

He popped the trunk and got out of the car. Looking up and down the road, he confirmed there was still nobody around. And then he lifted the lid and pulled up the fake floor of the trunk to get at the spare tire. And more importantly, the tire iron. He took it around to the passenger's side of the car, opened the door, and pulled out the box. Once it was on the ground, he inserted the edge of the tire iron into the gap between the wooden lid and the box and pressed. The edge slipped out, but he repeated the action and this time the lid creaked. He moved it to the right and wedged it in again before pressing the end down. The nails squeaked faintly and then the lid popped.

Otto dropped the iron and pried the wood up with his fingers. The door flipped up and over easily, skidding away on the rocky ground. Otto didn't notice. He was staring at the contents.

In the middle of the box was a handful of bones. Literally a handful – the tiny bones of an infant's hands and arms.

But that was all.

No ribs. Or legs. Or skull.

Just the arms and hands.

There was also a piece of yellow paper.

Otto reached down, picked it up and unfolded it. The words inside were typewritten and brief.

Congratulations. You have used your hands and learned to crawl. Next week, you will deliver another 250,000 euros at the same time. If you do that successfully you will be able to walk. I will tell you where to go next Thursday at 6.

Otto crumpled the paper up in as small of a ball as he could and then threw it in disgust into the bottom of the largely empty baby casket.

He was being strung along.

Lying in front of him was the proof that his blackmailer had the evidence…but the rest of the bones would be released little by little until the extortionist decided he'd gotten enough. How much would Otto be bled before this thing was closed?

"You fuckin' bastard," he whispered. "Whoever you are, I'll kill you, I swear I will."

CHAPTER TWENTY

Berger Mansion, June 13, 7:42 p.m.

"The doctor is here to see you," Ingrid said. The housekeeper had knocked first, but before Allyson could answer, opened the door to lean into Allyson's bedroom.

"I said that I didn't need a doctor."

Allyson lifted herself off the pillow grumpily. Even as she said it, she felt a twinge in her ankle. It had really swollen up since she got home.

"That may be," Ingrid said. "But your uncle insisted."

A shock of short white hair suddenly bobbed behind the housekeeper.

"Well then, let me see what's what in there," a warm and ingratiating voice said from behind Ingrid. She stepped inside to make room and the doctor materialized in the doorway.

"Hello there, Allyson," he said. "I am Dr. Testi, the Berger family physician. I understand we've had a bit of a slip and twist tonight."

"Yeah," she admitted. "But it's probably just a little sprain. I'll be fine."

Dr. Testi was a thin man with small silver glasses. His face was narrow and clean-shaven, but his eyebrows and hair were thick and slightly unruly. And white. He appeared older but still hale. And his eyes showed an intelligence that was both restless and querulous. He looked at her as if she were a question to be answered and he was determined to solve the puzzle.

She didn't want to be solved.

"Well, since I'm here, how about if we let me be the judge of that, hmm?" he said, and approached the bed. He leaned down and put his hands around the swollen ankle and gently pressed.

"Ow!" Her whole leg jolted.

The doctor smiled. "Indeed. This does not look like a happy ankle. Let me know where it hurts."

He proceeded to apply finger points of pressure at various spots on her leg and foot, repeatedly asking, "Here?", and if she shook her head, "How about here?"

Eventually, he took her foot into his hand and gently moved it up and down and side to side. She winced a little at certain positions, but he continued. Once satisfied, he rested a cool palm over the thickened knob of her ankle. "Sprained for sure, but I don't think anything's broken. Can you stand on it?"

She nodded. "I could earlier, but it really twinged. I think it's swelled more since I lay down."

The doctor's brow creased. "Mmm, yes, that will happen. We need to get some ice on top and some ibuprofen inside. But let's see how you do."

She slid her legs over the edge of the mattress and gingerly put her feet down. Holding the edge of the bed, she pushed herself upright. She wobbled there a second, and then stepped forward. Instantly, she pulled up the injured foot with a gasp. But then she forced it down again and managed to walk a couple steps without falling.

"That's enough," Dr. Testi said. "Lie back down now, let's not irritate it anymore."

He turned and looked at the housekeeper, who remained a dark shadow in the doorway.

"Ingrid, can you get us some ice and a towel to wrap it in?"

"Certainly, doctor."

"And, Ingrid, do you have any ibuprofen or acetaminophen?"

"Of course." She disappeared from the room.

Dr. Testi sat down on the edge of the bed next to Allyson. He leaned across her legs and grabbed one of the spare pillows from beside her head, and lifted her injured foot to slide the pillow beneath it.

"Let's keep this elevated tonight and put some ice on it every twenty or thirty minutes until you go to sleep. You'll be sore for a couple days, but I think this will pass quickly. You're young." He put his hand under her calf and squeezed slightly. It made Allyson uneasy. "And strong," he said, rubbing the underside of her leg gently before finally removing his hand. "Tell me, how do you like it here?"

"It's fine," she said, not sure what else to say. "But I miss my friends."

He nodded, as if he truly understood. "It's hard to leave home, for sure it is. Did you have a boyfriend back in England?"

She shook her head. That was a sore subject she didn't want to discuss. "No, but my girlfriends and I did a lot together."

"Yes, but girlfriends are not the same as boyfriends, eh?" He smirked and reached out to fondle her calf again. "A girl like you should draw the attention of plenty of boys. And they'll make you feel very, very good."

Allyson didn't like where this conversation was headed.

"Well, I don't know any boys here besides Martin," she said.

He laughed. "Ah, but yes, that boy is off-limits. He hasn't put his fingers on you, right? No kissing cousins, eh?"

"No, of course not!" Allyson was appalled at the suggestion. She shifted her legs a little farther away from the doctor's petting hands.

"I'm sure you had boyfriends back home, even if there wasn't one recently. You have had a nice boy make love to you by now, I'm sure?"

What business was it of this doctor's?

"What kind of a girl do you think I am?" she asked, avoiding the direct answer.

"A normal, pretty girl," he said with a shrug. "I am sure that plenty of boys have tried." He rubbed her leg again and she shivered, growing increasingly creeped out.

"Has your uncle been treating you well?" he continued to probe. "He's always nice to pretty girls."

"He's been great," she said. "He even took me to Munich."

"Oh well," the doctor said, making his eyes grow wide. "Taking the girl out of town already, eh?"

"It was for one of his political dinners," she said. "Martin came too."

"Mmmm, of course," he said.

"Everyone has been very kind here," she said. "But I don't know anyone outside of the family."

"Well, you'll get to know a new group of friends," he promised. "Otto needs to make sure you get connected in Hildegard. I'll speak to him."

There was a rustle in the hall and then Ingrid's stern face was at the bed as she leaned down to put a tray on the nightstand.

"Here we are, doctor," she said. "Ice, towels, some water and some painkillers."

"Excellent."

He leaned over and spread one of the towels out before using the ice tongs to lift several pieces out of the silver tin they rested in. Once he was satisfied there were enough, he twisted the towel around them, and tied a quick knot in the end to keep the pieces inside.

"Let's just hold this here for a bit, shall we?"

He slid one slim palm under her leg and then gently held the impromptu ice pack on top. Allyson realized that as long as this man was in her bedroom, he was not going to take his lecherous hands off of her.

"Thanks," she said. "But I think I can hold it there myself." She sat up and put her hand on the towel, brushing his away.

The doctor looked amused. "Yes, but it's always better if someone does it for you, don't you think? A girl deserves proper pampering and attention."

She was opening her mouth to rebut when suddenly her uncle appeared in the doorway.

"How is our girl doing?" Otto asked, addressing Dr. Testi. Allyson thought his face looked drawn. Tired.

"I think she is going to be just fine in a day or two. But, Otto, you need to get this girl out and about. Introduce her to some people. She can't sit out here alone in this remote island like you. She needs to meet people."

Otto glanced at Allyson, as if to ask, "What have you been saying?", and then looked back at Testi. "Yes, yes," he said. "We will get her introduced. I'm sure Martin has some friends she will meet."

"I just don't want to see you take in a flower and then shelter her so that she withers," Dr. Testi said.

"Indeed," Otto said. He rubbed his forehead and looked at Allyson. "I want you to be happy here," he said. Then he looked at Dr. Testi. "Thank you, doctor, for coming out here on such short notice. Ingrid will take care of your bill."

Otto nodded at both of them and withdrew. Allyson silently wished for him to stay.

Don't leave me with this creep.

But it was too late. Her uncle was gone.

"I guess this is goodbye for now," the doctor said then, and she instantly felt relief. He wasn't going to keep fondling her.

"I will stop by tomorrow to check on you, but I think you'll be just fine. Keep icing it every twenty or thirty minutes while you're awake. Go easy on it when you get out of bed. I don't think you'll need crutches, but if it's worse tomorrow, just tell Ingrid and I'll bring you some."

"Thanks, Doctor," she said. "I'll do that."

He smiled and eyed her up and down. "I know you'll be just fine. And I will be around to make sure of it."

He reached down and ran his hand across her ankle, slipping it under the ice. His touch continued up her calf until it reached her thigh. It lingered there a moment, and then slid even farther up until her eyes began to widen. He gripped her upper thigh and squeezed, looking at her over the rim of his glasses.

"German boys will be very excited to meet you," he said. "You'll be happy here, I know it."

And then the doctor finally pulled his wandering fingers away and packed up his bag.

"Good night," he said, and she echoed his words back to him.

Allyson had never been so happy to see someone walk away as she was when Dr. Testi's white hair disappeared through her bedroom door.

CHAPTER TWENTY-ONE

Outside Hildegard, June 13, 9:20 p.m.

Ella pulled around back of the four-story roadside hotel and parked. Richard liked meeting here as it was unlikely anyone would recognize either of them at the pastoral inn. Surrounded by rolling fields, it was between Munich and Hildegard and a perfect place to steal a couple of hours, if not a night.

Although, he could rarely manage a night. His wife didn't buy the business trip angle very often. And Otto had sabotaged their Munich liaison a couple days ago by taking Allyson instead of Ella for some reason. Perhaps he had begun to get suspicious of where she disappeared to on excursions.

She walked around to the biergarten deck where a couple of old men sat nursing pints and arguing football under the warm lantern light. It reminded her of the heated conversations among the jocks in the school cafeteria on game day, and Donald, the nerdy American transfer student who used to always call it soccer. He did not score any points with the others for that. *Gasthof Neubau*, a wooden placard read on the whitewashed façade.

Richard had a thing for hose, so she'd worn black nylons with a seam that was patterned in floral vines up the back. She'd worn a short black jacket to hide the fact that the black minidress dangerously exposed her cleavage, but she knew she'd draw eyes if anyone took a moment to notice her. She hurried past the old men, hoping they'd keep their attention on whatever match they were arguing over.

Speed didn't save her.

The conversation abruptly stopped before she reached the door.

"I'll have one of those," a voice announced crudely.

"One sweet dessert," enthused another.

Ella rolled her eyes and moved quickly past the front desk inside before one of them tried to corner her and offer a drink. And something more. Something old and hairy and warm.

She shivered and raced up the back stairs to Room 314.

She got enough old and hairy and warm back at Berger Mansion. Richard was young, trim and hot. He answered her knock wearing nothing but a long, blue silk robe, sashed loosely at the middle. Cosmopolitan.

He didn't say a word before yanking her inside and slipping his tongue down her throat. Ella answered his anxiousness with some grabbing of her own, enjoying the tight curve of his buttocks through the light silk barrier.

The door closed and they moved slowly inside, without breaking their lips apart. Some called it a French kiss, but with the two of them it was often better described as tongue wrestling. They were always so anxious to touch that they tried in all the ways they could to climb inside the other, to merge and meld and own the other with their bodies, every limb, every pore.

Finally, they called a truce, and leaned back from the embrace, breathless and grinning. Her lips were wet and hot. Ella let her jacket fall to the floor. Richard ran his hands up and down her sides, clearly enjoying the sheer cover of the upper half of the dress.

"You like?" she whispered.

"You knew I would."

"I try to dress for success."

"Ah, but then I undress for sucks and sex."

"Crude."

"And you love it."

She smiled. She did love it. Richard had met her in Munich when Otto had taken her along as eye candy on one of his political jaunts. But as with his son, once her usefulness was over, he'd abandoned her to schmooze with his supporters. Always panhandling, Otto was.

She'd slipped away eventually to the upstairs hotel bar, choosing a seat near an attractive dark-haired man in a quiet but slick gray suit. He had a short dark beard and a face with just a hint of ruggedness. She liked that in a guy. Handsome, but not prissy. The kind of guy who could probably drop the suit coat and rebuild a car engine just for fun.

He hadn't made a move right away, but eventually he struck up a conversation and bought her a drink. When she'd told him what she did, he made a move to back his stool away.

"You probably shouldn't be seen talking to me, then," he'd apologized. "I'm afraid I'm the competition. I'd like to take that parliamentary seat away from the old guard and actually move things into the modern age here in Germany. I was at the event earlier tonight just to gauge who Berger's supporters were. Where his financial streams were flowing from. Taking notes, you know?"

Ella had smiled and reached out to pull him back closer to her. "I work for him, I'm not married to him," she laughed. "And he will probably be talking downstairs for a couple more hours at least. He won't see me with you."

They'd talked more and by the fourth drink, he'd looked at his watch. "Honestly, I don't think it would be good for you if your boss found you with me," he said. "He's bound to end up here eventually, don't you think?"

She frowned. "Yeah, probably. When the party down there winds down, he'll continue with his biggest funders at a bar somewhere."

"Would it be unseemly if I suggested taking one last round up to my room?"

"I'd like that," she had said, raising her glass with a smile.

Ella had not left his room until the next morning at dawn, just before joining Otto for a business breakfast.

* * *

A year later, here they still were, meeting furtively in hotel rooms. And if anything, their heat had only grown. They could never seem to get enough of each other when they could carve out the time to be together. And they made plans for the future. Plans that did not include Otto or Richard's wife.

Once he was elected, Richard promised that he would divorce, and she would join him on the public stage. Until then, she occasionally passed him bits of intelligence that helped the cause. Key funders and PR strategies that Otto planned to use to secure his seat once again. "We need to find a way to take money away from Otto Berger if that's ever going to happen," he'd said.

"I know," Ella had said. And she'd looked for ways. They'd discussed so many possibilities.

★ ★ ★

"I can't wait until we can be with each other every night like this," he said, running his fingers through her hair.

"The election is soon." She opened her purse and pulled out a white sheet of paper. "These are the ones he's worried about. He tried to get all of them to his Munich dinner. Putting the screws to them."

"Then we know where a counter-pressure may be most useful." He grinned.

Richard tossed the list on the nightstand and ran his hands over her back and the sensual curve of her butt.

"I've missed you," he whispered.

The sash of his robe had loosened further and his emotion was erect and obvious beneath the knot. She grinned and reached out to pull the end of the sash so the loose knot released all the way. And then she slipped her hand over that smooth hard flesh that made her crave him so much in the darkest hours.

"I can tell."

Her minidress was soon on the floor, along with her black shoes, as they wrestled their way down to the low mattress on a pale wooden bed.

Her stockings stayed on.

CHAPTER TWENTY-TWO

Berger Mansion, June 14, 8:33 a.m.

Ingrid finished putting the breakfast dishes in the dishwasher. The family had been strangely quiet at the table this morning. As if everyone was wandering in their own worlds, deep in thought about things they weren't willing to talk about with each other.

Otto sat next to Ella as always, but the two of them never made eye contact, which was unusual. They always seemed like they were silently speaking about something with their sidelong looks and body movements. Otto 'grew' when he was near her. He sat taller, talked louder, and acted more dominant. Ella's presence always made him seem more sure of himself. Ingrid knew that the woman was more than a secretary to Otto, but didn't understand how Ella put up with his wandering eye.

Then there was Aunt Ida. The old woman usually poked her nose in everyone's business, anxious to know who was doing what, where and to whom. Her quizzing grew tiresome every morning, especially before coffee, but this morning, she simply scooped herself some eggs, buttered a biscuit and ate, silent as a stump.

Martin never shared much at breakfast, just made snarky comments on whatever anyone else said, but nobody offered anything to snipe at and he left the table early. As for Allyson, their little refugee, she looked more brooding than usual. Maybe because of the pain in her ankle. Or maybe because of something else. Who knew?

She didn't know what was on everyone else's mind, but she knew that she had some secret thoughts that she didn't intend to share. And an itch that really needed scratching.

Whatever the rest of the family was pondering on didn't matter to her in the end. She had her own priorities. And this morning... she thought she might be able to take care of one of them. Everyone was quiet and nobody asked anything of her. She could afford, then, to disappear for a couple hours. And now that she'd put the last dish in to rinse...that time was now.

Ingrid smiled, wiped her hands on her kitchen apron, and pulled it over her head. She had things to take care of.

Private things.

And clearly, nobody was going to miss her. That was a blessing.

The housekeeper opened the door to the back stairs leading to the second floor and walked up. She shouldn't be missed for a while. And she needed to do something so badly her thighs ached with every step.

Something of which Otto would absolutely not have approved.

When she reached the second floor, Ingrid moved with silent speed down the hall and felt a tingle of anticipation as she reached the room she wanted to disappear in...forever, if truth be told. Instead, she could only steal away here for short, secret dalliances. With Allyson camping downstairs, this was a perfect opportunity.

She twisted the handle and pushed the door open.

Stepped inside.

And smiled at what awaited her.

CHAPTER TWENTY-THREE

Berger Mansion, June 14, 9:33 a.m.

Allyson looked up from her book when the doorbell rang. She had been reading in the front sitting room off the foyer since breakfast. She knew it was going to be slow and painful going up and down the stairs today, so she'd brought her book and phone, intending to stay downstairs for the morning. But now she frowned as she stared at the front door. Should she try to hobble over to answer it, or would Ingrid show up? She set her book to the side in case nobody came.

When the doorbell rang a second and then a third time, she began to lever herself upright. But just as she was on her feet, the sound of rapid steps on tile sounded from behind.

"Stay put, I've got it," Ella said, motioning with her hand for Allyson to sit back on the couch. She came from the hallway to Uncle Otto's office, and she sped across the tile as if determined to reach the door before the door chimes rang a fourth, impatient time. Her hair looked askew and she paused a moment just before opening the door to adjust her skirt.

A familiar face waited outside. Allyson recognized him immediately. The pointy-nosed police officer who had been here twice before over the past week.

"Come in, come in," Ella said, stepping aside so he could enter the foyer.

He removed his cap once inside but his voice remained formal. "Can you tell Mr. Berger that Officer Wagner is here to see him?"

"Yes, of course," Ella said. "Let me go find him for you."

"Thank you," he said, but made no move to enter the sitting area.

Ella didn't wait to see what he did; she hurried down the hall toward Otto's office.

"You're welcome to sit in here," Allyson announced, addressing him from across the foyer.

"Thanks," he said. "I'll wait here."

He stared straight ahead, not meeting her gaze.

Damn. That's one stick-up-his-butt formal cop.

It only made her wonder more why he was here.

She found out a minute later when Otto came striding out of the long hall from his office suite with a concerned look on his face. Ella did not reappear.

"Officer Wagner," he said as he crossed the room. "I didn't expect to see you again."

"Nor did I expect to be here," the cop said. The two exchanged handshakes.

"I'm guessing you're not here with good news," Otto said.

The cop shook his head. "I'm afraid not," he said. "I regret to inform you that your solicitor has been murdered."

Otto actually backed up a step in shock. "Wilhelm?" he said.

Officer Wagner nodded. "Mr. Schmitt was found dead in his office this morning."

Across the room, Allyson stiffened in her chair. She quietly set the book aside.

"How did it happen?" Otto asked.

"He stayed after hours last night. His secretary said he sent her home around five thirty and promised that he'd lock up. When she came in this morning, she found the door unlocked and Wilhelm dead in his chair. Someone shot him in the head, point blank. Based on the coroner's initial report, he was probably killed not long after she left last night."

Allyson sucked in a breath. She'd been in his office just an hour earlier. And then someone had chased her. Had that same someone gone back to kill the lawyer? But why?

"Do you have any clues?" Otto asked.

"The other tenants of the office building claim that they all left shortly after five p.m. at the end of the workday, so nobody saw or heard anything unusual."

"Was it a robbery?" Otto asked. "Perhaps somebody who broke in after hours and was surprised to find Wilhelm still on the premises?"

"It was a robbery, I believe, of a sort," the officer said. "Though probably not the kind you're thinking of. A cabinet was ransacked and there were files strewn about on the desk."

"So maybe it was somebody who had a grudge against him for a case gone wrong," Otto suggested.

"Maybe," Officer Wagner said. "But I have reason to believe that the grudge involves you and your family."

"What makes you think that?"

"Because Wilhelm Schmitt was found with a broken doll on his chest, similar to the porcelain dolls that were left on the body of your gardener and on the body of a woman who I believe used to spend some time at this house many years ago – Lita Von Helm. I'm sure you read about her death in the papers."

Otto looked taken aback. "I...I did read about that," he said. "But the newspaper said nothing about a doll."

"No," Officer Wagner said. "We didn't tell them."

He pulled out a plastic bag that held a white chunk of broken ceramic from his pocket. It appeared to be in the shape of a man's head. There were red dots on the face of the doll that clearly were not part of the original finish. "Does this mean anything to you?" Wagner asked, holding it out for Otto to take.

Her uncle declined to take the bag from the officer's hand. Instead, Otto stared at it a moment before answering. He almost looked afraid to get too close to it.

"No," he said finally. "I don't know what it would mean. I don't think Wilhelm collected dolls."

Officer Wagner shook his head. "No, we have no reason to believe that. But clearly there is significance to the dolls for the killer. And that suggests that all three victims were related in some way. The Berger family is the only link that I can see."

"I knew them all, of course, but that's meaningless," Otto said. "I know half the people in Hildegard at this point. It's a small town and I'm a public figure."

"Indeed," Officer Wagner said. "However, there's another link between this killing and your house."

"What do you mean?"

"Wilhelm Schmitt's last appointment of the day yesterday was with your niece, Allyson."

Otto's face wrinkled a bit, but he said nothing.

"And we believe whatever the killer was looking for in the files was related to her. Allyson Neumann's file was left open on top of all the others."

Across the room, Allyson's eyes widened.

"Think again, Mr. Berger. Can you think of any possible meaning of the broken dolls? The bloodstained dolls?"

CHAPTER TWENTY-FOUR

Berger Mansion, June 14, 9:42 a.m.

Allyson brushed her book aside and pushed herself up from the couch. She teetered for a second as she put weight on the bad ankle, but then muscled forward and took a step toward the front door.

"Someone tried to kill me when I left Mr. Schmitt's office last night," she announced, interrupting her uncle's discussion with the cop. Officer Wagner's brow creased as he turned his attention from Otto to focus on her. His unblinking gaze moved slowly from her head to her hips; she could almost feel his eyes sizing her up.

"Did they now."

Otto interceded. "Sit down. You know you should not be walking on that ankle."

Allyson hesitated for a second and the policeman took it as the opportunity to step past Otto and into the sitting area.

Wagner was in front of her almost instantly. Otto trailed behind, clearly not sure what to do at this point. He looked extremely uncomfortable.

"You must be Allyson," Officer Wagner said.

When she nodded, he asked, "What's the matter with your ankle?"

"After I left Mr. Schmitt's office last night, someone chased me down the street. I thought he was going to kill me so I ran as fast as I could. I ended up twisting my ankle in a hole in the pavement, but by that point, I was around a group of people, so he disappeared."

"I see," Wagner said. "Did you file a police report?"

Allyson shook her head. "No," she said. "Nobody saw him but me and…he ultimately didn't *do* anything. I didn't even get much of a look at him, so I really didn't have anything to report."

"Indeed. So why did you go to see Mr. Schmitt?"

"Well, he called me," Allyson said. Suddenly, she felt nervous. This wasn't something she wanted to discuss in front of her uncle. But how could she avoid it now?

"And what did he want to discuss exactly?"

Otto now stood next to the man. Both of them stared straight at her, one urging her to tell everything, the other clearly wishing for her to stay quiet.

"He had some…things to go over regarding my mother's estate," she said, stalling.

"What sort of things?"

She looked at Otto, who now looked as interested as the policeman in what she had to say.

"Just inheritance stuff," she said. "No big deal at the moment but he said with my mother's death, he had to show me."

"I see," Wagner said. "Was there paperwork that he went over with you?"

She nodded.

"Did you sign anything?"

Again, she nodded.

The cop made a note in his notepad and then looked at her with what seemed a patently fake friendly smile. "I'd like to talk in a little more detail about this," he said. "But I'd like to have it on the record. We'll need to file a full report about the incident, since it relates to a murder. Would you be able to come down to the police station this afternoon and do that for us?"

"I don't have any way of getting there," she said, motioning toward her foot.

"I'm sure your uncle would bring you," the officer said pointedly. "We'd like a statement from him as well."

"Of course," Otto said. He did not sound pleased.

Wagner slipped his notepad back into a vest pocket. "I'll look forward to it."

And with that, he turned and walked back to the foyer.

"Until this afternoon," he said and let himself out.

For a long moment, Otto just stood there, one hand on his head, as if considering what to do.

"We'll go down after lunch," he said. "Maybe around two o'clock. I have work I need to attend to until then."

Without another word, he quickly disappeared down the long hall to his office. A minute later, she heard a door close sharply.

Allyson leaned back on the couch and thought about what the policeman had said. It gave her the creeps to think that an hour after she'd been talking to the stodgy old lawyer, someone had shot him in the head right near where she'd been sitting. What if she'd still been there when the killer had come in? She might be dead now too.

But…why? And what was the deal with the broken dolls? She remembered then what Ivan, the strange, blue-eyed man in Munich, had said to her.

"Have you sat for your doll?"

CHAPTER TWENTY-FIVE

Berger Mansion, June 14, 10:35 a.m.

The doorbell rang.
Allyson laid the book down in her lap and looked around. She'd been reading for almost an hour since the cop had left. The house had remained strangely quiet the whole time. Nobody had walked through the main hall since Otto had disappeared back to his office.
She waited a few seconds for the familiar sounds of Ingrid's marching steps. But none came.
Where *was* the housekeeper this morning?
Frowning, Allyson stretched her legs out to the floor and carefully eased herself up off the couch.
The doorbell rang a second time before she'd managed to go two steps. It made her pause; would Ingrid come running out from somewhere this time?
The house remained quiet.
Whatever.
Allyson slowly made her way across the foyer, wincing each time she put her left foot down. Her whole body tensed with every step. She did not want to fall on the tile. Maybe she *should* have had Dr. Testi bring back some crutches. Her mind answered that thought instantly.
No.
The last thing she wanted was to see that creep again.
Somehow, she managed to limp her way across the foyer, avoid falling and get to the door before the doorbell rang a third time. When she opened it, she was expecting to see an older man in a suit. Or maybe the cop again.

But it was neither.

A young guy with curly, tousled dark hair and a lopsided grin stood just outside, holding a box that looked as if it threatened his balance. He had a dark complexion but a light in his eyes that made her instantly warm to him.

"Hi," she said.

"Hey," he answered. "My name's Anthony, from Capaldi's. I've got your groceries here. Is Ingrid around?"

"Um, no, I haven't seen her all morning."

"Crap," he said. "I'm a bit early, but I figured she'd be around. She always is."

Allyson thought the same thing but said nothing. The housekeeper had been oddly absent today.

"What does she normally do when you come?" she asked. "Maybe I can help?"

Anthony grinned. "You're the new girl, aren't you?"

"Yeah, I guess so."

"Ingrid mentioned you."

Allyson wondered what the housekeeper had said exactly. Probably something like, "We have a new ingrate staying with us from London."

"I hope she said good things," Allyson said, not believing for a moment that she had. "Just tell me what you need."

"I just need to take this stuff to the kitchen, honestly," he said. "Your stuff's all on account, so if you can sign that I delivered it, I'll be good."

"Easy enough," she said. "Do you know the way? I hurt my ankle yesterday and can't walk very well."

"I got this," he said and flashed her a grin as he took that as his cue to enter. "You stay right here, and I'll be back in a flash."

Allyson still had her hand on the doorknob as he took off down the tile and disappeared into the dining room. She hoped Ingrid wouldn't be mad that she let the boy into the house, but he had clearly been here before and knew the way. He hadn't hesitated at all.

"All right, that's trip number one," a cheerful voice announced. A second later, an empty-handed grocery boy emerged from the dining room. "But there's plenty more to come."

Allyson smiled as he walked past her and out to an SUV sitting just outside. He disappeared to the back and returned almost instantly with another armload of a box.

"I'm sorry I can't really help," she said.

"No worries," he said. "This part is my job. It's why I get paid."

Anthony smiled and wound his way past her and back through the dining room to the kitchen again. She admired the flex of his thighs as he moved. He wore white shorts and a loose buttoned shirt covered in green floral patterns. The shorts only emphasized his olive complexion. She thought maybe he was Greek, given his jet-black hair. If not, he'd clearly spent a lot of time outside this summer.

When he returned, Allyson saw that his face was flushed. He had sweat beading on his forehead.

"Take your time," she said. "It's not a race."

"Well, that's where you're wrong." He grinned. "I've got five other orders to deliver before noon. I need to kick it."

"Well don't kill yourself in the process," she said.

He was stepping over the threshold but only took another step before he turned and said, "Thank you. Most people don't really care about the person or the process, they just want their stuff as fast as possible, you know?"

"Everyone's in a hurry all the time."

"Ain't that the truth," he said. "I've got just one more load and then I can hurry out of your hair."

She stood there and watched him as he rummaged around in the back of his old silver hatchback to retrieve another box. His smile was bright and white as he reapproached her.

"Is it you that ordered the milk chocolate bars?" he asked. "The Bergers aren't a big sweets house."

Allyson shrugged. "Not me," she said. "But I'll happily take them."

She made to reach into the box he carried but he instantly jerked it to the other side, out of her grasp.

"Nuh-uh," he said. "All groceries must be delivered to the mistress of the house. Otherwise, I don't get paid."

"What if I follow you and manage to scavenge them myself?"

"I am sworn to protect the groceries!" he insisted and darted ahead of her.

Allyson forgot herself in the moment and began to hurry after him. That was a mistake, because there were two steps down from the foyer into the sitting room. Somehow her ankle held for the first one, but when she stepped down on the main floor, something angry and hot shot up her leg and she yelped in pain. She pulled her leg up immediately, but that only sent the rest of her toppling to the ground.

She couldn't help but let out a shriek as she fell, slapping her rump and shoulder to the tile and rolling before pulling her leg back and grabbing at the lower end to massage the immediate pain away.

"Oh my God," Anthony said. He set the grocery box on the floor just outside of the dining room entryway and hurried back to help her. "What happened?"

He knelt down next to her and put his hand on her shoulder, trying to support her back as she gripped at her leg.

"Stupid happened," she said. "I twisted my ankle yesterday and shouldn't have been trying to follow you."

"Yeah, not a good look to kiss the tile before noon," he said. "Are you sure you haven't been sipping your uncle's J&B?"

Allyson didn't even think about it; she slapped him on the shoulder in response. "I'm not a drunk, I hurt my ankle," she said.

Anthony pulled back and rubbed his shoulder with a lopsided grin. "Just because you can't walk doesn't mean you should make me unable to lift boxes. Easy there, girl."

She had to smile at the exaggerated way he rubbed his shoulder. "Sorry," she said.

"If you put me out of commission, I won't be able to help you up and over to the couch," he said.

"How do you know I wanted to go to the couch?"

"Well, it looks like that's where your book and orange juice are," he said, pointing to her things. "And I'm assuming you don't want to go to my car right now."

"No, why would I want to do that?" she asked, as he slipped his arm around her back and slowly pulled her up off the ground.

"Well, to go see a movie," he said. "Maybe get out of this house. But there's nothing playing until tonight."

"Oh," she said. Her tongue suddenly tied and she wasn't sure quite what to say. Then it occurred to her that she had to go with her uncle to the police station later and didn't know when she'd be back. "I don't think I can tonight," she finally said.

"Well then, tomorrow?" he pushed. As he said it, his arm tightened around her shoulders and back. Supporting her. Or...embracing her? The motion seemed suspect but...she had to admit she didn't mind. His arm was strong. She leaned in and let him half carry her across the room to the couch.

"I don't think I have anything..." she began.

"Then that's settled," he said. When they reached the couch, he turned her around and looked into her eyes with a mischievous grin than screamed both humor and hunger. "I can pick you up at six tomorrow. Seven if you already have dinner plans."

"Six is good," Allyson said. She realized her heart was pounding so hard, she wondered if he could hear it.

"All right, then," he said. He put both of his hands familiarly on her waist and helped ease her down to the couch cushion. "I think you better stay put here for a while."

"Yeah," she agreed. "I just hope I can walk better tomorrow night."

"No worries," he said. "If I need to carry you and the popcorn, I'm good with that."

She smiled and felt a blush creeping up her neck. "Just make sure you don't drop the popcorn," she warned.

Anthony laughed. "I'm glad Ingrid was busy today," he said. "Sadly, I have several other deliveries I have to make so…we're going to have to continue our conversation tomorrow. At six."

"Deal," Allyson said softly. He looked her up and down with a smile and then walked across the foyer to retrieve his box. He disappeared with it into the dining room, returning empty-handed a few seconds later.

"I almost forgot," he said, hurrying back across the foyer. He reached into his pocket to pull out a rumpled grocery receipt. "Can you sign for this?"

Allyson nodded and took the paper and the pen he offered, and then scrawled a loopy A and an unintelligible slash meant to represent l-l-y-s-o-n on the line at the bottom. When he took it back from her, he looked at it and grinned.

"I like your signature."

"Why, because it's unreadable?"

He laughed. "Tell Ingrid I was here?" he asked.

When she nodded, he added, "I will see you tomorrow."

"At six," Allyson answered.. A moment later, he disappeared with a wave out the front door.

"What just happened?" Allyson whispered to a room that suddenly felt very empty.

CHAPTER TWENTY-SIX

Berger Mansion, June 14, 10:56 a.m.

Ella bent to pick her panties off the floor. A sheaf of rolled-up papers promptly slapped against the creamy curve of her bare ass.

"Hey!" she yelped, jumping forward and almost missing the panty scoop in the process.

"You work better without those," a male voice said.

"Maybe so," she said, dodging out of reach and then arrowing one long leg into the hole of the sheer pink silk. She liked these because when she pulled them up, they clung just right and it took no imagination to see the dark triangle of her bush beneath. "But you know if I don't get some of those papers filed – without water stains – I will be in big trouble tonight."

"That's your problem, really," the man said.

"You're an ass."

"You have a great ass," he answered. "So, I guess we're two of a kind."

"Do you want to talk about the 250,000 euros?"

"Do you want to get tied up and left in a wooden box in old man Klosbier's barn as it burns to the ground?"

She shot her persecutor a deadly glare and then reached down to scoop up her equally sheer pink bra. Shrugged it on.

"I guess there are some things I don't need to know."

"You *can* learn." His voice dripped sarcasm.

Ella nearly tripped when the slap stung her now-pantied ass once more.

"I'm glad," the man said. "Because I have to admit I like having you around. And you know too much already about my affairs. I need to know my secrets are safe. If I ever found out that you were violating the trust we have. Well…I'd hate to see you get burned."

Ella swallowed, and faced away from him as she buckled the clasp. "I'm here to serve you," she said. "Night and day."

"Yes," he said. "But what about dawn and dusk?"

CHAPTER TWENTY-SEVEN

Berger Mansion, June 14, 11:03 a.m.

"Still a couch potato, eh?" a voice said from behind her.

Allyson craned her head around and saw Ingrid descending the last two stairs. "Can't do much else," she griped.

"Hmm," the housekeeper said, as if in disapproval but not providing any suggestions for what Allyson *should* be doing while she couldn't walk. Most likely because she had none, but couldn't admit that. Ingrid walked past her and strode up the steps to the front door. She opened it briefly to peer outside.

"The boy from the grocery store was here," Allyson offered.

"What?" Ingrid exclaimed, turning in surprise. "Why didn't you call for me?"

"I mean..." Allyson began, wondering if she was really supposed to have screamed Ingrid's name in the foyer until she got an answer.

"Never mind," Ingrid said, seemingly flustered now. "I just hope he put everything away. I don't need anything spoiling."

The housekeeper shut the front door and moved with driven purpose down the two steps and across the foyer to disappear into the dining room on her way to the kitchen.

For Anthony's sake, Allyson hoped he'd put everything in the right places.

★ ★ ★

Allyson had barely returned to her book when the doorbell rang again. She rolled her eyes and put the bookmark back in. At this rate, she was only going to get through one page of her book per hour today. The house had not had this many visitors in one morning the entire time she'd been here.

"I'll get it." Ingrid's voice preceded her. A second later the housekeeper came striding fast out of the dining room. As she took the two steps up to the door, Allyson noticed that a long strand of black hair had escaped her normally pristine bun in the back. She'd apparently been in a hurry when she pulled that coiffure together this morning.

"And how are you this morning, lovely Ingrid?"

Allyson froze at the rich German voice. It raised hackles on her neck. And then that face appeared. Thin and birdlike. A shock of disheveled white hair and a gaze that seemed to disrobe her even as he greeted her.

"Good morning, young Allyson," Dr. Testi called across the room. "How is our Judas ankle this morning?"

He looked very much the formal doctor in dark slacks and a gray jacket. A garish pink handkerchief poked out of his breast pocket. His blue-striped shirt was locked up by a thin gray tie.

"It's a little better," she said, slipping her legs off the cushions and preparing to get up.

"Good, good." He motioned with his hands for her to stay put. A second later, he was crouching down on one knee in front of her. Ingrid remained nearby, watching.

His eyes bore into Allyson's as if he could hold her hostage with the demand of his attention. "You iced it frequently last night, yes?"

She nodded.

"Well, then, let's feel."

And then his long, cool hands were kneading their way across her ankle and calf. Her skin goose-bumped at his touch. When his hand reached the underside of her knee and seemed inclined to keep moving up, ridiculously far from her injury, she shifted, pulling away. The doctor smiled faintly and brought his fingers back down.

"It is bruised, for sure," he said, as his hand continued to stroke up and back again. Then he began to press with his fingers in one spot after the other, gradually narrowing in on the ankle.

"Tell me if anything hurts greatly."

He applied pressure all around her black and blue flesh. She drew a sharp breath a couple times, but only made noise when he pressed right on the center.

"And you were able to get down the stairs okay?" he asked.

She nodded.

"Have you been back up since breakfast?"

"No," she said. "I didn't want to stress it out."

"Good," he said. "A couple days of resting it and you should be good as new."

The doctor put both of his hands on her leg then, one on either side, and slowly ran them up her calf, putting gentle pressure on her flesh. Again, his fingers traveled beyond her knee to knead her thigh. They went even farther than before. If they got much higher, they'd be under her loose shorts and pinching at her panties. The thought made her shiver. And not in anticipation. In disgust.

"I'm all good," she said, shimmying away from his touch to smash her back harder against the cushions. "I don't think you need to check on me anymore. I'll be fine."

The doctor's face crinkled in secret humor. "I am always checking on my patients," he said. "Your well-being is my life."

His hands lingered a moment longer, stroking the inside of her thigh before finally withdrawing.

"Ingrid," he said. The housekeeper still stood nearby with her arms folded. "Fetch our girl some more ice. While she's sitting down here, she might as well continue to keep the swelling down. She'll be better tomorrow if we keep that ankle cool."

"Certainly," the housekeeper said. "Is there anything else?"

"Is Otto around? I'd like to speak to him if so."

She nodded and pointed down the hall. "In his office, I believe. Best knock, though. Ella might be in there."

"Just Ella, hmm?" he asked and then, with a strange laugh, looked back at Allyson. "I want you to have Ingrid phone me if you have any discomfort. For today, though, do try to stay off it and keep it on ice now and then. Take some ibuprofen and get a good night's sleep. I look forward to seeing you up and about. Those legs should be strutting, not aching."

Somehow, she thought she knew what his vision of strutting was, and she did not intend to ever do that. And it bothered her that this doctor saw her as an object who would. If she did any strutting for him, it would be to plant two high heels on his chest for being such a dick.

Instead of voicing that, she nodded and held her tongue.

Dr. Testi flashed her a grin that only made her more uneasy.

"'Til we meet again," he said and walked past her down the hall to her uncle's office.

Allyson prayed that she'd never meet him again.

Ingrid returned from the kitchen with a towel twisted in a knot to hold some ice cubes inside. She offered it to Allyson without comment, and as soon as she took it, Ingrid turned away and disappeared again.

The housekeeper did *not* like her for some reason.

Whatever.

She didn't want to see Ingrid or the doctor again today. So, after touching the ice to her ankle for a minute or two, she slid her feet to the floor and eased herself up. She was not going to be here when Dr. Testi came back. Her ankle twinged when she picked up the ice and her book and began to hobble toward the stairs, but it got easier with every step. Maybe she just needed to walk on it a little more instead of lying on the couch and letting it swell. Regardless, she was getting out of the line of fire until she had to drive downtown with Otto.

At least that's what she thought.

But as she reached the base of the stairs, she was faced with a new challenge.

Martin.

His face lit up when he saw her.

Allyson's stomach sank.

"Well, well, well," he said, hurrying down the steps. "If it isn't our little gimp."

He reached her before she'd ascended two steps.

"I thought you were staying put for the day," he said, putting his hands on her shoulders.

"I just want to go back to my room for a couple hours," she said, and moved to the next step to pass him.

"Let me help you," he said, and slipped an arm around her back.

"I'm good," she insisted, trying to shrug him off. That turned out to be a mistake. She put pressure on the bad foot and that sent a pang of pain up her leg, which made her wince and pull her leg up from the step. That only unbalanced her and all of a sudden she was falling backward.

Martin's arm caught her and held her upright.

"I don't think you are," he observed. "Come on."

He gripped her shoulder with a hand that seemed rock hard and guided her slowly up the rest of the steps. When they reached her room, she turned the doorknob and tried to propel herself through the doorway alone. But he did not let go.

"I don't need you taking a spill as soon as I walk away." He held on to her all the way to her bed.

"So, this is where our princess sleeps."

She ignored his wide grin. As she slipped her butt onto the mattress and pulled herself up, he patted the bed and nodded.

"Seems like a perfect spot for a princess and a pea," he said, referencing the old Hans Christian Andersen fable. He slipped a hand under her mattress. "I wonder if you can feel this?"

In fact, she could. He was punching his fist up and down beneath the mattress.

"You'd have to be dead not to," she observed.

"I'm glad to know you're not dead," he said.

"Really?" she said. "I thought you wanted me dead."

"Dead girls are boring," Martin said. "Just ask my dad."

Allyson made a face of shock, and Martin just laughed.

"Don't act all freaky," he said. "You'll understand if you stick around long enough. But my advice to you...."

Martin thought better of whatever he'd been about to say and stopped talking. He stepped away from the bed.

Allyson wondered what his advice was but didn't want to seem eager to ask. She opened her mouth, but held her tongue.

When he reached the door, he stopped and looked back. "Lock your door," he said.

And then he was gone.

CHAPTER TWENTY-EIGHT

Berger Mansion, June 14, 4:54 p.m.

"I'm very sorry you've had to experience this in your first few days with us," Otto said. "Normally things at Berger Mansion are pretty quiet. Just ask Martin. He's bored stiff usually. For me, it's a respite. I'm often in the midst of business and political meetings and to come back home to a place in the country where everything is quiet and easily controlled is...refreshing. But I could see how it might be boring for a young person."

Otto was driving them home from the police station. They had both given statements and Allyson had felt only a little uncomfortable talking about her time with Wilhelm Schmitt and the strange aftermath of the chase. She'd really seen nothing that would help identify the man who chased her so...she wasn't sure what good her statement was really. But she told her story and then waited for them to release Otto from whatever interrogation he was undergoing. And then they had walked down the uneven cobblestone streets of Hildegard to where the car was parked outside of an old pharmacy to drive home across the empty country roads.

"It has been an experience," she said, giving up very little. It had been more than an experience. The past two weeks had been a living hell for her, if she was honest.

"I just want you to know that things are not normally so difficult here," he said. "It will all calm down and I hope you'll enjoy being a part of our Berger family."

"I'm sure I will," she answered, not feeling that way in the slightest. She didn't think Germany would ever feel like home. And as soon as she could, she wanted to find a way to go back to England. But that wasn't going to happen anytime soon. So, she needed to find her way with Uncle Otto until she could.

The car was silent for a few kilometers. Allyson watched the landscape blur by. The roads in the country were calming; she felt like she might be asleep at this rate before they reached home. But then Otto made the strains of sleep slip away.

"So, what did you tell them?" he asked.

She stopped staring out the window and saw a serious, perhaps worried, expression on her uncle's face.

"The same thing I told you last night," she said. "About how the guy chased me."

"Did you describe him for them?" he asked. "Maybe tell them something identifiable so they can track him down?"

She shook her head. "No, like I told you, I couldn't really see his face."

He grunted, turning his attention back to the road. But then he asked, "What about Wilhelm? Did you talk about the paperwork you signed? I know it's not my business but, what was it, anyway?"

Allyson cringed. She'd avoided telling him any real details about what Mr. Schmitt had wanted to go over with her.

"Well, it kind of *is* your business," she said. "He told me that my mom was basically a half-owner in your company and the estate with my aunt, but that she'd never taken advantage of that."

"No, she didn't," he said. "She didn't want to be involved, so Ellen and I managed and built the company into what it is today. She would really have no claim to it any longer."

Allyson didn't say anything to that.

"What was it that you had to sign?"

"Just some papers that said I had been told about all of this and that I understand that I would have a claim to the company once I reached legal age if I continued to live in Germany. He said it was part of his duty to ensure I was informed."

"Did he now?" Otto said. "I wish he had spoken to me first. At this point, I don't believe that your mother *would* still have any stake in the company we built. Perhaps there would be a token payout if she had come back to live in Germany as your grandfather's terms stipulated, but we've turned the company around and spent two decades expanding since she left here. With every year she was not contributing, her right diminished." He paused a minute and then asked, "Tell me, are you interested, then, in learning about the business?"

He stared at her intently, barely glancing at the road. It made Allyson extremely nervous.

"No," she said quickly. "Not at all."

"Well then, perhaps we can look at things again when you are of age, if you are still here at that point and see if there is an appropriate payout that can be made. Something to give you a nest egg to start life on your own. I will have to find a new solicitor to handle my affairs now that Wilhelm is gone and I'll make sure that he reviews the situation carefully."

"I...didn't mean to cause any problem," Allyson said. "You were very kind to take me in like you did. I only went to talk to Mr. Schmitt because he called."

Otto shook his head and stared straight ahead, focused on the road.

"I understand," he said. "Don't worry, you will be taken care of."

Somehow, the way he said those words did not bring her any comfort.

CHAPTER TWENTY-NINE

Berger Mansion, June 15, 5:59 p.m.

"Well, you're looking much better," Anthony said when Allyson opened the door. She'd been waiting in the foyer, anticipating his arrival for half an hour. That meant she could answer it before Ingrid intercepted her date.

Anthony stood on the stone pavement outside with a wide grin on his face. He wore dark jeans with black shoes and a deep blue button-down shirt. In his right hand, he held a single red rose.

"Are you saying I looked like crap yesterday?" Allyson asked, putting her hands on her waist in feigned offense.

He laughed. "No, but I thought I might have to carry you to the car tonight with your ankle."

She raised an eyebrow. "Who's to say you won't?"

"Touché," he said, and held out his hand. "Here, this is for you."

Allyson accepted the rose and felt the skin of her cheeks warm. "Thank you," she said. "Do you want to come inside for a minute?"

"Who's there?" a voice called from just behind her. Allyson turned to see Ingrid standing at the foot of the steps. The housekeeper looked annoyed. She probably didn't like it that Allyson had touched the doorknob ahead of her. A second later, annoyance turned to confusion when Anthony stepped into the room.

"It's Saturday," Ingrid said. "I didn't call for any—"

He shook his head. "It's my day off. I'm not delivering anything today, Ingrid. I'm picking up."

"Anthony's taking me to dinner." Allyson smiled. Then, taking advantage of Ingrid's unease, she held out the rose to the housekeeper. "Would you mind putting this in water for me while I get my purse?"

Ingrid accepted the rose but shot a dirty look at Anthony before she began to walk back to the kitchen. "Don't be late," she called over her shoulder. "Nobody may be up to let you in."

Allyson stifled a smile. She had a sudden vision of coming home late after a banger of a night and pounding on the door at two a.m. with her blouse unbuttoned, hair disheveled, and lipstick smeared. When Ingrid appeared in her nightdress with a face full of disapproval, Allyson would grin and tell her that she had had the best night ever before staggering drunkenly up the stairs.

That would certainly set the tongues of the house a-wagging.

"Careful," Anthony warned, as she felt a bit of a twinge and her walk to the couch turned into an awkward limp. Allyson sat down, slipped her feet into her most comfortable pair of shoes and then accepted Anthony's arm to stand upright again.

"It's a lot better than yesterday, but I may take you up on being carried," she joked.

He answered by slipping a strong arm around her back and reaching down to put his other behind her knees. As he started to lift her off the ground, she pounded at his back.

"No, no, I was kidding," she complained, but she was also laughing so hard the words barely came out.

Anthony ignored her protests and whisked her across the tile and up the stairs to the door. But before they could leave, Ingrid reappeared from where she'd no doubt been lurking in the dining room.

"What's going on out here?"

Anthony looked down and met Allyson's gaze with exaggerated, 'oh no, we're caught' eyes. She grinned and widened her eyes back.

"Sorry, Ingrid," Anthony said. "I'm just making my pickup, like I said. Won't bother you anymore."

He turned his body to try to grab the doorknob while still holding Allyson in his arms, but she reached out and twisted it for him.

"Teamwork," she said softly.

"Go team," he answered, and lofted her over the threshold and out into the warm breeze of a perfect summer evening.

★ ★ ★

"I think Ingrid was pissed," he said, as they wound down the country roads back to Hildegard.

"I think Ingrid's always pissed," Allyson answered. "Have you known her long?"

"A few months. I started the delivery shift at the grocery after New Year's because I needed to pick up some easy cash. Turns out… it really is easy cash, so I just kept doing it on the side."

"On the side of what?"

"I'm going to film school at Tovoli Academy."

"You want to make movies?" she asked. "That's so cool."

He shrugged. "I have always loved the camera. It would be good to be able to make a living with it, you know?"

"I don't know what I want to do," Allyson said. "But I know I don't want to just sit on my butt at Berger Mansion for very long."

Anthony shot her a sidelong glance before agreeing. "Yeah, the big old Berger estate is more the place you go to end your life, not start it."

"What do you mean?"

"I don't know…just…that it's a big, mostly empty place in the middle of nowhere. Not exactly the heart of things, right? Aren't you from London?"

"Yeah," she said. "How did you know? Was it the accent?"

He laughed. "That. And people talk. We don't get a lot of big-city girls around here. Munich's a hike and I don't know that anyone from the UK has been here in a long, long time. Hildegard's pretty backwater."

"Uncle Otto seems to like it."

Anthony snorted. "Everyone needs a hideout."

"What's he got to hide from?" Allyson asked.

"What doesn't he?" Anthony replied. "I'm sure there are plenty of people here in town that he doesn't want to run into."

"That doesn't sound good."

Anthony wound the car down narrow cobblestone streets and turned left. "Politicians and businessmen always make enemies," he said as he maneuvered the car into a street parking space. "Your uncle's both."

He shoved the gear shift into Park and killed the engine. "Ready for the finest beer cheese soup you have ever slurped?"

"I never slurp," she answered coyly.

"You've never eaten here."

Anthony got out of the car and quickly came around to open the door for her. She was about to do it herself but then realized what he was doing...so she waited. When the door opened, he extended a hand.

"Would you like me to carry you to the pub?" he asked with a stilted formality that was both charming and silly.

She used his hand to pull herself up and out of the car, but then brushed it away when he began to bend down to scoop her up.

"I've got this, thanks."

Anthony laughed and held out his arm instead. "At least let me make sure you don't embarrass us both by falling at the feet of the doorman or hostess."

"Deal," she said, and slipped her arm through the crook of his. His skin felt warm and smooth where her fingers rested. She tried to will away the butterflies that thought gave her, but her whole body felt fluttery at the moment. Maybe it was good that he was encouraging her to lean on him a bit. The funny thing was, it wasn't her ankle that was threatening to turn to pudding.

They walked down the street past a couple of small shops until they reached a sprawling pub on the corner. The building dominated the area with its four-story-tall A-frame roof and its whitewashed walls crisscrossed by dark wooden slats and window frames bordered by fairy-tale shutters. *Bertel Haus* was written in cursive wooden lettering above the lower-floor windows. People sat on a large patio area around the corner, but Anthony led them through the old wooden doors.

Inside, it felt as if they had stepped back to the nineteenth century. A dozen or more wide, flared glass lights that glowed a dull yellow to paint the space in cozy shadows hung from the ceiling. The walls were papered in some kind of faded red and cream swirling design, but you could barely tell. Every square centimeter was overlaid with framed black-and-white portraits, mirrors, Guinness and König and Löwenbräu brewery signs. There was a grandfather-style wooden pendulum wall clock and a long shelf that stretched from one end of the room to the other that held a wide array of bric-a-brac, from statuettes to glass steins to a manual typewriter. There were three different sitting areas that surrounded the bar, and old polished wooden railings cordoned them off from each other. Between the rails and the well-decorated walls were a series of round and square wooden tables, most of which were filled with groups engaged in animated conversations. If they weren't talking, they were tilting back large steins of golden beer.

This was absolutely a classic German beer hall. But Anthony had promised that it was more than that. He scouted them a table near one of the ornate railings and held a chair out for Allyson before holding her arm and easing her into it.

"I hurt my ankle," she complained. "I'm not a grandma."

"I wouldn't have brought you here if you were a grandma," he quipped, taking his seat.

"So, you've got something against older women?"

He shook his head. "I didn't say that. But I'm pretty sure I prefer you to them."

That brought a flush of heat to her cheeks. Allyson turned her face from him to study the plastic-sheathed single-page menu that was propped on the table next to the salt and pepper shakers. Before she could actually start to read it, a peppy voice broke the bar buzz right next to their table.

"What can I get you?"

A bosomy brunette with a barbed-wire heart tattoo on her shoulder and a dark skirt that flared dangerously high stood there smiling, notepad out and a pen at the ready. "Forgive the paper," she said when she saw Allyson notice it. "I'd rather get your order right the first time. My memory sucks." She flashed a disarming smile again. "Can I start you with something to drink?"

"I'm not sure yet…" Allyson began. But then Anthony leapt in.

"Can we each get a pint of the Bertel Märzen," he said. "And two bowls of the beer cheese soup to start?"

"What is it with German guys insisting on ordering my beer for me?" Allyson asked when the waitress finished scribbling their order onto her pad and walked away.

Anthony looked injured. "Just trying to make sure you get the best." He waved his arm at the crowded bar and tables around them. "This place is known for certain things – and with good reason. I wanted to make sure you tried them. Hildegard may be backward, but it has its charms."

"Oh, now you're singing its praises?" Her mouth crinkled in amusement. "A little while ago you were talking about how this place is too backwater for a big-city girl like me."

Now it was his turn to be amused. "All true, but I hope you'll find enough of interest here that you stick around awhile. So, it's incumbent on me to make sure you see those things."

He wanted her to stick around?

The waitress reappeared and slipped two golden mugs onto the table in front of them. "Soup will be right up," she said and disappeared.

Anthony lifted his mug and held it out across the table, ready to clink and toast. She accommodated and tapped his glass.

"This is one beer you will want to come back for," he promised.

She brought the glass to her lips and took a tentative sip. She hadn't drunk a lot at home, and when she did, it was rarely beer. But, as the liquid trickled a cool tingle down the back of her throat, she realized that this one was pretty good. Before answering him, she took a bigger gulp and savored the feeling as it went down.

"I was right," he gloated.

She licked a trace of foam off her upper lip.

"It's not bad," she teased.

"Liar. You love it."

She raised an eyebrow and drained a quarter of the glass before setting it down with a heavy "ahhhh."

"Careful," he warned. "Or we'll be back to the 'me carrying you' business again."

"Would that be so bad?"

His face brightened, but before he could answer, the waitress returned with their soup and a loaf of fresh bread.

If the beer was good, the beer cheese soup was exceptional. The table grew quiet for a few minutes while both of them made short work of the hot soup along with the help of some homemade – and still steaming – bread. Allyson took a deep breath to savor the yeasty scent as he cut them each a thick slice.

Anthony quizzed her on life in England while they waited for his other must-try recommendation – the currywurst. She told him about the hustle and bustle of a rarely sleeping city and the tiny apartments and budget nights out to see free bands in the park or second-run movies at the theater that went hand-in-hand with a low-income, one-parent family. Once the main course came, however, she turned the tables on him.

"Your turn! Tell me what's it like growing up in the hinterlands," she asked. "Tell me why I should love it in Hildegard, aside from this crazy-good sausage."

He smiled. "I knew you'd like it."

Anthony looked thoughtful for a minute. "Look, there are good things to living here, don't get me wrong. People are usually pretty friendly and most people know each other…or at least have mutual acquaintances. So that's comforting at times. But it's also stifling. I think sometimes you can feel more trapped in an endless field of corn or wheat than in the middle of a crowded city where you're surrounded by towering buildings and pushy throngs of people. I've dreamed about getting out of here and moving to Munich or Berlin or, yeah, even Paris or London, all my life. But I'll never do that tending bar or running orders at a grocery store, or working a farm, like so many out here end up doing. I want to be in the middle of it, you know?"

"I get it," Allyson answered. "I think maybe the answer is that you need a little of both. I mean...look at my uncle. He's involved in the national political scene and runs a big business, so he's around people in busy places all the time. But he says he likes to have his home off the beaten path so he can have some peace and be away from it all sometimes."

Anthony chewed his sausage slowly instead of answering her immediately. He met her eyes, and looked as if he was poised to say something...but then took another bite instead. Maybe he was savoring his currywurst. Or maybe he was intentionally staying silent.

After a bit, he tilted his head back, scanning the bar around them before looking back at her. "If you ask me, your uncle has a place in the country so he can get away with murder and not have anyone notice."

Allyson's mouth dropped in shock. "What are you saying?"

"I don't want to freak you out or anything, but I gotta say, there've been a lot of bad things that have happened at the Berger Mansion over the years. Hell, you know about one – the gardener there was just murdered."

"That happened here in Hildegard though," Allyson said. "Not at the mansion."

"Convenient," Anthony said, watching her reaction.

"You're not saying Uncle Otto actually had him killed?"

Anthony shook his head and spooned a healthy dollop of mashed potatoes into his mouth before finally answering. "No, probably not. But I also doubt that it wasn't *related* to your uncle, somehow."

"Why would you say that?"

Anthony paused his chewing and looked at her closely. "You know that they discovered a casket buried under a tree at the Berger Mansion not that long ago?"

"Yeah," she said. "I had just arrived the night it happened."

"Well, all I'm saying is that there are skeletons buried at the Berger Mansion. And the proof is right there. They just found one."

"Actually, they didn't," Allyson said. "There weren't any bones in the little casket."

"And don't you think that's suspicious all by itself?"

"No," she said. "Who knows why someone put a little mini-casket under a tree twenty years ago."

"I bet Otto does," Anthony said.

"He seemed genuinely surprised that night," Allyson said. "He's been really nice to me so, I don't know, I just don't see him being like, a 'bad' guy somehow."

"Of course not," he answered. "If the bad guys were obvious, we'd be able to catch them all easy, right?"

"You *are* jaded, aren't you?"

"Look, I bet if we rooted around in the old rooms or up in the attic of Berger Mansion, we'd find all sorts of interesting things. Possibly incriminating things. Maybe we'd even find those missing bones."

"I do *not* think there are bones in the house." Allyson laughed. "I think you've watched too many horror movies."

"And you, maybe not enough detective films."

Allyson chewed for a minute, using the food as an excuse to think. Could her uncle really be involved in bad things? He *was* a politician. One thing she'd learned watching the news is you could almost never trust them all the way.

"And what are we going to do if Ingrid finds us snooping?" she asked. "You'll be out of a job."

"You'll think of something to tell her. Maybe you were looking for a place to put your luggage?"

"That's ridiculous." But then as she took another sip of the Märzen, the idea suddenly sounded a little enticing. Skulking around with Anthony sounded like a lot of fun, actually. Even if they were supposedly doing it to find bones. Or something awful.

"I have wanted to explore the mansion a little," she admitted. "Ingrid didn't show me much when I arrived. She just told me not to go in some rooms because Uncle Otto didn't like people to go there."

"Ha," Anthony said. "Then there's our first stop. He's hiding something, I'm telling you."

"Well, you come over and find a time that Ingrid's not spying on us, and we can take a look," Allyson said.

"What are you doing tomorrow?"

Allyson pursed her lips and made her eyes go wide. "Sneaking around an old mansion?"

"That's my girl," he said. Then he rose from the table. "If you'll excuse me a moment, I need to visit the little boy's room."

"You don't seem like a little boy."

"All men are little boys in their hearts," he said with a grin, and then began to thread his way through the tables to the back of the bar.

Allyson watched him go, noting all of the animated conversations going on around them. But when her eyes reached the back of the hall, where Anthony had disappeared, something made her stop. She frowned, not accepting what she'd just seen.

There were several people standing around talking back there but she knew that she'd seen....

And then she saw him again.

A man in a black jacket and dark pants. And ice-blue eyes. He was lurking just behind a floor-to-ceiling wooden post. He held a stein of beer but appeared to be alone.

He also appeared to be staring right at her.

The hair stood up on the back of Allyson's neck. It was the same guy that she'd seen in Munich. What was he doing here? It couldn't be a coincidence. Why was he following her?

She glanced at the hall where Anthony had disappeared to the bathroom, but didn't see him. A rushed waitress with a busboy close in tow came hustling out, but no Anthony.

She looked back to the pillar and the blue-eyed man....

But he wasn't there.

CHAPTER THIRTY

Hildegard, June 15, 7:12 p.m.

"We need to go," Allyson said when Anthony returned to the table. The jaunty smile on his face disappeared in an instant.

"What's the matter?"

"There's a man here, somewhere. Watching me. I saw him while you were gone."

"Well, I can totally understand why a man would want to look at you, but why is that a reason to leave? My beer is still half full."

"He's following me. I want to get out of here."

Anthony looked briefly confused and then put his hand up. "Back up a little. Tell me what you saw and why you think he's watching you and not just hanging out at the pub?"

Allyson quickly recounted the story of the blue-eyed man who approached her in Munich when Martin had been gone. And of how she spotted him again just a few yards away tonight.

"Are you sure it was him? Lots of guys in Germany have blue eyes, you know. More than lots!"

"I know, I know," she said. "But it was him. I recognized the face, not just the eyes."

Anthony nodded and slowly scanned the bar. The tables all around them were filled with animated groups engaged in myriad conversations, and there were clusters of people standing by the bar, but none in black jackets. And none with ice-blue eyes.

"Look," he said, "I get that you want to get the hell away from him if he's stalking you, but…if we leave now, he'll know for sure you spotted him. It might actually be better if we don't leave, and he's unsure. If he's following you, the last thing he wants is for you to know it. So, let's not let him think that he's spooked you. Do you know what I mean?"

"I do, but…what if we wait until it's dark and then he knocks us over the head when we walk back to the car?"

"Look, he came right up and talked to you in Munich. If he wanted to knock you off, he could have done it easily then."

Before Allyson could answer, their conversation was unexpectedly interrupted.

"Well, well, well, what have we here?" a male voice said from just behind Allyson's ear. "A grocery man and a leg of lamb."

Allyson turned around and glared. "What are you doing here?" she demanded.

"I have just as much right to suck down a good sausage as you do." Martin said. "But I think the one I'm gonna be eating will be a lot tastier than the one you're gonna be eating."

Allyson couldn't help it. She turned around and slugged him in the shoulder.

That only brought a big grin from her antagonist.

"Beating up on your cousin is harsh," Martin said. "My dad might start questioning what kind of scorpion he's taken in when he sees the bruises."

"Will you just get lost?" Allyson hissed.

"Sure," Martin said. "I don't want to get between you and the delivery man." He winked in Anthony's direction and then tapped Allyson on the head before turning away and strolling to the bar.

"Now I *really* want to leave," she said.

"And now it's even more important that you don't," he answered. "You don't want him to think he was successful in running you out, do you?"

Begrudgingly, she shook her head.

"Good, then I'm going to order us another beer." He held out his hand and a moment later their bosomy waitress appeared with her notepad in hand.

"We need to wash that currywurst down," he said. "Can we get more of the Märzen?"

"Easy enough." She disappeared to the bar.

"What the hell is Martin doing here anyway?" Allyson said.

Anthony shrugged. "It is the best place in town so...he probably just decided to come. Not because of you. But he definitely likes to tease you."

"Yeah," she said. "And I'd like to cut out his tongue."

"Tssk, tssk. I think there's been enough cutting in this town of late."

She gave him a glare but the words rang true.

Anthony reached out a hand and gently squeezed her shoulder. "Let's just ignore everyone else and get to know each other more, what do you say?"

Allyson slowly nodded, and then got an playful glint in her eye. "What's your favorite color?"

"Blue."

"What's your favorite band?"

"VNV Nation."

"What's your favorite movie?"

"*The Care Bears Take Manhattan.*"

"Liar. There's no such movie."

"But if there was...."

Allyson laughed.

"Okay, my turn," he said.

"But you didn't answer my film question."

"Would you believe *Suspiria*?"

"Well, at least it's a real movie. It is, right?"

Anthony's eyes widened. "You haven't seen it?"

She shook her head.

"I have a new mission in life," he said. "Okay. What's your favorite sports team?"

"Manchester United."

"Football girl, huh?" He grinned. "Bayern Munich will crush them."

Allyson opened her mouth to protest but he pushed on. "Favorite comfort food?"

"Hmmm...I love a good mash but...honestly...I love a corned beef hash with some jalapeños and a lot of cheese on top."

"A spicy girl, huh?"

Allyson nodded. "Gotta do something to warm you up in the winter."

"A couple of tall dunkels can help with that."

"Curry or some jalapeños are more direct."

Anthony smiled. "Touché. Okay, would you want your vacation to be on a beach or ski slope?"

"Neither. I sunburn too easy and I hate snow. I'd rather be in a dark club listening to some great bands every night for a week. I'd never go outside at all."

Anthony nodded. "Fair. Favorite band?"

Allyson thought a minute, pursing her lips and staring into space. "That's hard. I love VNV Nation too...but I probably listen to The Smiths more."

"The Smiths whine too much," a voice interjected, and they both looked up to see their bosomy waitress standing there, notepad in hand. "More Märzen?"

Both of them looked at their nearly empty glasses and then at each other.

Anthony was still staring directly into her eyes, as he said, "Yes, we'll have another, thanks."

They continued to quiz each other for the next hour, until the bar began to empty out. Allyson didn't want the night to end; her fears of the blue-eyed man and irritation with Martin had been all but forgotten as she pried into Anthony's head and he into hers. The buzz of many beers had long ago overtaken her senses. But when Anthony suggested it was time to leave, she agreed. "I don't want Ingrid to lock me out," she said with a frown.

"Well, you could always stay with me," he offered.

Allyson felt a heat spread across her face, and not from the beer. "I appreciate the offer, but I wouldn't want to get a bad reputation my first month in Hildegard."

He pursed his lips and thought a moment. "Okay, what about your second month?"

She laughed and slapped his shoulder without answering. And then realized she was a little unsteady as they began to thread their way through the still-crowded tables toward the entrance. As they walked, Allyson began to feel uneasy. As if someone was watching her. Suddenly the fuzzy warmth turned to a chill. A chill that made no sense in a bar room heated by a hundred competing conversations. Just before they reached the door, she stopped following Anthony and turned around to stare back at the bar.

Starting at the empty table they'd left, she slowly scanned the room. There was a group of people standing in the back at the edge of the bar, but nobody appeared aware of her at all. People laughed, waved hands in the air, and hunched over tables to tell private stories in low voices.

Silly girl. Jumping at shadows now.

She turned back to follow Anthony...and froze.

The man was right there, just a few yards away. He leaned his back against the end of the bar and stared at her with eyes that glinted ice-blue. There was a faint smile on his face as he did something with his hands. He was turning something, maybe a pint glass, around and around in his fingers.

Then she got a better look. He wasn't holding a beer.

The blue-eyed man was holding what appeared to be...a doll.

Allyson bolted for the door.

CHAPTER THIRTY-ONE

Hildegard, June 15, 10:44 p.m.

"Let me go back in there and find out what he wants," Anthony said. "You can point him out and...."

Allyson shook her head. "No, I don't want to see him again. Plus, I don't want to get you involved in...whatever *this* is."

"I can call the police," he offered.

"And tell them what? That a guy with weird eyes was looking at your date?"

He didn't have an answer for that.

"Just take me home. I want to be far away from here now."

They got in the car, and he quickly pulled out onto the empty street. After the town had fallen behind them, and the dark shadows of rolling fields passed like ghosts beyond their windows, Anthony finally spoke again.

"That guy has something to do with the Berger family," he said. "Mark my words."

"And what if he does?"

"Then we need to figure out what. Unless you are okay with some weirdo stalking you whenever you're outside the Berger Mansion."

"Not really."

"Then it's a date?"

"What do you mean?"

"I think you and I need to do a little digging into your family's past."

"How is that going to tell us why there's a guy following me?"

"Find the skeletons in the closet, and all of the mysteries become clear," he said. "Or maybe I should say, find the missing skeleton from the casket."

The thought made her shiver and hunch back in her seat. "I'm not interested in finding any skeletons."

"I don't want to scare you but...I kind of think you might be in a situation where, if you don't find the skeletons, they're going to find you."

As he said it, the car pulled onto the long, winding road that led to Berger Mansion. And, it occurred to Allyson, it also led to another place.

A private cemetery filled with bones.

CHAPTER THIRTY-TWO

Berger Mansion, June 16, 12:03 a.m.

The wind was picking up. It flipped the hair across his forehead and into his eyes. He tossed it back and stifled a slight shiver. The temperature was dropping. But he hoped that what he was about to see would heat things up a bit. The old man was a kinky, twisted bastard. He'd seen the evidence before.

The photographer crept along the side of the house, careful to stay out of sight of any windows. There was only one window he wanted access to, and it was around the back. He'd been there before. And the reward had been handsome.

He patted his camera at the thought. Like a pet. This lens and this house had brought him a nice stack of euros and should be bringing a lot more. If tonight was like the last time, there should be a small fortune to come. Sometimes a picture was worth more than a thousand words. It could be worth a thousand euros. And euros were much better than words.

The back of the old mansion was dark and he used the light of his phone to guide his steps. The last thing he needed was to bang into some old statue or planter and wake the house. There was only one room that should be awake right now; he had it on good authority, or he wouldn't be skulking around in the dark. But he needed to get into position if he was going to capture the moments that counted.

The moments that paid.

Time was fleeting, unless it was captured on film. Or a digital hard drive, as it were.

He finally reached the back of the house beyond the chimney that rose three stories from the ground. And thank God it did. Because on the far side of the brick structure was a tall trellis that served as a home for grapevines.

It also served as a great way to get a leg up to the second floor.

He sought out a solid grip on the wooden slats and put his feet on two sections that seemed solid and well twined with greenery. And pulled himself higher.

It only took a minute, but he was breathing heavy when he set his feet down on the bedroom balcony above. As much from fear as from exertion. He was petrified of getting caught trying to photograph the dirty politician. But the paycheck was worth the risk. And this wasn't the first time he'd climbed that trellis.

He stepped slowly and carefully across the balcony, taking care not to kick something or be in easy sight of any of the nearby windows. This balcony wrapped around the back side of the house and a couple of the bedrooms had access to it. He was interested in the last one.

He pressed his back against the wall and sidestepped closer and closer to the light beaming from the window. The drapes, he'd learned, were never closed. Great for photos. Dangerous for getting spotted.

When his cheeks pressed against the decorative wooden shutters, he braved a peek inside. Just for a second, and then he pulled back.

A second was all he needed.

The view to the huge four-poster bed was unobscured. And it only took a second for him to process the fact that there was a naked woman trapped on that thick and lofty mattress. Her wrists were chained above her head to the thick, dark wood posts, and her ankles were likewise chained. She looked 'stretched' in all directions.

He hadn't noticed anyone else in the room, however.

Worth a photo or two, but not worth much if he didn't have the old man in the shot. He slid down the wall into a crouch and readied his camera. And then he twisted to put the bed back in view at the most discreet angle and hit the shutter twice.

Click.

Click.

He dropped instantly back to a crouch against the wall, his heart beating hard. He was not a fan of the secret agent stuff. But how could he turn down the money?

The girl on the bed was young (no surprise). And thin (ditto). She had black hair that curled over the bare skin of her shoulder. And a dark but very short triangle between her legs. She trimmed versus shaved. He appreciated that, though he wasn't going to get much time to savor the view. He'd be seen.

Time to get comfortable. He wasn't here to shoot the girl. He was here to get the old lech abusing the girl. And at the moment, the lech was missing. He settled down on his haunches and prepared to wait.

The wind was not going to make that wait comfortable. He shivered as it whipped across his face and neck.

After a few minutes, he risked another glance at the lower right corner of the window. The girl was still in the same place, eyes closed. Alone.

This might take a while.

Luckily, it didn't take as long as he feared.

A couple minutes later he heard a faint yelp from inside the room. And then a female voice crying, "No, please."

This was why he was here.

He twisted and slowly raised himself until the lens of the camera caught the corner of the window.

Click.

Click.

Click.

The lech had arrived. His naked back was covered in a pelt of silver hair. In his hand, he held a short leather whip. Hopefully one of those clicks had captured the man's hand in the air as the biting end of the leather connected with the poor girl's breast.

That had to hurt.

He held his back to the wall and took a few breaths, slow, waiting.

There were noises from within. The girl's voice, begging. The man's deeper voice, cajoling. Just the timbre sounded unkind.

He turned and snuck in another shot. This time he had the unpleasant view of the old man's wide, naked buttocks square in the center of his lens. The smooth white skin of the girl's thigh was trapped beneath him. It was like a scarred and battered whale had launched itself onto…and maybe into…a pretty girl on the beach.

It was disgusting. And the tears that coursed down the girl's cheeks didn't make it any easier to swallow. Some girls liked a little whip and chain action, but she clearly wasn't here because she wanted to be. He shot a few more action scenes, including a few seconds of video, trying to catch a solid profile of the man as he speared the poor fish beneath him.

The scene appalled him. He hoped that these photos ultimately put an end to this abusive asshole. He waited a few minutes, striving to catch one more decent shot before heading down the trellis.

And his patience was rewarded.

There was a shriek from within and he rose up. The man was slapping the girl around now. His palm hit her across the mouth and then the breast. And when she cried out again, he barked something and put his hand down hard on her face. Then he slid his heavy body off the bed and lumbered over to a small table against the wall. He returned with a key, which he used to unlock the chains around the girl's feet. He tossed the key back to the table and picked up what looked like a red rubber superball on a string.

It wasn't a kids toy.

The man gripped the girl's nose until she opened her mouth, and then slid the ball in between her teeth. He tied the string that ran through the center of the ball behind her neck to complete the rubber gag, and then retrieved the whip.

He pushed the girl until she turned over and put her ass in the air, crisscrossing the long chains that bound her wrists until she was hopelessly tight to the front of the bed.

Meanwhile, at the back, he began to flog.

The globes of her perfectly smooth young buttocks quickly grew red with the beating, and shook to and fro as she tried to angle her body away from the whip.

It was a futile exercise, because she couldn't really move much and the man could go anywhere.

Click.

Click.

Click.

And then the man ditched the whip and buried his groin between her thighs.

He wrapped his whole ugly body around hers, and slid his stubbled face against her perfect cheek. She turned away, trying to escape his touch, but could go nowhere. The motion gave him a perfect shot though.

Click.

Her dark eyes bugged out with pain and desperate longing for a savior.

Otto Berger's face, cruel and laughing, stared in the same direction.

They both looked toward the window, with wildly different expressions. A perfect cruel moment captured by his lens.

Click.

CHAPTER THIRTY-THREE

Berger Mansion, June 18, 6:35 a.m.

Otto stepped softly down the steps, taking care not to let his shoes click or clack. He didn't want to alert Ingrid that he was down here. Or Ida for that matter. The two of them were the early risers and he had no desire to discuss where he was going.

He walked through the foyer to the kitchen, and then let himself out the back door. He walked the stone steps around the side of the house and headed down the hill toward the cemetery. As soon as his head disappeared from view, a dark form rose from behind the hedge. Black face mask, black gloves, black boots. Dark as the house before dawn and just as quiet. The figure stole up the back step and opened the kitchen door that Otto had left unlocked. After a quick glance in Otto's direction, it slipped inside and eased the door shut once more.

* * *

Berger Mansion, June 18, 10:23 a.m.

The door chime had not finished ringing when Ingrid called into the front foyer.

"Allyson, could you get the door?"

Allyson set her book down on the couch and eased herself up. The ankle was better, but she could still feel the twinges a little, so she was trying to take it easy. Even so, she made it across the tile before the chime sounded a second time. "I'm on it," she called, lest Ingrid get irritated.

She opened the door and her face lit instantly.

"Well, hello there," Anthony said. His hands were hugging two bags filled with groceries.

"Shopping day again?" she asked.

"For Ingrid. Delivery day for me!"

"Do you want some help?"

"You could take this one," he said, shifting a bag forward. "It's not heavy."

"Are you calling me weak?"

"No. Would you prefer the heavy one?"

"Also no."

"Well, there you go," he said. "I read your mind."

"Nice save."

She led the way to the kitchen but was intercepted by Ingrid, who was toweling off her hands even as she reached for Allyson's bag.

"Thank you," she said. "I didn't think you'd mind answering the door this time."

Allyson heard the undercurrent in the other woman's voice. As if she were calling her 'slut' under her breath. *Whatever.*

Anthony brushed past her to follow Ingrid into the kitchen. And maybe more than brushed. His arm pressed against hers for much longer than it should have taken him to walk by. He caught her eye and raised his eyebrow knowingly before he passed.

Just like that, Allyson was standing alone in the dining room. She got the feeling that Ingrid didn't want her to follow. She began to walk back to the foyer.

Just as she stepped in that room, Anthony bustled past her again. His fingers slid across her shoulder, but he didn't slow. He was up the steps and out the door in a heartbeat.

Allyson followed him outside and saw him loading his arms with more bags from the back of the delivery vehicle.

"Want me to get something?"

"Naw," he said. "Ingrid likes to see me work for my tips."

"Wait, you get tips?"

He winked and bent back inside the SUV.

Maybe Ingrid just enjoyed watching him sweat, Allyson thought. She held the door open for him, but this time didn't try to grab a bag.

"Thanks," he said and continued quickly across the tile.

She stepped outside and took a deep breath of the late-morning air. It smelled summer warm and earthy rich, filled with life and health and the light humidity of a perfect blue-sky day.

"One more trip," Anthony huffed a minute later. He took the steps in a single stride and grabbed two more bags before slamming the back door shut. Then he rushed back in the house.

Allyson just stayed outside waiting.

Eventually, he returned. His forehead was damp with exertion. He flashed her a wide smile and let out a long breath.

"Sorry," he said. "Ingrid likes to get everything in fast. And I've got three more deliveries to make this trip. So...I can't really stay and talk. But, maybe we could have lunch tomorrow? I don't work on Tuesdays usually."

"Sure," she said. "What time?"

"High noon?"

"I'll be here."

"Can't wait," he said, and leaned down to kiss her forehead. "See you then."

And with that, he squeezed her arm briefly, opened the SUV's door and slid inside. A moment later, Allyson was standing alone. She really didn't want to go back in the house...but taking a long walk in the country seemed like a bad idea with her ankle, so grudgingly she stepped back in, closed the world and Anthony outside, and returned to her book.

She hadn't gotten through a page when she suddenly slammed the book shut and jumped to her feet.

Somebody in the house had just screamed.

CHAPTER THIRTY-FOUR

Berger Mansion, June 18, 11:00 a.m.

Allyson moved down the hallway toward Uncle Otto's office, which sounded like where the scream had come from. She hadn't managed twenty steps when Ingrid rushed past her without a word. Martin trailed right behind. By the time Allyson reached the office, both of them had gone inside.

When she turned the corner herself, Allyson found the two of them standing with Ella. The secretary's cheeks were damp and she was kneading her hands nervously, as if she didn't know what to do with them.

"That's fucked up," Martin said.

"Who would do this?" Ella asked.

Allyson moved closer and saw the reason for the commotion.

In the center of Otto's desk, with awful, glazed eyes staring at them all, sat a severed pig's head. A puddle of blood congealed around the ragged flesh of its neck.

"What does it mean?" Allyson asked softly.

"It means someone got into the house," Ingrid said. "We need to check all of the locks." The housekeeper looked hard at Ella. "Do you know where Otto is? I haven't seen him this morning."

Ella shook her head. "He was gone when I woke up. I came down here to find him."

"We should call the police and not disturb anything…but I would like to make sure that's what he wants."

"I'll call him," Martin said. He pulled out his cell phone and hit the speed dial. It rang for a while before Otto apparently picked up.

"Hey, Dad, are you near the house? We've got a situation." He said "yes" a couple times and then clicked off. "He'll be here in a few minutes."

A high-pitched, strangulated cough echoed from somewhere down the hall. And then the cat-scratch gargle came again. Nobody even looked up. Ida had announced her entrance.

"What is the party all about?" she said when she finally entered the now-crowded room.

"Just trying to figure out the best way to cook boar's head for dinner," Martin quipped.

Allyson saw Ingrid stifle a laugh.

"Well, this is a strange place to be doing it," Ida said. "And you need to get that thing off there now. That's going to stain Otto's desk. He won't be happy. Also, it seems very unsanitary."

"He was just joking," Ella said, and explained how she'd discovered the disturbing 'message' someone had left for Otto.

"Well, I don't think it's funny at all," Ida said, poking Martin with one bony finger. Then she went to stare closer at the pig. "Do you think you might roast it, Ingrid? Maybe with a honey glaze?"

"No," the housekeeper exclaimed instantly. "You can't be serious. We don't know where it's been!"

Ida stepped back, nodding slowly, before turning to Martin and poking him again. "Now *that's* funny," she said.

"Aunt Ida, you are bad," he said.

"And I'm old. I'll sit down while we wait for Otto." She shuffled across the room, let out a wheezing cough, and eased herself into a leather chair.

When Otto finally entered the room, he was wearing casual pants and a loose t-shirt. So, he'd clearly not been out at an early morning business meeting.

"What's all the commotion…" he began, but then trailed off on the last word when he saw the porcine stare.

"Someone from your fan club was here," Ida answered.

"Where the hell did that come from?"

"Ella found it," Martin said. "We think someone must have broken into the house."

"I can have the locksmith come to change all of the locks tomorrow," Ingrid offered.

Otto shook his head. "No need, I suspect. I am guessing whoever it was came in the back kitchen door."

"I always lock that," Ingrid said.

"Yeah, but I left it open when I went out for a walk this morning," he said. "Someone must have been waiting."

"But why?" Ingrid said. "And how did they know you'd be going out...or the way to your office?"

"I'd guess it is someone who has been watching me pretty close," he said.

"Otto, I'm frightened," Ella said softly.

He patted her shoulder. "Don't be," he said. "This is a message to me, nothing more."

"Well, what does it mean?" Ella asked.

"That, I'm not completely sure. But I'm sure whoever did this will let us know soon."

"Should we call the police?" Martin asked.

Otto nodded. "I'll call them. I seem to be getting on a first-name basis with the inspector of late. We'll need to leave this here until he can see it, I expect. You can all go about your business for now."

As they began to move toward the hall, Otto took a closer look at the pig. He shook his head, wrinkling his nose in distaste. Then he picked up the phone and began to dial.

★ ★ ★

On the way back to the foyer, Allyson walked next to Martin. "What do you think it means?" she asked.

"I think it means someone thinks my dad is a pig." He paused and pursed his lips. "They're not wrong."

CHAPTER THIRTY-FIVE

Berger Mansion, June 19, 11:44 a.m.

Allyson was already pacing the foyer as if Anthony was late, though he wasn't. Yesterday had been a train wreck with the pig's head and a police officer interviewing everyone about it, though there wasn't much to say – they'd walked into the office and found a decapitated animal head. Breakfast this morning had been uncomfortably quiet. She really wanted to get out of the house.

And apparently, she wasn't the only one. Everyone had scattered after breakfast. Otto said he would be out on business all day and had left in the car. Ingrid said she was going into town and Martin volunteered to go with her. She wasn't sure where Ella had disappeared to, but she'd already checked and Otto's office was empty.

The house was eerily quiet.

When the door chime finally sounded, Allyson practically ran to answer it.

"I am so happy to see you," she said when Anthony's face appeared.

"Well, the feeling is mutual, but you seem a little more animated about it. What's going on?"

"I'll tell you on the way to lunch," she said.

They walked out to Anthony's SUV and drove a kilometer or two down the road while she explained the events of the day before.

"That's kinda creepy," he said. "And it also supports what we were talking about the other night. Something is going on with your uncle. And it's not good."

She shook her head.

"What did they do with the pig's head?"

"Why, do you want to carve it up for pork chops or something? He laughed. "I mean...why waste?"

She grimaced. "They took it away for evidence."

"Maybe the butcher left fingerprints."

Allyson laughed. "Maybe. But.... Let's not talk about pigs anymore. Where are we going for lunch?"

Anthony hesitated and then dodged the question. "You'll see."

He drove them back into downtown Hildegard and pulled up outside of a quaint brown building with white shutters and a wide front window looking out at the street. The sign above the door made Allyson's eyes widen.

"Is this a joke?"

The sign read, *Das Kleine Schweinchen* (*The Little Pig*).

Anthony laughed, a little nervously. "Well, no. This is where I planned to take you...though your pig's head story kind of made me think twice. But this place has the best sausages and pork loin plates in town. I really wanted you to try it."

She frowned but said, "Well, as long as pig's head isn't on the menu...."

"I think they have head cheese but there shouldn't be any pig heads staring at you off a plate."

"Okay."

They entered and a waitress in a tight, white blouse and blue-checked skirt grabbed two menus and escorted them into a wide dining hall. It had a couple dozen long wooden tables. Nearly half of them were full. They were seated near one of the windows, so Allyson could easily look out to the street.

"Are you ordering for me again?" she asked with a grin.

"Can I? Because I'd like you to try the Schwenkbraten sandwich. It's a grilled pork sandwich and you can get fries or mashed potatoes or sauerkraut with it."

"Mashed."

"Good choice."

When the waitress came back, he ordered for both of them, adding mugs of Hofbräuhaus Weisse.

"I think you're gonna like this," he said.

"Well, you called it last time, so I'll trust you."

Allyson thought of the last time she was downtown with him and took a look around the room. There appeared to be no creepy men with bright blue eyes lurking in any corners staring at her. She felt muscles relax that she hadn't known had been tight.

"So, what's your favorite comfort food back home?" Anthony asked. They peppered each other with similar questions until they were suddenly interrupted by the waitress who approached the table with their plates on a wide brown platter.

"Oh my," Allyson said when she looked at the heaping sandwich on her plate. The top bun perched well over a handsbreadth off the table, it was stacked so high with slabs of pork, blackened on the edges from the grill, as well as thick, yellow grilled onions. "I don't think I can get my mouth around that!"

"Give it a good smoosh and you'll be fine," he promised.

She did as he suggested and then cut the sandwich in half with a knife. Somehow, she got her teeth around it and bit down. "Mmmmmm," she moaned as the juice of the pork and onions and whatever they'd dressed the sandwich with hit her tongue. Her entire mouth seemed to ignite with flavor.

"Told you."

Allyson dove into the sandwich but realized early she was not going to finish. She tried the mashed potatoes and they were rich in cream and garlic; another taste explosion! Eventually, she had to push the plate away and give up.

"I'm going to burst," she said.

"It is pretty filling," he agreed. "But also amazing, eh?"

"Yes, thanks for bringing me. But this Little Piggy was not at all little."

"Speaking of piggies.... How are you feeling about yesterday and your uncle?"

"I mean, it's not great, right? We think we know how the person got in but...to think someone was in the mansion while we were sleeping, putting that *thing* there...whew." She shivered.

"You lock your bedroom door at night, yeah?"

"Well, not always, but maybe I'll start."

Anthony nodded. "I would."

After another stein of weisse, Anthony paid the bill and they walked around the downtown area for a while. There were little clothes boutiques, a couple of bars, a jewelry store and at the end of the busy area, a candy shop that sold ice cream as well as chocolates and cookies.

Allyson was too full for ice cream, but bought a box of frosted gingerbread cookies to take home.

"Want to head back to the mansion?" he asked, once they were back on the street again. "You've really seen all there is to see here. And if Ingrid's still gone, maybe you can give me a tour."

"You haven't seen the place?" she asked.

Anthony shook his head. "Front door to the kitchen, that's all I know."

"I can show you around," she agreed. "The place is huge. And I haven't even been allowed to go in half of it. But why don't you want Ingrid to be there when I show you?"

"I don't know. I just get the feeling she doesn't want me inside the house. I'm the delivery boy to her and that's it."

"Well, she better get used to it," Allyson said, and looked up at him with wide eyes.

Anthony slipped an arm around her waist and walked them back to the car.

When they reached the mansion, Otto's and Ingrid's cars were both still missing. Luckily, Allyson had finally been given a key to the front door this week, so she used it for the first time and let them in.

"Hello?" she called as they stepped into the foyer and closed the door. "Anybody home?"

Light from the tall windows sent beams of brilliance across the room, lighting up the couches and floor in long beams of sunshine. But somehow, the place still seemed dark.

It was the emptiness.

Allyson led the way through the dining room to the kitchen, which was empty, as expected. The counters were shiny clean and the sink empty. It could have been the subject of a magazine photoshoot for a model kitchen with the granite counters and classic wood cabinetry.

"Well, this place you know," Allyson said, waving her hands around.

She pointed to a door at the side of the kitchen. "The servants' quarters – and Ingrid's room – is back there, not that I've seen it."

"Wanna take a peek now?" he asked.

"Not really."

She led them back down the first-floor hallway where her uncle's office was, opening a couple doors to peer into before turning the knob on Otto's door.

"Here's where Uncle Otto works a lot," she said, waving at the rich leather and wood furniture and the huge dominating desk.

"The seat of the empire, eh?" Anthony said. He walked around the room, running a finger across the shiny wood of the small bar on the side and staring for a moment out the window to the back gardens. Then he grinned and stepped behind the desk, pulling the big, black leather chair back and plopping into it.

"What are you doing?" Allyson asked, appalled. Her voice was a harsh whisper.

"I'm checking out how the big man lives," Anthony laughed. "Relax, he's not home."

"Still," Allyson said.

Anthony pulled out one of the fancy pens Otto kept in gold metal holders and then feigned searching for something. "Where do I sign?" he asked.

Allyson had to laugh at that, though it still made her nervous to be in here with him.

He put the pen back and wiped his hand across the deep rich wood finish. "Looks like they were able to get rid of the hog before the blood stained," he said. Then he opened the top drawer to his right and looked inside. He set a stapler and a few pads of paper on the desk and reached deep into the back of the drawer.

"Anthony!" she whispered. "Get *out* of there."

"Look," he said, holding up his hand, "apparently if negotiations are going poorly, he just locks people up until they agree with him."

He held a pair of silver handcuffs in the air and Allyson's eyes bugged out of her head. "Put them back!"

"Or maybe he uses them on his secretary when she misbehaves," he said, raising his eyebrows suggestively. "What's her name?"

"Ella. C'mon, let's get out of here."

He nodded and stuffed the cuffs and other things back in the drawer.

"All right, what's next?"

"There are some locked rooms down the hall here, and then the closed-off part of the mansion. But I can show you the game room upstairs."

"What about *your* room?" he said. "Could I see where you live?"

"That's a little forward, don't you think?"

"I've learned if you don't ask, you don't get."

Allyson smiled. "Okay, you get. But it's not that exciting."

She led him back down the hall and up the staircase. And then up to the third floor to show him the game room. He walked around, admiring the different areas.

"This is huge. I would love to hang out here in the winter when you don't want to be outside. So much to do."

She nodded. "It seems like a great retreat. I wonder if anyone uses it besides Martin."

They opened the outer door and headed out to the wrap-around patio. Anthony walked over to the edge and stood at the rail looking out across the gardens below and the slope of the hill beyond. He could see the broken ground where the tree had uprooted from here perfectly. It had been mulched over but it stood out from the garden areas and rich green grass that surrounded the house otherwise.

"Wow, something happened down here," Allyson said, leaning over the rail on the left side of the balcony to look down.

"What's that?" Anthony said, moving closer.

"Something broke the trellis right there," she said. She pointed to a wooden slat that hung down. The ivy that completely enveloped the wooden slats of the trellis was also missing from that spot; vines hung down the wrong way, with their under-leaves facing the sky.

"Looks like a cannonball went through there," Anthony observed.

"Or someone's foot," she said. Just saying that gave her a chill. Who would have climbed up the wall of the house? And why?

She led them back inside, feeling suddenly ill at ease. Maybe the pig-head guy had gotten in through the second floor, not the kitchen as Otto had suggested.

As her stomach digested that idea, she led Anthony back down the stairs to her bedroom door.

"This is it," she said, turning the handle. "Don't get too excited. Because...it's not that exciting. I feel like I'm still staying in someone else's room."

She stepped into the room and Anthony followed her. As soon as he was inside, he gently pushed the door closed behind him. Then he whistled. "This room is larger than my whole apartment."

"It is a little...big," she agreed. "But there you have it. There's my bed and the dresser and a nice view from the window actually. But I don't have a lot of my own stuff set up here yet. I don't even know if I will. I'm kind of like a guest still. Who knows if I'll end up staying here for a long time or not?"

"You shouldn't think like that," he said. "If this is your space for now...make it yours. And who *wouldn't* want this room?"

"I guess," she said, turning to walk back to the door.

"At the moment, there's something I'd like to make mine," he said. He reached out and wrapped both of his arms around her, pulling her close. His eyes were bright as he stared down into hers.

"I…um…" she said.

He didn't wait for her to figure out what she was going to say to cover the moment. He covered her lips with his instead.

She didn't pull away. His tongue slipped past her lips easily; she opened her mouth to him. Allyson had wondered if he would make the first move – had hoped he would, because she didn't want to be too forward, or do it at the wrong time. Anthony seemed like the kind of guy who liked to be in control, and she was okay with that. She wasn't that used to guys paying her any attention at all, if the truth be known.

His fingers slipped down her back and gripped her hips at her beltline. She held his shoulders and slid one hand up the back of his head to caress his neck and press his face tighter to hers. He was warm and smelled good and she wanted to melt into him so badly. Her thighs were hot against his and she groaned faintly when his hands slipped down and massaged her rear.

At the same time….

Allyson didn't want him to think they were just going to 'do it' because he stepped into her room on a second date. She didn't want things to move that fast. After a warm, wet, tongue-teasing moment, she slowly moved her hands from his back to his shoulders, and while she didn't really want to, she eased him back.

"Mmmm," she mouthed, as their lips parted. "Maybe not right now though?"

Anthony nodded. "I hear you. But this is a really soft bed." He pressed his hand to the mattress and pressed down.

"It is," she agreed.

"And it looks like it would hold two."

"It absolutely would," she said, and reached up to grip his cheeks. She drew his lips down and kissed him again, softer this time. And pulled away faster.

"But not today."

"Tomorrow?"

She hugged him but averted her mouth from his. Ramping it down, not up. She'd heard plenty of stories from her girlfriends about relationships that moved too fast. She felt a rush of heat inside that stretched from the erect tips of her chest to her moistening groin, but she was not about to let that take her over. She was not going to make those mistakes.

"Want me to give you the rest of the tour?" she said. Her voice was unintentionally husky.

"Not really the tour I'd like to take but…sure," he said. "I hope you'll invite me back here, though. I could help you decorate."

"I may take you up on that."

Allyson took him by the hand, *God, it's warm*, and led him back out the door into the hallway.

"I can't really give you the tour of these rooms," she said as they walked. "Here's where Martin's bedroom is, and Ida's, and Ella's… and Otto's."

"All the little Bergers, all in a row," Anthony said.

"I guess so."

He pointed at the first door. "So this is where your persecutor lives?"

She rolled her eyes. "Yeah."

He reached out and grabbed at the doorknob.

Allyson, in turn, grabbed his arm. "What are you doing?"

"I want to see what an asshole's room looks like."

Before she could stop him, he'd thrown the door open and stepped inside.

Allyson hadn't been in Martin's room before. It was laid out similarly to hers, but the colors were all masculine; his bedspread was a deep midnight blue and the throw rug on his floor was a similar color, with a gold design etched into the center and corners.

The walls, unlike hers, were decorated with framed posters from bands and films, most of which she didn't recognize. One in particular, though, drew her eye because it was so garish – it was for an Italian film whose title she couldn't read (the title started *Il Tuo Vizio È Una Stanza*…and kept going!). But the center image showed a giant keyhole with a frenzied woman's distorted face stretched out like a carnival fun house mirror. Not far from that, on the same wall, was a pinup calendar with a bosomy blonde who was demonstrating with no uncertainty that she was, in fact, a real blonde.

"Come on," she said. "We shouldn't be in here."

Anthony grinned, and slid into the chair at a small desk where Martin's laptop sat open. "Wanna look at your cousin's browser history?" He laughed, interrupting the laptop's revolving geometric screensaver.

"Absolutely not!"

"Yeah, probably me either." He opened the side drawer but closed it almost immediately, the contents of no apparent interest. Then he pulled out the main desk drawer and slid his hand in. A moment later, he came back with a package of condoms. "Bingo."

"Anthony, stop! I don't want to know. C'mon, we can't get found in here."

He nodded, but bent to look further inside the drawer. He held up a book of matches and a postcard with the logo of a very *adult* nightclub on it. And then he smiled and closed the drawer.

"Please," she said, starting to panic.

"Okay," he said. He stood, slipped one hand into his pocket, and with the other took hers and led her back out to the hall.

"What else can you show me where you won't have a heart attack?"

"Well, seriously? If Martin came back while we were in there? I don't want to think."

She pulled him forward and pointed down the hall.

"If you head that way, there's a door that leads to the other half of the building that they don't let anyone into. Then upstairs, on the third floor near the game room, is the door that leads to the attic."

"Well then, let's go open that one," Anthony said.

"Oh, I don't think we should. Ingrid said not to go up there."

"That's a perfect reason to open the door, then."

"You're a troublemaker."

"You know you want to see what's up there."

She stifled a smile. "I kinda do. I never lived anywhere with an attic."

Anthony took that as his cue and darted back to the third-floor stairway. Allyson couldn't help but follow. When they arrived at the attic door, Anthony took her hand in his and slowly stretched it out until it touched and then grasped the doorknob. Then he twisted her wrist and the door squealed open.

"Oh my," he said with false surprise. "I wonder how that happened. We should check it out and make sure everything inside is okay."

Allyson got into the groove with him. "Maybe we should."

"I love old attics," Anthony said. "You never know what you'll find in them."

"Dust, mainly, I think," Allyson said.

He rolled his eyes. "Sure, but also...old forgotten things. Let's see what the Bergers have been hiding."

Anthony pulled on a string that was latched near the handrail and a bulb lit at the top of the plank steps in front of them. They ascended the steps together, each plank creaking as they did. The floor above was an archive of the past. There were pieces of furniture covered with old spiderwebbed sheets and boxes stacked along the walls. It looked exactly like what Allyson expected really...slanted ceilings that descended onto piles of dusty, forgotten boxes and children's toys and old chairs and electronic equipment. There were bedposts and computers and even an old children's chalkboard that someone had written *Guten Tag* on.

"Doesn't look like a treasure trove or anything," Allyson said.

"Oh, come on," he said. "The hidden jewels aren't going to just be sitting there on a gold platter out in the open! You haven't looked in any of the boxes. And who knows...you might want some of the old pictures over there to decorate your room."

He pointed at a stack of frames piled against one wall. The first one was a black-and-white portrait of a dour-looking woman with a thick bun of hair and a broad collar that appeared to be from the nineteen twenties. Probably the ones behind it were much the same.

Allyson made a face. "I think I'll just leave those up here."

Anthony moved down the wall, picking up odd things that had ended up gathering dust in the storage floor of the mansion. Hairbrushes, small statues of frogs and cows, wine glasses and empty bottles. There was even a stack of forgotten VHS tapes which he rifled through quickly. Mostly dramas and love stories, but he pulled out one that had a woman's face on it, her eyes bugging out in fear, with two hands pulling her mouth wide on either side. Inside her mouth was a skull with equally bugged-out eyeballs. Below the mouth was the film title, *Dead Alive*. It claimed to be 'The goriest fright film of all time'. He grinned and held it up. "Date night movie?"

Allyson saw the cover and laughed. "Looks highbrow. Think you can find a VHS player?"

"I'll keep looking."

In one corner of the room, he found a strange contraption consisting of a rough, unfinished wooden box with electrical leads that emanated from an enclosed area in the center and connected to an array of metal clamps. An old brown plug trailed from the box on the floor that looked dangerous to touch if you were plugging it in. Much of the plug's metal was exposed.

"Looks like a good way to get shock treatment," Anthony said, holding up one of the silver metal clamps.

"Yeah...put it down."

He lifted a sheet and a cloud of dust puffed out into their faces. Allyson sneezed and fanned her hand through the air.

"Blech."

There was a bureau beneath the dusty sheet and he opened the doors to look inside. It was filled with clothing – a man's sweaters and shirts were piled inside.

"Maybe you can find yourself a new wardrobe," she suggested.

He lifted a red-and-blue-checkered shirt and held it in front of him. There were a half dozen holes in the chest area. "No, I think the moths have worn these a little too much."

Anthony tossed it back and closed the door and reset the sheet. They continued to walk along the wall. Allyson hit the keys of an ancient typewriter and Anthony found a BB gun that looked vintage. He aimed it at a mirror that leaned against a pile of boxes.

"Do not even *think* of causing us seven years' bad luck," Allyson said, and pressed the barrel of the gun down.

He dropped it back on the floor and walked a few steps to where there were bundles of magazines and notebooks and file folders stacked on top of a couple of wooden file cabinets.

"Looks like a bit of family history over here," he said, and pulled open one of the file drawers. It was packed tight with folders and papers. "You could probably find out a lot of interesting things about the Berger family here."

"It would take a year to find a needle in that haystack," Allyson said.

He closed the drawer and pulled the overflowing stack of folders resting on top of the cabinets closer.

"How about these?" he asked, picking up a stack of files that did not seem to have nearly the amount of dust on them as the rest of the things up here. "Probably more recent stuff."

Allyson looked at the handwritten labels. They said things like 'Electric, Construction, Medical'.

"I don't really care about Uncle Otto's bills," she said.

He picked up another handful and his face lit up. "These may be a little more interesting. Here's one for someone named Ellen. And Ida. And a bunch here for 'Catherine'."

"What?" Allyson said. "That's my cousin. Or…was my cousin. She died. There's a gravestone in the backyard."

"Nice to keep your family buried close to home."

"Yeah, it's a little creepy but…whatever. Let me see."

He handed over the files and Allyson flipped the tab open. There was a thick stack of papers within, which, from what she could read, seemed to talk a lot about *mental stability* and *baby* and *psychosis*. If she was going to make a word cloud, those would have been in the center.

Allyson leafed through the papers inside the folder. There were school transcripts and art pieces clearly created by a child, along with police records and…medical records. Those were the ones she focused on.

One of them was labeled 'Camino Mental Health Center' in German and she pulled that out to look at. But while she knew some German, she didn't know enough to read some of it. She held the papers out to Anthony and asked him to translate.

He took the papers and looked over the first page before flipping to the next.

"There's a lot of administrative gibberish but the important areas are all about psychiatric issues. The gist seems to be that the girl was admitted to an insane asylum after multiple issues, including a suicide attempt."

"Whoa," Allyson said. "Nobody has ever mentioned that."

"It was a long time ago. The paperwork says she was admitted just before Christmas in 2008." He riffled through the papers some more and said, "There are a series of reports after that talking about a psychiatric condition caused by mental and physical trauma, including, um…rape. The earliest ones called her 'unreachable' while later ones simply stated, 'condition unchanged'. The most recent one was dated 2018 and says, 'Patient remains withdrawn on most days but does interact with others inconsistently.'"

Allyson's eyes widened. Catherine had been alive not that long ago. Maybe was *still* alive!

Then why was there a gravestone outside that said she'd been dead for over fifteen years?

"This is crazy," she whispered.

"What's that?"

"Uncle Otto said Catherine is dead. There's even a gravestone in the cemetery outside for her. But according to those reports, she's been living in a psychiatric hospital since 2008. Or at least, that's where she was five years ago."

"Sounds like your uncle doesn't want anyone to know that she's alive," Anthony said.

"But why? She's sick, that's all."

"It sounds like something horrible happened to her. Maybe he doesn't want anyone to know what that was. Might hurt his business or political career."

"I wonder what. It had to have been pretty bad if it's been covered up all this time."

"I guess you could just ask him about her."

"How would you suggest I do that? He's already told me she's dead. I'd have to tell him I came into the attic and was snooping through his stuff and found proof that she isn't."

"There is another way," he said. He pulled out one of the later reports on Catherine's condition, and then set the folders back where they'd come from.

"What's that?"

"We could pay your sick cousin Catherine a visit."

CHAPTER THIRTY-SIX

Camino Mental Health Center, June 19, 2:55 p.m.

The Camino Mental Health Center was about a forty-minute drive from Hildegard, on the road to Munich. Allyson kept folding and unfolding the paper they'd taken from the attic with the institution's address on it the whole ride.

When they'd exited the attic, there was still nobody home. The hallway and front foyer had been silent.

"I'd love to explore the other half of the house," Anthony had said, gesturing to the door at the far end of the hall.

"Not today. Someone is bound to be home soon," Allyson had replied. "Let's go before anyone gets back and we end up with questions."

They'd gotten back to the car and out of the drive without seeing anyone, which eased Allyson's nerves. But the closer they got to the psychiatric center, the more her heart began to pound. What if they didn't let them in and called her uncle?

"You're family," Anthony insisted. "Visiting from England. They will let you in."

She tried to believe him, but as they pulled off the main road and onto a winding path that led up to an impressive brick building at the top of a small hill, she balked. "Maybe this is a bad idea," she said. "What are we going to find out and…what does it matter anyway?"

"Oh no," Anthony said. "We've come this far, you can't back down now. And maybe Catherine's story will shed some light on why your uncle has pigs' heads being left on his desk and empty caskets popping up in his backyard."

"Maybe we don't want to know," she said.

"That is also a possibility."

Anthony pulled the car up and around an oval entryway and then parked nearby.

"All right," he said. "Let's go meet your cousin."

Allyson took a deep breath and opened the door.

They walked up an old stone path with large oval planters spaced every meter. They were filled with greenery and topped with yellow and purple blooms. A long, perfectly groomed hedge blocked their view of the grounds beyond. After a few yards, they took a flight of wide steps and found themselves in front of the imposing three-story institution. It was a classic German structure with stone block walls and a sloped tile roof. They ascended a set of steps and Anthony pulled open the large wooden door.

"After you."

Allyson stepped inside.

The lobby was small but ornate, with granite flooring and a bronze bust of somebody with an impressive mustache. Probably the founder. A nurse station was just beyond, and a blue-uniformed woman with a white bonnet called to her in German. "*Fräulein, kann ich Ihnen helfen?*"

Allyson nodded and approached the reception area, hopeful that she appeared outwardly calm. Because inside, she was shaking.

"Do you speak English?" she asked.

The woman nodded.

"I'm visiting from England for the first time since I was a child, and I was hoping to see my cousin, Catherine Berger?"

The nurse typed something on her computer screen and then raised an eyebrow.

"Nobody has come to see her in a very long time," she said. "Do you understand her condition?"

"I know she doesn't always talk," Allyson said. "But I'd still like to see her. We played together as children."

The nurse nodded. "She has been having a good week, so you may get a word or two out of her. We shall see. Let me call an orderly."

She picked up a phone and spoke a few words in German before turning back to Allyson and Anthony with a clipboard.

"If you could just list your names here, I'll get you visiting passes. Visiting hours close at five, but you should have plenty of time. Don't expect a lot of reminiscing."

Allyson wrote their names on the sheet and filled in '3:05' for the time they came in. There was a sign-out column for when they left.

The nurse then handed them two visitor badges on strings. They slipped them over their heads just as a young, heavy-set man with blond hair and a serious smile approached.

"Catherine Berger?" he asked.

Allyson nodded, and he said something in German that she thought was 'this way'.

The orderly led them through a swinging wooden door and all at once it was as if they were in a completely different place. The halls were old linoleum and the lighting fluorescent and yellow. There were administrative offices along the way with people bent over keyboards at desks with piles of paperwork beside them. But the orderly led them to another door and flashed a key card across the electronic lock. Once inside, they passed a series of numbered rooms along the hall before arriving at 129.

The orderly said a few foreign words to them before pointing to a small nurses' station just down the hall.

"He'll be waiting for us right over there when we're through," Anthony translated.

"Figured, thanks."

The orderly looked inside and said, "Catherine, *du hast Besuch*."

Then he turned and let them step inside.

A thin woman with long, unkempt blonde hair sat in a chair with avocado-green vinyl cushions. She wore a powder-blue t-shirt and long, loose white pants. She had been watching something on television, but the volume was so low Allyson could barely make out the words. Clearly Catherine had just been focused on the pictures.

Catherine looked up at them with an empty gaze. She didn't blink.

"Hello, Catherine. I'm your cousin, Allyson."

Catherine's head nodded faintly.

"I have wanted to see you, but I lived in England all these years. I am here now though."

Catherine blinked.

"This is my friend, Anthony."

"It's good to meet you," he said, and held out his hand.

Catherine did not shake it.

He looked at Allyson and raised his eyebrows. This was not looking promising.

"My mom died, so I am living with your father now," Allyson said.

The word 'father' got a reaction. Catherine drew up her legs and hugged her arms around them tightly. She moaned faintly.

"What's the matter, Catherine?" Allyson asked. She leaned forward and patted her cousin's arm.

Catherine frowned.

"Do you not want to talk about Uncle Otto?"

"My baby," Catherine said. Her voice was almost a growl. "Not his. *My* baby." She squeezed her arms across her chest, as if hugging herself. Or a child.

Allyson looked at Anthony, unsure of where to go with this.

"Catherine, what about the baby?" Anthony asked.

"I did what he asked me to," Catherine said. "It's not fair. I was a good girl. He told me every night."

"Who told you?" Allyson said.

"Father said I was his good girl," Catherine said. She patted her own arm and then began to stroke it as she spoke, petting herself. "He said, 'Just like that, yes, yes,' when he came to my room. He told me, 'You're my good girl. My very good girl.'"

"But what happened to the baby?"

Catherine balled up her fists and punched the chair. "They took it away. My very own. Not just his to take. Then they took me away because I wasn't Father's good girl anymore."

"Who took it away, Catherine?" Allyson asked softly. She patted the woman's arm some more, trying to calm her. Coax her.

"In the kitchen they have knives, you know. Very sharp knives."

Catherine looked up from her knees and her eyes grew wide as she met Allyson's gaze. "Knives draw blood. Knives kill."

"Who took the baby, Catherine?" Anthony asked, trying to help.

"All the doctors in the world couldn't put it back together again." The woman turned her eyes away from them. A tear trickled down her cheek.

"Dr. Testi said it would be all right, but he lied."

Allyson's eyes raised at the mention of a familiar name. "Did the doctor take the baby?" she said.

Catherine looked straight at her. "He promised. He said my baby was better off. Rain would wash the pain away."

"So, he did take it."

"Everything. Took my everything."

"Why did you come here?" Anthony asked.

"Not his good girl now. He has other good girls."

Tears ran down Catherine's face and the woman seemed to suddenly deflate. Her face went slack. Her hands slipped away from her knees to hang limp at her sides.

"Catherine, why did your father bring you here?" Allyson pressed.

"Blood is so red. More red than you think."

Catherine turned her face away from them to stare at the television.

"Goodbye," she said.

"Are you happy here?" Allyson asked.

Catherine didn't respond.

"Would you like to go home again?" Anthony asked.

Catherine continued to stare at the screen. They prodded a couple more times, but the woman refused to speak anymore.

"I think she really meant goodbye," Anthony whispered.

Allyson nodded and stood.

"It was good to meet you, Catherine," she said. "Thanks for talking to us."

The woman's eyes did not budge from the screen, where a herd of gazelle were apparently running away from a lion. Allyson didn't need the sound of the narrator to know how this ended. The weakest and slowest would lose the race. And the lion would spill its blood and gorge on the gazelle's pain.

Just like Otto apparently had on Catherine. She felt sick to her stomach.

* * *

They left the room and found the orderly, who escorted them back to the front desk to sign out. The nurse smiled at Allyson as she handed over the visitor's pass.

"I hope you had a good visit," she said.

Allyson nodded. "She didn't say a lot, but it was good to hear her voice."

The nurse gave a sad smile. "So many of our patients here have lost theirs forever." She motioned at her head and mouth. "The connections are just gone. Burnt out."

"It's horrible," Allyson said. "Like a prisoner in your own head."

"We try to make their days comfortable," the nurse said.

"Thank you," Allyson answered, and then turned to leave.

"Come back again," the nurse called. "Catherine could use her family. Often, they are really the best cure."

* * *

Anthony didn't say anything until they were on the road back to Hildegard. But his face looked deep in thought. Finally, he looked at her and said, "Well, I guess we got what we came for."

"Yeah," Allyson said. "Maybe it would have been better not to know."

"I think we may have solved the mystery of the baby casket."

"Maybe," she said. "But where are the bones?"

CHAPTER THIRTY-SEVEN

Camino Mental Health Center, June 19, 9:23 p.m.

The man watched the last of the day staff walk from the asylum to their cars. There were only a few other cars left in the staff parking lot; he'd been watching the place clear out one by one for an hour through tinted windows from the safety and obscurity of his black Volvo.

When the last car's taillights turned onto the street, he got out of the car and walked up the path. He headed to the side door the staff had exited from and pulled a tool from his pocket. He'd looked at the lock earlier and didn't expect it to be a tough one to crack.

It wasn't.

The door led to a room that he quickly realized was the 'changing room'. There were shelves on the right stacked with scrubs, and two doors marked Men and Women just across from them. It wouldn't hurt to be in uniform, he thought, and grabbed the XXL shirt and pants. He was pulling them on over his clothes, not changing. He shrugged the bulky blue shirt over his own, and then stepped into the baggy blue pants.

There. If anyone was watching the halls at the front desk, they'd see a tech they might not immediately recognize…but they'd see the uniform. That should be enough.

He pressed the door open to enter the main part of the facility. A vacant nurses' station was just down the hall. The lighting was low; there was basically just a nightlight on in the nurses' station. The important thing was…the computer there was still on; a screensaver that displayed a slideshow of mountains was available for his fingers.

He slid into the chair and clicked the mouse. The nurse's monitoring program was still live, with patient alerts and vital signs graphics next to a list of names. He located the search bar and typed in 'Berger'.

The number 129 appeared on the screen.

"*Danke schön,*" he murmured, and stood. The room numbers appeared to be ascending to the right, so he turned to the left and passed by 147 and 145 and 143. When he turned the corner, he found himself just three doors down from 129. But he also found himself staring at the back of someone walking down the hall. He stepped around the corner and flattened himself against the wall. One hand slid into his pocket and brought out a black-handled straight razor. He flipped it open and waited.

After a minute went by with no action, he peered back around the corner. Satisfied, he flipped the razor closed again, and walked down the hall, stopping at 129. After reaching down to turn the knob, he stepped inside.

The woman was snoring.

He pulled the door closed behind him and carefully walked to the bed. He pulled out the razor again. Flipped it open. He stood there for a second, studying the face. It had been a long, long time. A pity to end her life this way, but living all of her adult years in an asylum, had she really had a life anyway? No. There was no sadness in this dispatch. It should have been done a long time ago. She should have been buried with the baby.

He brought the razor close to her throat, the silver edge primed for the kill. And then some sixth sense woke the girl. Her eyes popped open and she stared at his face, still visible thanks to the LED light of her clock in the darkness.

"You," she said. "Why...."

He pushed a black-gloved hand over her mouth to silence her.

"You were a bad girl today, Catherine," he said. "You were telling stories. But those stories need to die. Like you."

Her eyes widened and he drew the razor across her throat, pressing down as hard as his arm had strength. There was no reason to make her suffer any more than necessary.

The blood spurted like a jet to drench the white sheets with Catherine's life.

She struggled beneath him, but with his hand on her mouth and his knife hand on her chest, he held her down long enough that she never managed to kick her way off the bed.

Her deathbed.

When he finally took his hand away from her silent lips, her feet had stopped kicking and her arms lay limp against the mattress. Her eyes still stared at him, angry accusation locked in their gaze.

"Sweet Catherine," he said, and wiped the switchblade clean on the bedsheets.

From his pocket, he removed a small statue of a young girl. He broke it in half, almost tenderly between his hands, and dropped the pieces on her blood-drenched chest.

"This bedtime story is finally over."

CHAPTER THIRTY-EIGHT

Berger Mansion, June 20, 8:23 a.m.

It was another quiet breakfast. Until it suddenly wasn't.

"So, tell us about your boyfriend," Ella said. She was staring across the breakfast table straight at Allyson.

Allyson had a forkful of pancake poised to go into her mouth. To buy herself a second, she plunged it in.

"You were gone all afternoon yesterday, and out with him a couple nights ago, so I'm sure everyone's curious," Ella prodded.

Ingrid answered for her and managed to make it sound dirty and suspect.

"She's latched on to our grocery delivery boy. So, if anything is missing from the kitchen, I'd guess we know why. Distraction."

"His name is Anthony," Allyson said. "He's really nice."

Otto looked up from his plate. "He'd better be. I will have a talk with him if he doesn't treat you well."

"He's a gentleman," she said.

"He's a grocery boy," Ingrid emphasized.

"Interesting," Martin said. "Has he offered you any frozen pizza?"

Allyson glared at him. "No, he took me out for sausage and pork."

"Mmmm. Yeah, we all know about what a little sausage porking is like. I hope it's a big sausage, actually, for your sake."

"Martin," her uncle admonished. "Mind your tongue."

"Sounds to me like our Ingrid might be a little jealous," Ida suggested.

"Jealous!" Ingrid said, her nostrils suddenly flaring. "I couldn't care less. I just don't want our service to diminish. If she wants to slum with the grocery boy—"

"I'm not slumming with anyone," Allyson snapped. "Anthony is really nice and he's going to be a great filmmaker."

Martin laughed. "What kind of films? Will they need a wardrobe department?" He wrapped his napkin around a spoon, and then with two fingers yanked it off and dropped it to the table, laying the spoon down and then dropping his fork on top of that, miming utensil sex. "No, probably not."

Allyson wanted to hit him, but instead she only glared and decided not to answer at all. Conversation quieted, and as soon as she finished her plate, she excused herself and went back to her room. She didn't understand what Ingrid had against her for going out with Anthony, but she'd been even more bitchy for the past week since she had.

She lay on her bed for a while and texted her friend Megan in London. But no dot-dot-dots appeared in answer. Megan was not looking at her phone apparently. She tried reading her book, but found that she was reading the same paragraph over and over. She couldn't concentrate.

All she kept thinking about was Anthony…and the trip yesterday to the insane asylum. She pictured Catherine living here as a teenager. And then she pictured Catherine lying in bed late at night, and her uncle walking into the room and sitting down on the edge of the bed and….

No. She couldn't think about that. She hadn't been able to meet his eyes at breakfast at all. But she knew something for sure since yesterday. She might stay in Germany, but she wasn't going to stay at Berger Mansion for very long. She understood now why her mother had refused to come back here. However, if what the lawyer had said was true…maybe it was worth sticking around a little while at least.

Allyson surfed on her phone a bit, but then finally rolled off the bed. She needed to take a walk. She was antsy and had absolutely no place to go.

She walked out into the hall and started toward the stairs. But when she reached the fourth step she stopped.

What was she going to do down there? The family had disappeared from the first floor; everything was quiet. Ingrid was probably back in the kitchen somewhere. Martin had either gone out or locked himself in his room. Otto and Ella were probably locked in his office. Maybe Ella was handcuffed to the desk by now. Allyson shivered. More images she didn't want to imagine.

She thought about their visit to the attic yesterday, and wondered what other things were hidden in this house. Like...what else was behind those doors that Ingrid had told her were off-limits?

Allyson decided that maybe it was time to find out. This was her house too now, right? She walked down the hall past her bedroom. There was a door on this floor that she'd wondered about. Just across from Uncle Otto's room. She stopped there and cocked her ear to listen. She didn't think he was up here but....

Nothing.

Good.

She reached out a hand and twisted the doorknob. It opened onto a teenager's room.

A teenager from the mid-2000s.

There were posters on the walls on either side of a white dresser – Arctic Monkeys and the White Stripes and Daft Punk. The mirror of the dresser also had band photos. She recognized a photo of Foo Fighters amid a series of clipped images that were stuck into the grooves on either side of the mirror. Her cousin had liked music, clearly.

The wooden floor had thick, plush white rugs to cover it, and a wide, tall bed dominated most of the room beyond the dresser. There were framed photos on the dresser, which showed a young Catherine grinning in the center with a couple of other girls at what looked like a carnival. The other was a picture of a woman with blonde hair and pretty eyes, who grinned at the photographer as a young Otto stood next to her with his arm on her shoulder. Catherine's mom, Ellen?

So. There was no real reason not to come into this room except that it was a private shrine. The room looked to be preserved exactly as it had been when Catherine had lived here.

And...right across the hall from Otto. It would have been easy access for him to walk over to tell his daughter what a good girl she was.

The thought made Allyson's skin crawl. She opened the door and peered into the hallway to make sure it was empty.

It still was.

She let herself back out, closing the door quietly behind her.

Just a little farther down was another room that Ingrid had forbidden her from entering. Emboldened, Allyson decided she was going to open that door, too. Time to break down all the taboos.

She glanced both ways in the hall and, seeing nobody, turned the knob and stepped inside. She pushed the door shut behind her and turned to face a thousand eyes.

The room was filled with dolls.

Every wall was covered in shelving and on every shelf were rows and rows of fake human eyes. It felt as if they were all staring right at Allyson.

There were small porcelain figures, and larger china dolls. There were Raggedy Ann-style dolls with red-and-white-striped legs that hung over the shelves. On either side of the door, there were person-sized dolls. Store mannequins that had been dressed and wigged to look fully human. When Allyson turned to study them, she felt her skin goose-bump. It was as if their dark-painted eyes were staring right back at her.

What was this place?

She had never seen so many dolls. So many different kinds all in one place. But who had put them here? Surely Uncle Otto didn't collect dolls?

Then she remembered the words of the blue-eyed man, Ivan. "Have you sat for your doll?" he'd asked. "Don't let them break you."

On the right side of the room were three shelves dedicated to porcelain dolls. They were painted as men and women and children, with gold locks and dark black hair and even one that was bald.

Were those the dolls that Ivan had meant?

The hair on the back of her neck stood up. What the hell was going on in this house?

Something thumped against the wall to her right and the dolls rattled.

Now what?

She did not want to be discovered here.

Allyson cracked the door open and peered out. The hall was still empty. Her exploring for today was done, she decided.

Allyson slipped out of the room, pulled the door shut and nearly sprinted down the hall to her room. When she got inside, she started for her bed but then stopped, turned back, and flipped the lock on her door.

Anthony may have had a point.

CHAPTER THIRTY-NINE

Berger Mansion, June 20, 11:42 a.m.

The door chime downstairs sounded. It was faint, but she could still hear it in her room. Allyson set her phone down and listened. Megan still hadn't answered her last text but she'd been scrolling through Instagram memes to take her mind off the fact that there was a museum to an insane girl across the hall and a museum of dolls a few doors beyond that.

The chime downstairs sounded again, and she sat up and decided to see who was here. Maybe Anthony was making a surprise delivery? A girl could hope.

She unlocked the door, stepped out into the hall and walked halfway down the stairs before she saw a familiar face.

But not the familiar face she wanted to see.

It was the thin, pointy mug of the police inspector. Officer Wagner.

What the heck was wrong now?

She hung at the top of the stairs and listened as her uncle invited the inspector in. The man looked serious. Not that he didn't always look serious when he turned up, but...more so than ever. She couldn't help but eavesdrop. The acoustics of the tile foyer with high ceilings meant that she could hear conversations from the stairs almost as clear as if she were standing right next to them.

"Mr. Berger, I believe there is a gravestone in your family cemetery for your daughter, Catherine, isn't that right?"

Otto nodded.

"And is it also true that if I excavated that grave, I'd find the coffin that was buried there with some ceremony is, in fact, empty?"

Otto's face looked stunned. "I don't know…why would you.…"

"Your daughter has been at Camino Mental Health Center all these years, not underground, isn't that true?"

Otto clearly knew he'd been trapped, though he didn't know why. He hung his head. "That is true, Inspector."

"Is there a particular reason that you faked her death, put an obituary in the newspaper, and advertised the funeral proceedings as a private family ceremony all those years ago?"

Her uncle turned away from the inspector and began to pace the foyer. "It was a difficult time," Otto said. "I was running for office and my competition was, shall we say, ruthless. It was clear that Catherine was lost to us. There was nothing I could do to help her and I didn't want her condition to be able to be used to weaken my candidacy.…"

"You thought that if the newspapers got wind of your daughter in an asylum, your opponent would use that situation to question your own faculties?"

"Yes, that's it exactly," Otto said, a relieved expression taking over his face. "What difference does any of this make to you?"

"Mr. Berger, I have come here with bad news. I'm afraid that empty coffin out back can legitimately be filled at long last. Your daughter was murdered last night."

Allyson stifled a gasp and almost fell down the stairs. Her knees turned to water and she abruptly sat down.

Holy shit.

She felt as if someone had stabbed her in the chest. This was *her* fault. She had gone to talk to the lawyer and he'd been killed. She had gone to talk to her lost cousin and Catherine had been killed. What was going on?

"Oh my God," Otto said. "This is unbelievable. Unthinkable!" He held a hand to his forehead, shaking his head in seeming disbelief. "How…how did it happen?"

"Her throat was slit in her room last night after hours," Officer Wagner said.

"Who would do this?" Otto said. His eyes were wide with what Allyson believed to be exaggerated, feigned grief. According to the nurse, nobody had visited the poor girl in years. How heartbroken could he really be? He'd committed his daughter, told the world she was dead and seemingly washed his hands of her.

"We have good reason to believe that it was done by the same person who committed the other recent killings. There was a broken porcelain doll left on her body. Just like the others, its body was snapped in half."

"I don't know what to say," Otto said. "I think I need to sit down."

He walked across the foyer to one of the couches. Officer Wagner followed but did not sit.

"Mr. Berger, I'm concerned that all of the victims of this killer have had a close connection to you. Have you made an enemy that you can think of who might be behind all of this? Someone who is sending you very pointed, deadly messages?"

Otto put his head between his hands. "No, no. I cannot imagine."

"If you think of anything, anyone, please call me at once. I am very sorry for your loss. The Camino Mental Health Center will be in touch with you shortly, now that I've let you know the circumstances, so that you can make arrangements. I am guessing they will be very private."

Otto nodded, but said nothing.

"Again, my condolences," Wagner said. "I'll let myself out."

As he walked to the door, Allyson eased her way up from the stairs to return to her room before Otto saw her. On the couch just below, her uncle leaned his head back and stared for a long while at the ceiling.

She couldn't imagine what was going through his mind. But she knew what was going through hers.

Fear.

Someone was following her and killing the people she talked to. How long would it be before the killer came for her? And what about Anthony? Was she putting him in danger too?

The ring of the cell phone on her nightstand made her jump. Maybe Megan was calling her back finally. She hurried to answer it but when she picked it up, she froze. The screen said:

Hildegard Police.

CHAPTER FORTY

Berger Mansion, June 20, 12:05 p.m.

"Miss Berger, this is Officer Wagner."
"Yes?"
"I saw you at the top of the stairs, so I would guess you understand the reason for my call. Would you be able to come down to the station this afternoon and talk to me about your...excursion... yesterday? I thought it might be best to discuss this privately."
"Um, yes, I guess...if I can get a ride to town."
"Please do, or I'm afraid I will need to come ringing your bell again. And then our conversation may not be private at all."
"I'll find a way."
"Good. Until later, then."

★ ★ ★

Well bollocks, how was she going to get downtown without saying why?
The answer came instantly. She had been about to call him anyway to warn him that he might be in danger. Anthony.
She quickly dialed his number and paced the room anxiously waiting for him to pick up. He did on the fifth ring.
"Sorry, Allyson, I was making a delivery. What's up?"
She felt strangely cautious about saying anything while she was in the house. What if Martin was listening at her door?
"I...um...need to tell you something really important. But I want to do it in person. And...I need to get downtown this afternoon. It's urgent. Would you be able to pick me up?"

"Actually, I'm not far from you right now and need to go back to Hildegard anyway so…sure. See you in ten?"

"Deal."

She hung up and looked in the mirror. She teased a wild strand of hair back and shook her head at the pink t-shirt that redundantly said PINK on it. Not great, but it would have to do. She grabbed her shoes and purse and rushed out to the hall and down the stairs.

Otto had disappeared and the house seemed ominously still.

She hadn't seen Martin or Ingrid in a couple hours. So much the better. Nobody to ask her where she was going.

Allyson slipped out the front door and waited for Anthony in the driveway. It didn't take long, although it felt like an hour to her. She grabbed the passenger car door handle before he had fully stopped the car and shot herself into the seat.

"Whoa, girl, what's the hurry? And what is it you couldn't tell me over the phone? I feel like I'm driving the getaway car."

"You kinda are," Allyson said. "I need to get away from this house right now. And I need you to take me to the police station."

"Police station?"

"Somebody killed Catherine last night after we left."

He hit the brakes and the car abruptly stopped halfway down the driveway.

"What? No way." He turned to look at her as if she might take back what she'd said.

But she didn't.

"Yes. Slit her throat and left another broken doll on the body. Anthony, somebody did exactly the same thing to Mr. Schmitt, the lawyer, after I visited him."

"It's gotta be a coincidence," he said. "I still think somehow this all has something to do with your uncle… but not you. That woman who was killed downtown had a broken doll left on her corpse too and you never even met her. So, it's not all about you."

"She's the only one," Allyson said. "I'm scared. I'm worried now that you might be in danger from being near me."

"Don't worry about me. I'm tough to catch."

He took his foot off the brake and the car began to creep forward again. "Why are we going to the police, exactly?" he asked.

"Right after he talked to Uncle Otto, the police inspector called me and asked me to come down to the station for a talk." She leaned forward to catch his eye. Her face was twisted in concern. "Anthony, he knows that we visited her yesterday. We are probably both suspects now in the murder."

"Oh, that's just great," he said. "I am not a fan of being on the Most Wanted list."

"I think you're jumping the gun there a little. And we didn't do it! But I bet I know who did."

"Who?"

"That creep with the blue eyes who was watching me in the bar the other day."

"You need to tell the police about him."

"I will, in just a few minutes."

Anthony shook his head and frowned. "That poor woman. If you're right, we led the killer right to her."

"I know," she said. "I've been feeling sick about that ever since I heard. She was fine all these years, and then we go sleuthing and… bam."

"Don't blame yourself. How could we know? But it is pretty horrible."

They were silent for the next few minutes as the road wound into town. Anthony pulled up in front of a tall, narrow old brick building that said POLIZEI in large letters above the door.

"Thanks for taking me," Allyson said. "I really didn't want to ask anyone at the house because then I'd have to tell them where I was going."

"I get it. And it's fine – I needed to come down here for an appointment anyway. Just text me when you're done."

She leaned over and gave him a quick peck on the cheek, and then got out of the car and watched as he pulled away.

"Time to face the music," she whispered to herself. She walked up to the wooden doors that felt ominous to her, inset within an arched entryway.

* * *

The woman at the front desk was older, but Allyson was pretty sure she'd take down most of the room in a bar fight. She was a thick-set woman with broad shoulders and a chest that threatened to pop the buttons of her blue uniform. Beneath the straight-cut white hair at her temples glared a broad face that looked ready to attack at any opportunity. There were lines around her eyes and a jagged scar that led from her left cheek to her chin. Maybe she *had* been in a bar fight or two.

"*Guten Tag*," she said, and looked at Allyson expectantly.

"I'm here to see Officer Wagner," she said. "He called me."

"Hmm. Name?"

"Allyson Neumann."

"I've got her, Gertrude," a male voice said from Allyson's left. She looked and Officer Wagner stood there holding a door open for her. "Please step inside."

She followed him down a hall past a couple of desks and into a private office. He motioned her in and then closed the door behind her.

"Have a seat."

Officer Wagner sat behind the desk and took out a notepad.

"A couple hours after you visited Catherine Berger yesterday, she was killed."

Allyson swallowed hard.

"Nobody has visited Catherine Berger in the past five years," Wagner said. "Don't you think it's odd that she was murdered almost immediately after you spoke with her?"

Allyson nodded. "I still can't believe it."

"I'm going to guess that your uncle does not know that you saw Catherine yesterday."

"No, he doesn't," she said. "How did you know?"

"Because he has maintained that Catherine has been dead since 2008. I can't imagine why he would tell his niece, new to the country, that she had a cousin still alive that he'd been hiding."

She shook her head.

"Tell me, then, how did you discover that she was alive?"

"I was looking around in the attic and found some papers from the asylum."

"You were looking around. *Just* you?"

Allyson hesitated.

"I know you were not alone at the Camino Center," he said. "Were you alone in the attic?"

She shook her head again. "No, my friend Anthony was with me."

He nodded. "I'll want to speak with him as well."

Allyson's stomach clenched. She hated it that Anthony was being dragged into this. That *she* had dragged him into this. He had just been trying to help her.

"So, when you discovered these papers suggesting that your cousin was alive, you didn't ask your uncle about it?"

"No."

"Why not? Seems like that would be a simpler step than driving to another town to check."

"Because he told me that she was dead."

"Hmm," he said, writing something on his notepad. "So, you didn't trust him to tell you the truth."

"I didn't say that."

"But it's true?"

She didn't answer and he scribbled something else.

"Tell me about your visit with Catherine," he said, switching gears. "What did she say to you?"

"She wasn't really all there," Allyson said. "She just kept talking about someone taking her baby away. And knives. And how they draw blood."

"Who did she say took her baby?"

"She didn't directly say, but she mentioned Dr. Testi and said he told her it would all be okay. She said she wasn't 'Father's good girl' anymore."

"Did she say what they did with the child?"

Allyson shook her head. "Just something about rain washing the pain away. She was really scattered."

"That's why she's been institutionalized all these years. What else did she tell you?"

"Honestly, nothing. At first she didn't answer us at all, and then when I brought up her dad, Uncle Otto, she got really distraught and started talking about 'them' taking her baby and knives and blood and not being a good girl."

"I see." He wrote in his notebook for a minute or two. "You can't think of anything else that she said? Anything, really, could be a clue as to her killer."

"Not really. She said her father always told her that she was his good girl, every night. But that he has other good girls now. And then she said goodbye and wouldn't talk to us anymore."

"I can understand why you wouldn't talk of this to your uncle," he said, after a moment of quiet. "And while I can't promise that the information about your trip to Catherine won't come out eventually, I'll keep it in my private file as long as I am able. Please let me know if you think of anything else."

"There is one thing," she said.

His eyes looked down and he set his pen on the desk. "What's that?"

"I think I might have actually seen the killer."

That made Wagner look up fast.

"When Uncle Otto took Martin and me to Munich for a dinner, a man came up to me when I was alone at the Hofbräuhaus for a few minutes. He said his name was Ivan and warned me to be careful. He asked if anyone had made a doll of me yet. And then he said something I'll never forget. He said, 'Dolls are made to be broken. Don't let them break you.'"

Wagner looked very interested in this. "What else did he say?"

"Not much — Martin was just away at the bathroom, so he only had a couple minutes. But he really creeped me out."

"I am sure. What did he look like?"

"He was tall. Pretty in shape. Strong shoulders but a normal-looking guy really, except for the eyes."

"What about them?"

"They were super blue. Really piercing. Like, when he looked at you, you felt like he had x-ray vision and could see right through to your spine."

"Interesting. And he just came up and asked you about this doll thing out of the blue."

She nodded. "In a bar a long way from home. But that's not all."

He raised an eyebrow.

"I saw him again just a few days ago. He was watching me from across the room here in Hildegard when Anthony and I had lunch at the Bertel Haus."

"Did you speak to him then?"

She shook her head. "He stayed in the back of the room, kind of lurking behind groups of people."

"Are you sure it was him?"

"Oh, it was him. I saw the eyes."

Wagner jotted something down. "Can you describe anything else about him? Age? Some characteristic other than eyes?"

Allyson squirmed a little, trying to remember. "I mean…he was dressed in dark clothes both times I saw him. He has kind of a big nose, not a perfect complexion? And heavy eyebrows. I think that really makes his eyes stand out more. His hair was dark. Maybe he's like forty or fifty years old? It's hard for me to judge people's age if they're not in my generation."

He looked hard at her a second but said nothing. Then he wrote again in his book.

"So, what makes you think this man could be the killer? He has been watching you, apparently, but…it also sounds like he tried to warn you."

"I know," she said. "But he's clearly following me. And two people have been killed right after I visited them. Doesn't that sound like someone followed me and…killed them?"

"It is certainly a possibility. And I would very much like to talk to this man. If I showed you some photos, do you think you might be able to recognize him?"

"I think so," she said.

He smiled thinly and rose. "Come with me."

Wagner led her to a manila-colored room dominated by a wall of tall, bound books. He gestured for her to sit at a small, rectangular table in the center of the room and then selected a handful of the volumes and brought them to the table.

"Leaf through these," he asked. "They are a collection of men involved in violent crimes over the past few years. If you see anyone who looks similar to the man who followed you, mark the page with one of these Post-its and call me. I'll be just down the hall in my office, but I'll come back to check on you in a little while."

He dropped a pack of Post-its on the table and exited the room, pulling the door closed behind him.

Allyson turned the cover of the first book and was faced with a page of men all scowling at the camera. The faces came in all shapes, from thin and bony to fat and puffy. They looked young and old, and most looked somewhat mean. But none looked like the blue-eyed man.

She turned the page. And saw much the same thing.

Over half an hour went by before Allyson closed the cover on the last book. She'd looked at hundreds of pictures of criminals, but none had struck her as the man she wanted to identify. Though the longer she looked, the more difficult it was to know. The faces all began to blur together after a while.

The door opened and Wagner stepped in.

"How are we doing?"

"I literally was about to get up to come find you," she said. "I'm sorry, I didn't see anyone that seemed like a good match."

He pursed his lips and nodded as if he'd expected this.

"Thank you for trying," he said. "I'll see you out."

He motioned for her to follow and led her back through the police station to the lobby. He handed her a business card.

"Please call me immediately if you see this man again," he said. "I want to help you, but I can't if we can't get anything to help us identify him."

"Thank you," she said. "I will."

"And please tell Anthony I'd like to speak to him about your visit yesterday as well. Perhaps this afternoon, or tomorrow morning?"

"I will tell him."

"Please tell him not to make me come looking for him."

She nodded.

"And, Miss Neumann," he added, "please be careful."

Allyson flashed him a smile but did not feel in the slightest bit happy. Somehow, she felt more in danger than ever. She stepped out onto the sidewalk, and texted Anthony to see if he could come back to pick her up. She stared at her phone, praying that he'd answer quickly.

She really did not want to be alone in this town right now.

CHAPTER FORTY-ONE

Bertel Haus, June 20, 12:48 p.m.

Martin Berger was sitting at the back table in a corner. Away from the bar. Away from any windows.

As Anthony approached the table, he raised an eyebrow. "You showed up."

"Yeah, I told you I would," Martin answered. "You want a beer?"

Anthony shook his head and pulled out a chair. He hesitated before sitting, as if weighing whether he wanted to or not. But then a big-bosomed waitress with a blouse that did its best to display as much of her pale, milky chest as possible appeared.

"What are you drinking?" she asked.

Anthony didn't fight it. He sat. "Dunkel."

"Make that two," Martin said.

When she went away to place the order at the bar, Martin flashed Anthony a catlike grin. "You've been delivering more than groceries to our house lately," he said.

"That's none of your concern."

"You're messing around with my family. That's absolutely my business."

"Give me a break. You wouldn't have recognized her on the street a month ago."

Martin shrugged. "She's part of my house now. So, I'm interested in what you're delivering to her, delivery boy." He leered at Anthony across the table. "Does she make a lot of noise? I'm betting she's a quiet one. You know, little mouse squeaks and that's it. Am I right?"

Anthony looked as if he was about to haul off and slug Martin, but whatever he was about to do was cut short by the return of the bosomy waitress, who planted two steins of dark beer in front of them.

"Will you be ordering food?"

"I think Anthony's got his mouth set on something else," Martin said. "But I may order something later."

She smiled, though she didn't get the in-joke, and disappeared back to the bar.

"Cut the shit, Martin. I got you exactly what you wanted, and you welched. Pay up or I will make things very publicly difficult for the family you say you care so much about. You know that I can. I could blow your father up, so you don't even dare show your face outside Berger Mansion. Hell, an angry mob with torches might come storm the place before I'm done."

Martin raised his hand, looking around the bar. "Take it down a notch, friend. I said I'd get you the money, and I will. But you're going to have to give me a few days. The well seems to have gone nearly dry of late."

"I've got an insurance policy if the well stays dry," Anthony said. He picked up the dunkel and downed most of it in a few gulps. "I'll let you take care of this, my *good* friend."

Somehow 'good' didn't sound good at all.

Anthony didn't wait around for a response and headed back to the bar door.

CHAPTER FORTY-TWO

Berger Mansion, June 20, 3:09 p.m.

Allyson pushed open the front door of the Berger Mansion, praying that nobody would be there to see her come in. She really didn't want to talk to anyone. Thankfully, the foyer was empty, and Ingrid didn't come dashing out from the kitchen to ask questions. She took the stairs almost two at a time back up to her room. It was so good to not have to worry about her ankle anymore. Well...she worried a tiny bit because she anticipated it to hurt still when she set her foot down... but the truth was, it didn't.

She headed up to her room and ditched her purse and shoes. She had seen nobody on her way up and that emboldened her. There was a place in the house she really wanted to go after talking to Wagner. She'd realized that the one thing she'd neglected to say to him was that there was a room in the Berger Mansion filled with dolls.

And...dolls seemed to be a thing around here of late.

What was the connection between the murder victims and dolls? She had a feeling that the answer was somehow right here, in this house. Just a few doors away, in fact.

Allyson decided to walk down the hallway and look around a little closer this time.

She passed Martin's door and slowed for a second, listening extra hard. Was he in there?

Hearing nothing, she kept going and arrived at the room she'd been thinking about ever since she'd run out of it.

Why was it here?

Take another look, the voice in the back of her head said. And she listened. Allyson turned the knob to open the door and stepped inside.

Dolls.

So. Many. Dolls.

She looked at the porcelain section, which was all stacked on shelves along the wall to her right. The wall directly to her left had Raggedy Ann-style fabric dolls.

Allyson stepped forward and took a closer look at the shiny glass dolls. There were a bunch, but really not that many. And there were some spots on the glass shelving where there clearly had been a doll that was missing now. As she drew near, she realized that where there were empty spaces where dolls clearly once had been, there were small pieces of tape.

She leaned closer and saw there were names written on the tape. *Kate. Ginger. Maia.*

Weird.

She lifted up one to the right of a vacant spot. The doll had dark, short hair and a sharp look in its narrowed eyes.

The sticker on the shelf beneath it read, 'Ingrid'.

Allyson's eyebrows shot up and she abruptly put the doll back down on the shelf with a click.

Could that really be a doll commemorating the current Berger housekeeper Ingrid? If so…that was creepy and begged the question, who were Kate, Ginger and Maia?

There were other vacant spots on the shelves. They were on a higher tier than the Ingrid doll and she couldn't read the labels. She looked around and saw a small round garbage can on the far side of the room. It would do.

She walked over, grabbed the empty can and turned it upside down so that she could step up and get a boost.

And she almost fell off the shaky can when she read the labels that were exposed on the second shelf.

Lita.

Wilhelm.

There was a blank space on the third shelf a ways over and she twisted and craned to see what the label said there.

Kurt.

Kurt the gardener? she wondered. It had to be.

There was also a blank spot on the first shelf. Allyson stretched hard to the left to read it. The dolls up there seemed older, more detailed and refined maybe. As if a very different hand had crafted them. But artistry was not why she was looking. The blank space drew her eye. She didn't think it had been blank before.

And the label said something that chilled her heart.

Catherine.

That sealed it. She knew who Kurt and Catherine and Wilhelm were, and it was a damn good bet that Lita was the whore who had been murdered downtown.

All of the victims of the killer had had dolls on this shelf. And those dolls were all missing now, broken into many ceramic shards on the bodies of the victims they represented. The question was, who had taken the dolls off this shelf in a room in the Berger Mansion and then taken the lives of the dolls' namesakes?

There couldn't be that many suspects. This house wasn't exactly bustling.

There were a couple other empty spots on the shelf, and she could see the spots where a label had once been. She reached over to touch one and it was vaguely sticky to the touch. She saw another empty spot on the third shelf, at the end of a whole row of dolls with blonde and vaguely red-haired heads. It was too far for her to reach, so she stepped down and moved her impromptu stool to the right.

When she stepped back up, her eyes snapped open wide.

Oh shit.

The words of the blue-eyed man came back to her full force, as she read the name on the piece of tape over and over again.

Allyson.

CHAPTER FORTY-THREE

Berger Mansion, June 20, 4:12 p.m.

Otto Berger grabbed the phone in his office and dialed a number. The connection crackled for a moment before the ringtone stopped and someone picked up.

"I need you to liquidate the Angston holdings," Otto said. "And I need the cash at my house tomorrow afternoon. I have a business deal I need to close and that is the funding mechanism that needs to close the deal."

"You're slaughtering Angston?" the voice said. "That's a cash cow I don't think you want to touch right now. You've got other assets, I'm sure."

"That's the one I'm sacrificing," Otto said. "Because I know you can make it happen in twenty-four hours."

"I can," the voice said. "But you're going to regret this. It's going to be five times this in a year or two, I'm telling you. Are you sure you won't reconsider?"

"Get me the money."

CHAPTER FORTY-FOUR

Berger Mansion, June 20, 6:31 p.m.

Allyson had made sure she was at dinner on time that night. She didn't need anyone asking questions about where she was. She was not the first at the table – Ida almost always seemed to beat her, which made no sense since the woman could barely walk! – but she'd beaten Martin by at least two minutes. And when Ella waltzed in, the secretary seemed oddly distracted. She stared in every direction *but* at the people at the table, and after a bit, she wiped her eyes with a tissue and then pulled a compact out of her purse and touched up her makeup.

Otto strolled in with a scowl on his face, but forced a grin once he'd sat at the head of the table. "I trust everyone had a productive day," he said.

"If by productive, you mean profitable, then no, I can't say that I did," Martin sniped. That only drew a glare from his father, but any rebuff was interrupted when Ingrid came out of the kitchen with a silver platter that boasted a steaming heap of pink meat. A petite brunette followed just behind her, wearing a short black skirt and white knee-high stockings.

As Ingrid set the meat on the table, she smiled and addressed the group. "Everyone, it's about time for you to meet Karin, our new house girl. I've been training her in the kitchen for the past few days, but she still has plenty to learn so go easy on her, eh?"

"Glad you finally got some help again," Ida said, just before wheezing out a cough that made Allyson grimace. Nobody else seemed to take notice.

"It's been a difficult few weeks," Ingrid agreed. She nodded at Karin. "This is the family."

"Hi," Karin said in a voice that sounded just shy of quavering. "I'm happy to be here."

"Is she living with us like the others?" Martin asked. "Hope she'll be around longer, if so."

Otto shot his son a glare that said, *Shut your mouth or I'll come over there and shut it for you.* Martin lifted his glass of water and held it in the air. "Welcome to our merry band, Karin," he said, and downed half of the glass with exaggerated relish.

"She's in the servant wing on the first floor, in Maia's old room," Ingrid said. "But don't go bothering her at all hours."

"Oh, I'm sure nobody in this house would do that," Martin said. *What was up with him?*

"I'm sure you'll enjoy your time here," Ella said. "Ingrid will train you well. And there's plenty to learn at Berger Mansion." She twisted her fingers together as if holding herself still against her will. "I trust you won't need me to work late tonight, Otto?"

Otto shook his head, not even meeting her eyes. Instead, he flashed the new girl a broad grin. "It was very good to meet you last week and I am glad…*we* are glad…you are here," he said. "I look forward to getting to know you better."

Ella said something into her napkin as Otto waved at the table. "Let's eat."

★ ★ ★

After dinner, the dining room emptied quickly. Martin was thumbing anxiously at his phone and suddenly stood and disappeared. Ella pushed her plate back half-finished before anyone else was done eating and abruptly excused herself. She looked as if she might cry at any moment. Allyson wondered what was up.

Ella had only been gone seconds before Otto threw down his napkin on top of his half-eaten pork and gravy and stomped off to follow.

Allyson suddenly felt like she was being watched and turned to find that, in fact, she was. Ida stared at her. The old woman was leaning on the back of her chair. "Stick around too long and Ingrid will have you washing dishes," she warned, before turning and coughing her way out of the room.

Allyson's phone buzzed then. A text notification was on her home screen. "Can I see you tomorrow?"

Anthony.

She grinned and quickly answered. "Sure, what time?"

"I have to work but I can pick you up at eight."

"Perfect," she wrote.

He asked how her night was and they went back and forth a couple more times before saying good night. She looked up and realized the new girl was standing at the threshold in the kitchen. Probably waiting for her to get up so that she could clear the table.

"Come in," she said, and motioned to her. What was her name? Carol? Kristin? And then it came to her. Karin.

The girl hesitantly stepped into the room.

"I'll get out of your way here in a sec. My name is Allyson, by the way."

The girl smiled. "I'm Karin. Happy to meet you."

"Are you from Hildegard? I just moved here from London," Allyson said.

Karin shook her head. "No, I grew up on a farm in a small town outside of Frankfurt. But I came out to Munich with my boyfriend a few months ago."

"This is a hike from Munich," Allyson observed.

The girl looked embarrassed. "I woke up one day and he was gone. So, I hit the road looking for a job. I liked the idea of a live-in maid, at least for a while, since I had no place to go. And Mr. Berger hired me on the spot at the end of our interview."

"Congratulations," Allyson said. "A happy ending!"

"It won't be if I don't get these dishes back there," Karin said ruefully, and began to stack the plates.

"I can help," Allyson said, smiling inwardly as she remembered Ida's warning.

"Oh no, please don't," Karin said. "That would just tell Ingrid I can't handle it. But I can, I know I can."

Allyson nodded. "Believe it. If you really won't take a hand, I'll get out of your way."

"Thanks," Karin said. "It was good to meet you."

"I'm sure we'll be seeing a lot of each other in the coming days."

"That would be nice," Karin said. And then with a quick smile, she picked up the pile of plates and disappeared with them into the kitchen. No sign of Ingrid.

Allyson shook her head. *I guess when you get a helper, you don't have to touch dirty dishes yourself anymore.*

CHAPTER FORTY-FIVE

Berger Mansion, June 21, 5:59 p.m.

Otto sat in his office with his hand poised. When Ella poked her head in, he waved her away. "Not now."

His eyes didn't leave the phone. He'd had to make some painful choices this week to liquidate this money. Whoever was bilking him out of it had better call on time.

The phone rang.

His hand nearly toppled the receiver when he grabbed for it.

"*Guten Tag,*" he answered.

"Good, you're ready," the voice on the other end of the line said. It crackled and wavered a bit. Some kind of audio filter to disguise the caller's identity. Filter or no, Otto could still hear the smirk in the masked voice.

"I am ready," Otto said. "But this had better be the final time we have to speak."

"I was going to send you to another location to keep things interesting for you," the voice said. "But I think we'll visit the Klosbier Farm again. This time, however, I'd like you to go to the chicken coop. Do you know it?"

"Yes," Otto said.

"Of course you do. Birds of a feather...."

"The last time," Otto warned.

"Seven p.m. or your story is on the ten o'clock news."

Click.

"Goddamnit," Otto whispered. He could tell that the blackmailer was not planning on letting him off after tonight. But what choice did he have but to go ahead?

He picked up the black leather bag next to his desk and headed toward the garage.

* * *

The old farm came up like an ominous sentinel in a silent but now seemingly malevolent field. There was a time that pulling into that long drive had filled Otto with anticipation. He had enjoyed his hours with Karl when he was a younger man. His mentor had had so many tales to tell, and often poured them both more than a spot of whiskey in the telling. A smoke and a drink out on the sprawling back veranda just after sunset was one of his most favorite memories of his twenties.

But now the entry gate to Karl Klosbier's farm looked like a crooked jaw just waiting to swallow anyone foolish enough to turn onto its path. And the farmhouse was no longer a vibrant seat of power, but instead, a sagging structure that awaited the wrecking ball. Otto tried to put these thoughts from his mind as the gravel crunched under his tires, and he pulled the car behind the house and along the side of the old barn out back. He knew the chicken coop that his caller had directed him to. He'd pulled eggs from beneath some of the irritable fat hens that Karl had kept. And he'd gotten pecked plenty in the doing. One time an angry hen had stabbed him so fast with her beak that he'd bled all over the prize egg he stole from her.

Bitch.

Otto had great memories of the farm, but not of the chicken coop. He'd hated the miserable fowl.

He glowered at the little house as he stepped out of the car. Was his hand going to get bitten again after he went inside? Lord knows this trip was making him bleed. Speaking of...he reached back into the car and retrieved the black bag. Then he slowly pivoted, looking carefully at the landscape all around him. The bastard had to be here somewhere. Maybe with a telescopic lens, but still within viewable distance. The lone window on this side of the barn was dark, however, and what he could see of the house from here was also still. He stared at the house for a long while before looking out across the field.

Wherever he was, his tormentor was well hidden. Assuming he wasn't waiting just inside the chicken coop with a gun. The thought chilled his heart temporarily. But then again, if he was about to be strung along another week for another payment...well...he was physically safe for the moment.

Otto glanced at his watch.

7:01.

Time to face the blackmail.

He turned the knob on the coop door and pushed it open. The faint smell of chicken poop still colored the air inside. But all of the wooden boxes where the birds had once sat and laid were clear. There had been no eggs here in a very long while.

In the center of the stained gray plank floor was a small wooden box. He looked around the room, but even in the shadows there was no place here for someone to hide. This time, he was not as petrified of being gunned down, so he knelt next to the box and decided to open it right here instead of waiting.

He wanted to know what he was getting before he left the money.

The lid lifted easily.

Inside was a pair of long, white bones. They were attached to two more thin bones and those, in turn, married to small feet. But there was no pelvis...no ribs.

There was, however, a note.

Congratulations, you have learned to walk. Next week when we talk, I'll teach you about heart. Lord knows you could use one.

What the fuck?

His blackmailer was now taunting him as well as extorting. He'd get this bastard. He had resources. And friends.

He would get all of the evidence first, but then he'd make sure that this asshole ate dirt.

Hard.

Otto pushed the lid back down and stood up with the box in his arms. He left the black bag in its place as promised. It killed him to do so, but he had a suspicion that if he tried to walk out of here with both bones and cash…he'd find himself shot full of holes.

He could wait awhile for his revenge.

But he *would* get it.

CHAPTER FORTY-SIX

Berger Mansion, June 21, 11:53 p.m.

The girl lay face down on the bed. Her skin was beautiful, the little that he could see of it. Supple, creamy perfection. Trouble was, there was a hairy whale beached on top of her. A grunting, rutting whale. The grimaces on the man's fat face were stomach-turning to see as the pixie beneath him twisted in discomfort. She was 'taking it', but not without obvious distaste.

She couldn't really get away, regardless. The pig had tied her wrists to the headboard with thin black cord.

He lifted the camera slowly, waiting until he was sure the man would have his face in view, but not be staring directly at the window. When he was sure, he lifted and clicked three times before yanking the camera back down and out of view.

His heart was beating fast, but he forced himself to peer through the lower corner of the window.

The rutting continued. Good. He remained unseen.

He waited a minute, letting his heart rate slow.

That didn't last long.

A muffled cry came from inside.

He peered through the window again.

The setup inside had changed. The big man now stood next to the bed, the sweat of exertion glittering on the silver hair of his chest and groin. His erection was flagging but still obvious, as he lifted his hand in the air before bringing it down on the pure silken skin of the girl on the bed. He'd flipped her over, twisting the cords of her hands in an X. Her buttocks raised in the air as if she were trying to caterpillar her way to the head of the bed, but the force of his hand knocked them back to the sheets.

A red mark spread instantly across that delicate cream. He could see the tears on her face as she let out another cry when his hand came down again, wide palm slapping hard against her smooth, young ass. It jiggled beneath the force and the action was clearly exciting the whale again.

The camera readied and lifted fast for three seconds of exposure just as the man's hand came down on the poor girl again.

Click.

Click.

Click.

There were more cries from within, as the inevitable sodomy commenced. The camera made one more rise and fall, and then he slipped away from the window, careful not to so much as snap a twig in his furtive getaway. It was easier this time, since they were on the first floor.

He had gotten what he had come for.

Sadly, the girl trapped inside had clearly gotten a lot *more* than she'd come for.

CHAPTER FORTY-SEVEN

Gasthof Neubau, June 21, 11:57 p.m.

Ella slid behind the wheel and leaned her head back for a moment before starting the car. Richard had been amazing tonight. So good in fact, that as she stretched out her leg to touch the brake, she could feel a wetness spread across the inside of her panties. He had taken her three times in the short while they'd been able to squeeze in.

But she had to get back. Otto was suspicious and she was afraid to be away from Berger Mansion too long. And Richard's wife was apparently getting snoopy as well. He said he'd caught her scrolling on his phone the other day, supposedly just looking for a photo that they'd snapped the week before. He'd insisted there were no text chains still sitting on it from Ella but...not great.

Tonight, however. *That* had been great. And their scheme to funnel in some of Otto's campaign money to help Richard's campaign was paying off. He was going to be able to put up a television ad in the month before election now, which would be important. Part of her felt bad for helping Richard in this way; after all, it was Otto who had given her a job when she had nothing but her looks to sell her. But Otto had also certainly capitalized on that in a way she'd never believed would happen.

And then, after giving him every part of her, he'd had the nerve to bone the kitchen help when he felt a little extra pervy? She had slowly grown to hate him for that, all the while still spreading for his fat prick because, let's face it, she needed the job more than her purity. But she still didn't like sneaking around to be with the guy she loved. This had to end, and hopefully, would end soon.

Richard had planted the seeds – in more ways than one – to guarantee they could finally be together every day and night.

That thought made her smile, though it faded quickly as she reached out to thumb the START button to begin the drive home. She had no desire to return there. But she also didn't want Otto to ask where she'd been all night. She'd bet that he'd be taking his frustrations out on the new girl right now.

Ella put the car in Drive and turned onto the main road.

★ ★ ★

Behind her, a dark sedan pulled out on the road, headlights off. The driver let her get a ways ahead, and then turned on his lights and hit the gas. When he closed the gap, he got in the opposite lane and passed Ella, shooting ahead of her. He'd seen and heard what he needed to. There was no security in the hallways of the Gasthof Neubau and he'd been able to loiter right outside their door. The place wasn't soundproofed either.

The man glanced at the rearview mirror once to stare back at the woman driving behind him. His ice-blue eyes seemed to shine with their own beams of light.

Deadly beams.

CHAPTER FORTY-EIGHT

Berger Mansion, June 22, 12:21 a.m.

Ella entered Berger Mansion as quietly as she could, taking her shoes off immediately to walk barefoot across the foyer tile. The house seemed quiet and she prayed she wouldn't meet anyone on her way upstairs.

She paused outside Otto's door, leaning an ear toward the wood. Was that a creak inside? Something. If it was just him, it meant he was up and might come looking for her at any second. Ella hurried past and opened the door to her own room, then quickly shut the door behind her. She didn't even flip the light on – she needed to get out of these clothes quickly in case Otto came knocking. She pulled off her blazer and pushed it into the wardrobe and tossed her shoes in the corner. Then she pulled the dress over her head and buried that in the back of the wardrobe for the moment. She needed to lose the hose; that was more of a giveaway that she'd been out with another man than the lacy black bra and panties set.

She turned to put her foot on the chair of her desk as she peeled one leg down. That's when she saw the glint of two eyes watching her from the far corner of the room.

"Nice show," Ivan said, stepping out of the shadow. "But not as good as the one you put on earlier."

Ella's eyes widened as Otto's hit man approached her. There was nowhere to run.

"I think our boss is going to find that you're a very, very bad girl."

CHAPTER FORTY-NINE

Berger Mansion, June 22, 10:53 a.m.

Allyson needed to get a job. Sitting around the mansion all the time equaled boredom with a capital B. As she climbed the stairs after sitting for a while in the front foyer, she watched Aunt Ida shuffle back to her bedroom and wondered how the old woman could exist here, day after day, without ever leaving. At least Allyson got out of the house every day or two now thanks to Anthony. And he was picking her up again for dinner tonight.

That was great, but she didn't want to rely on someone else to constantly give her something to do. She needed to go make some money, buy her own car and be able to come and go as she pleased. And eventually get her own place. Uncle Otto had said she was welcome to live there for as long as she liked, but she didn't intend to be a permanent resident.

She opened the door to her bedroom and stepped inside, but after sitting down on the bed and checking her phone, she got up again and began to pace. She was restless. She didn't feel like reading anymore and shrugged away the idea of going to the game room and watching TV. She looked out the window at the gardens below but opted not to go outside. It was a gray morning. Really the perfect kind of day for staying in bed or lying on the couch vegging out but…she was antsy.

Well, the house had plenty of places to wander to. Maybe she'd even explore the closed section a bit, if nobody was around to see her slip past the 'do not enter' doorway.

Allyson walked back out to the hall. No sign of Ida or Martin or anyone. She started down the hallway away from the stairs, and passed the rest of the bedrooms. And then she saw a door that made her slow.

The doll room.

She had gotten spooked after seeing her name on the shelf and hadn't fully explored the various shelves in there the last time. Glancing behind her and still seeing nobody, she put her hand on the knob and twisted.

It opened.

She'd been afraid it would be locked, but…that was kind of foolish – like the rest of the rooms on this floor, the only way it would be locked was from the inside.

Allyson slipped in and gently shut the door behind her.

The gray light from outside gave the entire room a ghostly sheen. As if a wispy gauze was between her and all of the eyes that stared down from the shelves.

So many eyes.

Her stomach tingled as she realized how many pairs of eyes were watching her.

Sure, they were dolls. But some of them looked so…real. She could imagine the larger ones with flesh-tone plastic arms and legs slowly moving to their hands and knees on their shelves and then levering themselves over the edge to drop to the floor.

Stop it.

Allyson shook the image away. The dolls were just plastic and glass, and they had all been here, unmoving, for years.

Except.

There was something different on the low shelf of ceramic figures.

The space on the end where her name had been was no longer empty.

She walked over and stared at the new dolls that sat there. One of them had been placed in the spot where the tape had listed her name just a couple days ago. It had shoulder-length dark hair, just like hers, and wore a black t-shirt with a red rose on it. Someone had made a doll of her!

She shivered and reached out to pick it up. Slowly. She was almost afraid to touch it.

Her name remained taped on the shelf beneath it.

But who? Who had made a doll of her?

Dolls were made to be broken.

Allyson set the thing down. It clinked on the shelf. There was another ceramic figure next to hers that hadn't been there before either. This one was of another girl, but with shorter hair and large, brown expressive eyes. She lifted it up and there was a new label on the shelf beneath.

Karin.

Allyson's skin crawled. She set the figurine down gingerly and backed up a step. In another context, she would have been excited that someone had made a doll in her image. But seeing her face on the ceramic figure made her feel almost sick. Because lately, at least, the dolls in this room had been less homage and more voodoo-ish. Likenesses used to put the period on the end of a sentence of murder. She considered, for a second, pocketing her doll so that it couldn't be broken over her dead body.

"What are you doing in here?"

Allyson nearly jumped a meter in the air.

Martin stood in the doorway. He looked angry.

"I was just – just…looking," Allyson stammered.

"I'm sure Ingrid told you this room was off-limits, didn't she?"

Allyson shrugged. "What is this place?"

"My sister liked dolls," Martin said. "So, naturally, my parents gave her a thousand of them. My mom made some of them. I was too young to remember, but they say the dolls were especially helpful when she was sick. The faces helped her focus, the doctors said."

"I'm surprised they kept all of these once she was gone."

"My father doesn't let go of his possessions easily. That really goes for people as well as things."

"It seems like there are still new dolls being made, though," Allyson said. "If this was for Catherine, why would someone still be making dolls?"

"I don't know what you mean. This room has been like this for years and years."

"But there's a doll right over there with my name under its feet."

"Do you really think you're the only Allyson to ever exist?" Martin gestured for her to leave. "Come on, out you go. This room is not for you to play in."

"I was just curious."

"And you know what happens to curious cats," Martin said, cocking a knowing eye at her. "They get killed."

CHAPTER FIFTY

Hildegard, June 22, 6:02 p.m.

Ida watched on the upstairs terrace as the car pulled away from the house. Allyson was inside, off once again with the delivery boy.

God, she hoped the girl knew what she was doing. If she got herself knocked up, she'd need Otto's support more than ever, unless the boy was ready to take her on full-time. And as a college student and grocery driver, she really didn't see that in the cards.

Still, the boy at least gave Allyson a chance to escape these grounds. Things had been growing more frightening of late. People dying. Otto sneaking around early in the morning and leaving in the car at night, only to return twenty minutes later. You couldn't get to Hildegard and back in that kind of time. She'd heard some terse conversations emanate from his office. And even Ella looked less and less like his perfect angel-secretary of late. She'd once licked the front of his shoes as if she were a kinky shoeshine girl. But things seemed more tense between them lately.

And the kitchen girls.

That was another thing entirely.

Otto had a wandering eye, and hand, for sure. But you'd think they'd last longer under his attention than they did. Was Ingrid running them off, or Otto?

Sometimes Ida heard what seemed like screams in the night, and she wondered.

Go, Allyson. Find your steed and ride him far away from here before the plague on this house infects you too.

She slowly walked back to her room, coughing all the way.

An old woman with lungs like this won't be aging much longer.

Somehow, she'd like to make sure the poor girl was taken care of before she dropped. Lord knows she'd tried with Wilhelm, and look how that had gone. She hated to consider it, but maybe Otto had found out about the visit and put things in motion to destroy the evidence. And the thug had nearly destroyed Allyson in the process.

If it had been Otto behind it all, did he know that it was her who had pushed Wilhelm to tell the truth?

Things were tense.

People were wired.

And the more tightly wound things got, the closer they were to snapping.

She let herself back into her room and sat in her soft, pink-cushioned wooden chair. She knew things that could take Otto down. But was she up to that fight?

She stared at the phone on the table next to the bed. Tucked almost out of sight under the phone....

There was someone she could call. Someone she probably *should* call.

He could bring Otto down forever if he was brave enough to take on the Bergers.

But Ida didn't know that she'd survive long if she dialed that number.

CHAPTER FIFTY-ONE

Hildegard, June 22, 6:22 p.m.

"I want you to be in my movie," Anthony said. He took a sip of his Märzen, holding her gaze over the top of his stein.

He'd picked her up and brought her back to Bertel Haus for dinner. And he'd been all excited because he was finally starting down the path to shoot his first short film. He'd told her all about scouting locations this afternoon.

"So, you want your first film to fail?" Allyson shook her head. "I don't want to be the reason, thanks."

"I'm serious," Anthony said. He put his hand over hers. "I was thinking about it all afternoon while I was doing some of the establishment shots. I still don't have my leads cast, and I need an actress who is pretty but real, someone the viewer will believe and instantly identify with. And…. It hit me today that you're *it*. You're exactly who my film needs."

Allyson laughed. "I am absolutely none of those things. I'm not an actress. I'm not pretty, and I don't think anyone is going to identify with me. I've never exactly been a lightning rod that draws a crowd, you know?"

"That's what makes you perfect," he said. "You're not a model type, one of those plastic people that everyone looks at, but nobody believes is real. You are more the girl next door. But…the *cute* girl next door. Once someone sees you – really sees you – they can't look away."

"You're very sweet, but I'm not an actress," Allyson said. "I played a donut in a primary school play, and that's the extent of my stage experience."

"And I'll bet everyone wanted to eat you." Anthony laughed.

"I don't think that was the reaction. I think all the parents were forcing their smiles and sneaking glances at their watches to see how much longer it would be until they could go home. We were not good."

"Would you just come out one day and do a read-through with a couple of the other actors? Just try it on, see how it fits?"

Allyson rolled her eyes. She was not a camera girl. But she didn't want to disappoint him either. Film was his life and love. She knew it was important to him. But she also didn't think she could do it. He'd surely see that as soon as she tried.

"I'll think about it," she said. "But could we talk about something else for now?"

"Sure," he said. "What hot gossip do you have from the Berger Mansion?"

She raised an eyebrow. "I don't know about hot, but Ingrid's got herself a new lackey."

"Ah, they finally replaced Maia, huh?"

"Who was Maia?"

"The last scullery maid Ingrid hired."

"Ah, well, this one's name is Karin."

"Young, pretty, maybe a little naïve?" he asked pointedly.

"Sure, I guess," Allyson said. "She seems nice."

He snorted. "Don't get too used to her. She won't be there long."

"What do you mean?"

"Pretty girls never last long at Berger Mansion with your uncle pawing at them. Ingrid has griped to me about it before."

"Well, that's a bit rude, don't you think?"

He shrugged. "Just telling you the truth. There's apparently been a parade of girls through that kitchen."

"But why? I know Ingrid is a bit of a hardass, and Martin is a smartass, and Uncle Otto is...."

"Just an ass," he finished for her.

"I'm serious," she said. "It seems like a pretty easy place to work, honestly."

"Girls don't stay long, that's all I can tell you." He bit off a chunk of his wurst and made a faint moan of gastro pleasure. "How's yours?"

She nodded exuberantly. "Good."

The waitress stopped by their table and offered to refill their glasses. When she left with their drink order, Allyson pushed her plate away.

Then she leaned across the table and whispered, "Anthony, they made a doll of me."

"What?" He chewed faster and swallowed. "What do you mean?"

"In the doll room at the mansion. There's now a doll of me on the shelf."

"How do you know it's you? Maybe it's just a pretty girl with dark hair."

"My name is on the shelf underneath it."

He looked concerned.

"There's a doll for Karin there too."

"I take it you just discovered this. Nobody told you they were making these?"

"Right."

"Interesting. Well, as long as your doll stays safely on the shelf, I guess it's all okay."

"Yeah," she agreed. "But what if it doesn't?"

CHAPTER FIFTY-TWO

Berger Mansion, June 22, 9:41 p.m.

A light was on in the kitchen when Allyson got home. Was Ingrid still poking around back there? She wanted to grab a soda from the fridge but didn't really want to run into the housekeeper if she was still up. The woman always made her feel like she was trespassing when Allyson walked into the kitchen.

She almost kept walking to the stairs. But something made her stop. Maybe a piece of her instinctively knew that it wasn't Ingrid. Allyson peered around the doorway of the dining room. Just as she did, the new girl looked back at her from the opposite entryway.

"It's you!" Allyson said, surprised.

Karin looked happy to see her. "I was just finishing up."

Allyson walked through the dining room. "Why are you down here so late?"

Karin's eyes grew wide. "I know.... I put off cleaning up until super late. I promised Ingrid I'd do it, but I didn't say when."

Allyson laughed. "Nice."

"I was literally just finishing when you walked in. Do you want to have a glass of wine with me before bed?"

Allyson shrugged. She'd had plenty of beer already but.... "Why not?"

"Cool," Karin said. "I hate to drink alone at the end of the night."

She walked over to the fridge, pulled out a bottle of Chardonnay and set it on the counter. Then she pulled a couple of wineglasses from a cupboard and poured a healthy glass for each of them, before stuffing the cork back in the bottle and shoving it back in the fridge.

She held a glass out to Allyson. "Do you want to sit down for a minute?"

"Sure," Allyson said.

"C'mon then," the girl said, and led her to a door on the far side of the kitchen. The entrance to the servants' quarters. She motioned Allyson through and flipped the kitchen lights off before closing the door.

"My room is right down here," she said. "You'll be the first one to see it!"

They walked past a couple closed doors before Karin stopped and opened one. She hit a light switch on the wall and stepped inside.

Allyson followed her inside and pushed the door shut behind.

"This is really cute," Allyson said, looking around at the space. It wasn't a large room, but it had high ceilings and the walls were wallpapered in a pale pink and gray pattern that looked pleasing… if extremely dated. The room might have been decorated in the seventies, with its wallpaper, classic dark-stained desk and nightstand and sleigh bed. There was a window on one side with wispy flowered curtains and a wardrobe on the opposite wall.

"I haven't really had the chance to put up my own things yet," Karin apologized. "And there's not a lot of room for visitors, but you can sit on the bed."

"Thanks," Allyson said, and sat down on the edge of the mattress.

Karin hopped onto the opposite end, and drew her legs up ankles over knees like a human pretzel. She sipped her wine and closed her eyes for a second as she swallowed. "That goes down so good," she said.

Allyson took a sip of her own and the warmth in her throat was nice. "I'd guess they don't stock the cheap stuff in this house."

"No, that's for sure. Do you like wine?"

Allyson shrugged. "More of a pint-of-ale girl, if truth be told, but wine is nice too."

"Anything to wash the world out of your eyes."

"I don't know...I kind of like to know what's going on around me," Allyson said, and then chuckled. "I guess I want to keep the world in my eyes."

"Not me. The less I see, the happier I am. I don't want to remember or think about it."

"Well, you had a pretty shitty breakup," Allyson said, after taking another sip of her wine. It *was* pretty nice.

"Bad breakup, bad boyfriend, bad boyfriend before that, a shit of a dad…. Yeah, there's not too much I really want to remember."

"It will get better now that you're here," Allyson said. "A brand-new start, you know? I'm kind of in the same boat."

"Yeah, but you had a good life before and now you'll probably have a good life here."

"And so will you," Allyson said. She suddenly realized how damaged Karin was. In her head, she vowed to get her out of the house this week. She didn't want to add a third wheel to her dates with Anthony, but this poor girl clearly needed some companionship. She took a sip from her glass and realized it was almost empty. Which sucked. She'd been enjoying it more than she'd expected.

"Can I get you a refill?" Karin asked. She unfolded her legs and hopped to the floor.

"I don't want you to have to go back to the kitchen," Allyson said. Though actually, she kind of did. She did want a refill.

"No need," Karin said. "I put last night's bottle from dinner on ice for later. And…well…it's later!"

She walked over to a small trash can next to the desk and pulled a green glass bottle out of the ice inside. After she pulled the cork, she poured a healthy slosh of golden liquid into Allyson's glass before filling her own.

"And there's even a little bit more left." Karin's eyes sparkled when she smiled and Allyson wondered how such a perky girl could be so jaded inside.

"Wanna watch a movie or something?"

"What did you have in mind?"

"Nothing in particular," Karin said. "We can just surf Netflix for something?"

She picked up the remote from her nightstand and turned on the flatscreen TV perched on her desk. When the red logo swam onto the screen, Karin's face brightened. "We never had Netflix where I lived before."

She flipped through a few programs and they settled on a newer film called *Renfield*, a horror comedy with Nicolas Cage. As the movie began, Karin crawled across the bed and used a pillow as the cushion against the headboard. Allyson followed her lead and the two girls leaned back on the bed, still sipping their wine. It was like a classic girls' sleepover.

"Sorry I don't have any popcorn," Karin said.

"Doesn't really go with Chardonnay anyway."

"True."

As the film went on, and Dracula's servant, Renfield, joined a support group for people in abusive relationships and realized he needed to 'take back the power' and leave Dracula for good, the girls laughed at the modern twist on an old story. And Allyson felt increasingly warm and fuzzy from several glasses of wine.

It was all pretty perfect, until the abrupt sound of a door slamming came from somewhere nearby.

Karin shot up in the bed, her eyes wide. "That's him, I know it is." She looked around the room in a panic. "He can't know you're here." She looked frantic and flustered and then suddenly came to a decision. "Get in there." Karin pointed at a large wooden chest on the side of the bed next to the wall. It was the farthest point in the room from the door.

Allyson was confused at the sudden change in the girl. Did Karin really think she was going to get into a big wooden box? "I'm not going to hide," she said.

"Pleeeease," Karin begged. She grabbed Allyson's arm and squeezed. "For me? I will try to send him away, but he *can't* see you."

"Who?" Allyson asked, grudgingly slipping off the far side of the bed with her wineglass. She set it on the floor against the wall where it would be hidden from view by the bed. Karin opened the lid of the large, long chest. Inside, it was half full of comforters and blankets.

"He comes every night when you all go to bed," Karin whispered. "He calls me his 'good girl', but then he hurts me."

Those words sent a chill through Allyson's gut as she climbed into the chest. She'd heard them before.

"Who does this to you?" Allyson asked, crouching now on top of the blankets and holding the chest lid up with one hand. Karin met her question with a finger to her lips.

On the other side of the room, the door handle turned.

Karin jumped up from the floor and set her wine on the desk. With one hand behind her she motioned to Allyson to close the lid. On the television, Dracula was on a killing spree, blood spraying everywhere.

Allyson huddled down on soft blankets, her head and shoulder keeping the lid propped up just a crack. She wanted to try to see who Karin was so afraid of. Uncle Otto? Martin? Someone from outside?

Across the room, Karin said, "Please, not tonight, I'm begging you." But the only answer was a laugh.

Allyson could see Karin backing up and let the lid close to just a slit. She caught a glimpse of a man's black leather shoes and gray suit pants. And she saw the pale skin of Karin's calves crushed up against them. She had never changed out of her servant's clothes, so she was still in a black skirt.

"Please, no," the girl begged. Her voice came with a gasp for air, and then a thick hand connected with a resounding slap against her buttocks.

"You'll do as I say in my house," the familiar voice said. "You're drinking my wine, I see. Did I say you could have it? Well then, you need to work off that debt as I say."

Allyson's eyes widened. The man was Uncle Otto. And as the realization hit, the two pairs of legs moved out of view, blocked by the bed.

"We talked about this last week when you started," Otto growled. "Your service here is at my whim. I took you off the street so you wouldn't have to take in any ugly diseased monster just to let you pay the rent for another day. You'll serve me as I wish."

"Can we talk about this another time?" Karin asked.

Allyson let the lid close all the way as she tried to shift her weight in the box to get more comfortable. It was a long chest and the smell of cedar was rich and comforting but it still was very cramped. She hoped she could manage to stay in here until Karin said it was okay to come out.

There was a faint thump outside and she heard the tenor of Otto's voice rise. Karin answered something, but her voice was muffled and Allyson couldn't make out the words. Clearly, they were arguing.

Allyson took a deep breath and closed her eyes, resting her head on the soft comforter beneath. This was not exactly the way Allyson had expected the night to end.

Things quieted, but then she heard Karin's voice rise again. And the heavy rumble of Otto in reply.

Allyson closed her eyes and waited.

And then the tickle started.

Maybe it was the dust. Maybe the smell of cedar. Whatever it was, she had the horrible feeling that she was about to sneeze. And she could *not* make noise! Karin had seemed really afraid of what Otto might do to her if he found Allyson here, though she couldn't fathom what the big deal was. Would he fire the girl because she had someone in her room?

She didn't want to find out.

Allyson pressed her face hard into the mound of blankets beneath her, praying that she could stifle any sound of a sneeze. She stayed that way for what seemed like minutes, and amazingly, the sneeze never came.

Slowly she raised her head again. The voices outside had quieted, but there was some other noise. Something rhythmic.

Carefully with her head and shoulder she pressed the lid up a crack. Instantly the sound became clear.

It was the sound of flesh meeting flesh. It was the sound she'd heard as a child when her mother was angry and made her pull down her pants and bend over the bed to take her punishment.

The sound of spanking.

Allyson let the lid close again for a minute. What should she do? Did she leap out of the box and tell her uncle to quit spanking the help? Did she just let it pass so that Karin didn't endure any further punishment? She felt paralyzed, not knowing which way to go. Outside, she heard a cry that was clearly pain, and made up her mind. This was ridiculous and she wasn't going to just lie here and let it continue.

Allyson began to push the box lid up, but as she did, she realized the slaps and cries had stopped. She waited a moment, listening. And then Otto's voice finally broke the silence. He sounded…happy.

"That's my good girl. I told you to behave and it would all be good for you."

The bed creaked, and there was a thump on the floor. Suddenly Otto's stockinged feet were visible at the corner of the bed. He was saying something quietly to Karin, and then all at once he stepped away from the bed, moving closer to Allyson. She could hear every word he said next.

"You should have behaved like I told you," he said. "Now look at you."

He reached down for his pants, and Allyson let the lid close. Whatever had just happened was apparently over, so there was no point in leaping out like a Jack-in-the-Box now. She held her breath and waited, cracking the lid just the faintest amount once more to try to hear what was being said. Otto picked up his shirt and then retrieved his shoes. A minute later, he stood, apparently dressed. He turned around and faced the bed; she could see his knees. He stood there for a while before whispering, "Sleep deep, my bad little girl. Sleep deep."

Then he turned and walked out of the room.

Allyson let the lid close. She'd wait for Karin to compose herself from whatever had just happened. She'd probably open the lid in a couple minutes and fill her in on what a jerk her uncle apparently was.

She lay there waiting, but after a few minutes passed, there was still no motion from outside.

Had Karin forgotten about her?

Allyson decided to count to fifty. If Karin didn't come for her by then…she was coming out on her own. She was disappointed when she reached twenty and still, no Karin.

"…twenty-one, twenty-two, twenty-three…thirty-five, thirty-six…forty-seven, forty-eight, forty-nine…."

All right.

She opened the lid enough to confirm that it was safe to come out. Seeing no one, she pulled herself out of the box with a groan. She'd gotten stiff in there.

Otto appeared to be gone for good. As she stretched and straightened up, she saw that Karin was lying on her back on the bed.

Naked.

That's when she saw Karin's face. The slack jaw. The still, parted lips. The eyes wide open, staring unblinking at the ceiling.

Karin was gone for good too.

"Holy shit," she whispered, leaning forward to touch Karin's cheek. It was already cool to the touch. "He fucking killed her."

CHAPTER FIFTY-THREE

Berger Mansion, June 22, 11:22 p.m.

Allyson ran through the kitchen and up the stairs, tears streaming down her face. She couldn't believe what had just happened. How had this night gone from a dream to a nightmare so fast? How was any of it possible?

Back in her room, she paced back and forth, the muted sounds of arguing and spanking playing over and over in her head. The beer and wine and shock combined to make everything around her seem hazy. She felt guilty and fuzzy and angry and frightened all at the same time. She sat down on the bed and cradled her head in her hands but that didn't stop it all from swirling around inside. Almost immediately, she stood back up.

Maybe Otto didn't even realize he'd killed her. Maybe he'd left thinking he'd just roughed her up. Taught her a lesson.

She had to confront him. Make him realize what he'd done. Give him the chance to turn himself in to the police.

The anger that surged over her as she thought of that cleared the fuzziness from her brain a bit. She clenched her jaw and headed toward the door.

Allyson walked down the hall to the bedroom she knew was her uncle's, though she'd never actually been inside. She stood in front of the door and raised her hand to knock.

Are you sure you want to do this?

There was a slight tremble in her wrist...and then she brought her knuckles down on the wood.

And waited.

When nothing stirred within, she knocked again.

And waited some more.

If he didn't come back up here after leaving Karin's room, where else could he be?

Her mind was fuzzy, but the answer was obvious.

She turned and hurried down the stairs, around the corner and down the hall to his office.

This time when she knocked, a voice answered her almost instantly.

"Come."

She turned the knob and stepped inside.

At night, her uncle's office looked as warm and cozy as a Christmas postcard. The furniture in the corners were cloaked in shadow, but he had a small fire going in the fireplace and the desk lamp and table lamps gave off a low, orange-yellow glow. The man himself sat behind the desk, phone in hand.

"Excellent," he said to whoever was on the other end. "Thank you for that. And now I have other business to attend to. Yes. Goodbye."

He hung up and turned to face her. "You're up late, my dear. How can I help you?"

He looked so calm, as if nothing traumatic had happened just a short while ago.

"How could you?" Allyson said. Her voice quavered but she pushed through. "She did nothing to you except say no. You're a monster."

Otto's brow furrowed. "What are you talking about? Did you have a bad dream?"

He would dare to pretend that he didn't know what she was talking about?

"You killed her," Allyson said. "I know that you did. I was there. I heard you beat her. I heard her crying for you to stop."

"What on earth are you talking about?"

"Karin," she said. "You killed the new kitchen girl Karin just now."

"Did I?" he asked. "And where did I do this exactly?"

"Please! Stop pretending. You ripped her clothes off and killed her in her own bed after you had your way with her."

Otto's eyes widened in disbelief. "Oh, Allyson, I think you may be sleepwalking or something. I wonder, how much did you have to drink tonight on your date?"

"Don't try to tell me I dreamed it," Allyson said. "I saw her body right after you left. It was...awful." She choked at the memory.

"I am disappointed that you would think so poorly of me after I took you in," Otto said. "Karin is a darling girl, and I would never hurt her."

"Well, you did," Allyson said. "Maybe you thought you left her unconscious, but you left her dead. I can show you."

"Can you now?"

She nodded. "Come on and see what you did."

His face looked extremely put upon, but with a grunt he pushed himself up from the chair.

"If this will help you to wake up and come back to this reality, all right," he said resignedly. "But I do not appreciate this behavior. Not at all."

Allyson led the way down the hall and through the dining room to the back hall of the servants' quarters. Otto trudged along heavily behind her, not saying a word. But she could hear his breath.

When she reached out to grab the knob of Karin's bedroom door, a knife of ice stabbed at her heart. Her hand froze on the cold metal. She did *not* want to go back in there and see the poor girl. But she had to. Gulping down her fear, she turned the knob and stepped inside.

"Look what you did," she said over her shoulder. And then she turned to face the horrible sight of her new friend's corpse.

Only....

It wasn't there.

The bed was made, the pillows perfectly set and the spread draped unwrinkled over the mattress.

"And what is that exactly?" Otto asked. "What am I supposed to be seeing here? It looks to me as if our Karin is out tonight, perhaps enjoying herself at some bar in Hildegard."

"No." Allyson looked frantically around for any evidence of their night. "No."

The wine bottle was missing, as was Karin's wineglass. What about hers? She remembered that she'd left it on the floor against the wall behind the bed. She stepped around the foot of the bed prepared to triumphantly retrieve it.

But the floor was bare.

"She was here!" Allyson cried out. "I heard you rape her. I heard her die at your hands."

"All right, that's enough now," Otto said. "I've let your little fever dream go on too long. I want you to go back to your bed right now and sleep this off. And in the morning, I will expect an apology. And I'll be honest, I don't know if that will be enough. I have enough drama in my life without some little transient girl coming into my home to manufacture more." He pointed to the door. "Come on, let's get you upstairs."

Allyson didn't know what to say. There was no evidence in the room that Karin or she had been here just a half hour before watching *Renfield*. Even the television was off, its screen an unhelpful black.

She followed his finger and walked ahead of him once again, this time in shame and confusion. Could Karin really have been alive, and gotten up after she left? Where could she have gone?

Otto followed her all the way to her room and stood behind her as she opened the door. When she stepped inside, he pushed his way in behind her, and closed the door.

"I don't know what's come over you tonight," he said. "Please sit down."

He pointed to her bed, and she did as he said. For the first time since confronting him, she began to worry about her own safety. Shut into a small bedroom with him? Alone? She'd been shut in a room with him before less than an hour ago and someone had died.

Otto reached over to her dresser and lifted the phone from its cradle. He held up one finger at her, warning her to wait until he was done.

Allyson said nothing, but gauged her chances at running for the door. Could she get past him, get the door open and get out to the hall without him catching her?

She didn't think so. She'd have to pass within a meter of him. And he'd see her moving three or four steps before she reached that gap.

No way.

"Allyson needs some help getting to sleep tonight," he said. "Yes, if you could come up immediately, I'd appreciate it."

He hung up the receiver and then turned to look at her.

"Sometimes the stress of a situation gets the best of us, and the mind plays tricks," he said. "Things can happen when you're not in full control of your faculties. Bad things. So, I think it's best if we make sure that you're comfortable tonight. No more walking the house."

"I know what you did," Allyson said. "I saw you enter her room. I heard it all."

"You need sleep," he said. "When the light of the morning comes, you'll see that this was all some strange fever dream. And you know that when the sun comes, the darkness of dreams fades away until we forget it all."

"It wasn't a dream," she insisted.

"I went to the room with you," he said. "We stood there together. There was no body. Surely you are not so delusional that you saw that."

"Yes," she said. "I saw that. But I know what I saw *before* that."

She met his gaze and did not blink. His eyes were hard. Allyson had always thought he had a kindly, if distant look to his eyes, but now she realized otherwise. It wasn't distant.

It was cold.

There was a knock at the door then, and Otto simply said, "Come."

The door opened and Allyson sucked in her breath at the smiling figure who stood behind Otto now.

Dr. Testi. What was he doing here in the middle of the night?

The bedroom light glinted off his small spectacles and made it look as if his eyes were searchlights as he stepped into the room carrying a small black bag.

"What have we here?" Testi said in an ingratiating voice. "Someone having a bit of a time with the Sandman? I brought my bag of tricks to lure him in, and we'll have you safely to morning in no time."

"Our little girl was wandering the house and thinks she saw a dead body," Otto said.

"Dead body, oh my," Testi said, staring at first Allyson and then meeting Otto's eyes. "That would be unsanitary indeed. I don't believe Ingrid would allow that in the house for a minute."

Otto laughed. "No, my friend, you're right there. But Allyson is having some kind of waking nightmare. I thought you might be able to help her get through the night and then we can see how she's feeling about things in the morning."

"Yes, yes, of course," Testi said. "I've got just the thing. My patients always say this makes them sleep like a log but wake in the morning without any aftereffects."

He pulled out a syringe and a small clear vial. After plunging the needle in and drawing a small amount of fluid, he held it up and tapped the glass with his finger to draw any air out.

"You should get a good night's sleep and wake feeling yourself again," he promised and moved toward Allyson.

She held up her hands. "No! I don't want any drugs."

"It's perfectly safe," Testi said. "Trust me, it has amazing effects."

"I can sleep on my own, thank you."

Otto stepped closer, standing next to Testi and blocking her escape. "This is not an offer," he said. "I insist. It's for your own good. We can talk again in the morning."

Testi took her arm by the wrist, and Allyson flung his hand with the needle away. The doctor nearly dropped the syringe.

"Please, my girl, this will help."

"I will hold you down, if necessary," Otto warned.

Allyson could see she was not going to get out of this, and slowly offered her arm.

"That's better," the doctor said. "This will just pinch a tiny bit and then...."

The needle bit her and something cool erupted below her skin.

"See, no problem at all."

The doctor withdrew the needle and walked over to his leather bag to place it inside. When he came back, he put his hand to her forehead, and then took her hand in his and put two fingers on the underside of her wrist.

"How do you feel now?"

"I'm fine, just like be...."

Allyson's tongue suddenly realized it couldn't make another syllable. She frowned and her eyes rolled. Her throat gargled a little, but no more words came out.

"Let's get her comfortable, eh, Otto?"

A moment later, she felt fingers at her waist, and then her jeans were slipping down her legs. And then someone was tugging at her sleeve, and the skin of her tummy was suddenly goose-bumped as the cool air of the room kissed it.

She tried to keep her eyes open, but the doctor kept getting larger and smaller as she stared at him.

"Otto, pull back the sheet there and we'll tuck her in."

The doctor's cool and too-familiar hands lifted her calves and slipped them across the bed. The sheet covered part of her legs then, but didn't come all the way up, as those long, thin fingers massaged and fondled her inner thigh. They moved up and down, gently caressing her skin, with each stroke moving closer and closer to the edge of her panties. And she couldn't stop him. She couldn't lift her arm or open her lips as his fingers slid across her most private part.

"She's a lovely girl, Otto, really she is."

Otto's voice came deep and raspy from a long way away.

"That she is," he said. "She's a good girl. My very good girl."

CHAPTER FIFTY-FOUR

Berger Mansion, June 23, 4:16 a.m.

Allyson's eyes flickered open in the dark. She felt weird. Like she was floating. The sheets were warm, wet and heavy against her skin, as if the bed itself was weighing her down. She threw them off to the side and a cool rush of air washed across her chest. Her nipples instantly hardened. That's when she realized that all she had on were her panties. *How?*

The events of the night suddenly came back to her all in a rush. Her uncle and Dr. Testi had stripped her after they drugged her. A pang stabbed at her heart. Had they done anything else to her?

She stretched her legs apart and slid her fingers across the panties. Nothing was sore. Or wet. Thank God. Small favors. If only Karin could say the same.

Poor Karin!

The image of the girl's face staring sightlessly at the ceiling would haunt her forever.

She had *not* imagined it. There was nothing Otto could say and no drug that was going to make her believe she hallucinated a whole evening of watching a movie, drinking wine and then lying oblivious in a trunk while her new friend was being raped just a meter away. She felt horrible now that she had not realized the full extent of what was happening outside the chest. She should have come out and beaten Otto in the back to get him to leave. But Karin had been so adamant that she couldn't be seen…and she hadn't thought that his abuse would end the way it did.

After he'd left the room, he must have come back and gotten rid of the body. Or had someone else do it. Maybe that's who he'd been on the phone with when she reached the office. He'd thanked whoever was on the line and it was well after 'business hours' at that point. Who had he been talking to?

More importantly, what had they done with the body? She hadn't heard anyone at the front door or any cars starting up outside…and at that hour, the house was silent enough that she would have heard every sound.

Where could they have put her?

Allyson slid her feet over the edge of the bed and the world moved sideways. She felt very unsteady. And her mouth tasted like metal. She needed water. Booze and drugs did not make for the best head cocktail. She looked at the clock and saw that it was after four a.m. Nobody else would be up yet. She decided to go to the kitchen and get something to drink…and then check Karin's room again.

She pulled on a t-shirt and a pair of sweatpants and padded barefoot down the stairs. The house was still pitch black, the light of the moon reflecting eerily in through the front windows to cast beams of faint light on the couch and chairs of the front room.

She walked slowly through the dining room, waving her hands a little in front of her to make sure she didn't crash into a chair. Once she got to the kitchen, there was a nightlight that gave enough illumination for her to see her way. She took a glass from the cupboard and filled it with cold water from the tap. She drank the entire glass without taking a breath, and then gasped for air as she put the cup right back under the faucet to fill it again. She was incredibly thirsty.

She set the glass down in the sink finally and wiped her mouth dry. Her body still felt weird – artificially light – but the water helped a little. She opened the door to the servants' quarters and walked down the dark hall, counting the doors to reach Karin's room. One. Two. Three.

Allyson turned the knob and opened the door. She stepped inside and turned on the light.

The room was just as it had been when she'd dragged Otto back here. She shook her head. There had to be something….

On a whim, she picked up the TV remote and powered it on. When the screen came to life, she saw options for most-used apps, and a live TV program schedule. She also saw a picture of Nicolas Cage with the word RENFIELD overlaid. Beneath the image was a progress bar that looked to be at about ninety percent and the words 'Continue Watching'.

There. There was her proof that she had not imagined it. She'd been here.

She flicked the TV off.

What had they done with Karin? Had someone driven the body to dump in a lake while she'd been drugged? Or was it still here while they decided how to dispose of it?

She walked out into the hallway and decided to check the adjoining rooms. She opened them one by one, using the flashlight on her cell phone to quickly look inside. A couple were set up as bedrooms, but they clearly were not used. A couple others appeared to be storage rooms; one was an extra pantry for the kitchen.

At the end of the hall was a door to the old wing. Allyson had managed to avoid going into that side of the house in her explorations up to now. But that seemed like a perfect place to stash a body temporarily. She tried the knob and it turned easily. The 'other side' looked much like the hall she'd just left, only the walls were older and painted a different color. The floor was laid in rich, dark wood planks, and the doorframes were also varnished wood, instead of painted, as they were on the 'used' side of the house. Honestly, it looked nicer over here. More classic.

The first two doors she tried opened onto rooms that were completely empty.

The third, however….

She turned the knob. Even before she brought the light up to spy on the contents of the place, she just had a feeling. The air smelled different. Warmer somehow. Used. There were a lot of things inside, dark shadows of furniture.

As soon as she raised the light to see that it was, indeed, decorated as a bedroom with a bureau and nightstand and bed, she pressed her hand against the light to hide it.

There was someone in the bed!

Was it Karin?

She let the light peek out between her fingers again slowly and raised her phone once more.

Again, she yanked it back. Her heart pounded like a jackhammer.

It wasn't Karin's body lying on that mattress.

There was a man in the bed. His body was mostly hidden by the sheets and his face was turned away from the door so she could only see the back of his head covered in dark black hair with traces of silver. She stood there frozen for a second, hiding the light in her hand. He didn't seem to be stirring.

Slowly, she took a step backward. And then another.

Carefully she pulled the door shut in slow motion, praying that it would not squeak or click.

Allyson stood in the hallway measuring her breath. Trying not to make a sound as her insides pounded with fright. She had not expected to find anyone living in the closed section of the house. Who the heck was it?

Were other people living here too?

She finally forced her feet to move and walked to the next door. This time, she turned the knob much slower and eased the door open a centimeter at a time. When she brought the light up, she saw that, again, this room was decorated as a bedroom. It had a masculine flair, with framed pictures of sensual artwork, and a dark blue comforter covering the bed.

There was nobody in it at the moment. But like the other room, something in the air just said that this room was at least occasionally occupied.

She pulled the door closed and moved to the final door on the opposite side of the hallway. The hall itself appeared to empty into some kind of large ballroom or open area. She could see a bronze statue in the shadows beyond and it looked as if there were some framed pieces of art and photos on the walls. But before she went exploring that, she slowly teased open the final closed door.

This room appeared to be mostly empty as she brought her flash up. There were some metal shelving units along the wall closest to the door filled with boxes and old radios, TVs and other equipment. There was also a sink, with some small paintbrushes drying in a dish holder on one side and an unpainted, unfinished clay doll sitting right in the middle of the counter next to it. Behind the doll were a series of small paint bottles. Just to the right of the sink was a squat appliance that Allyson recognized as a kiln.

So this was where the dolls were made.

And as she turned, she saw an old wooden dining room table that had been retired. It was no longer holding food. At the edge of the area illuminated by her flash, there was a pair of bare feet.

She focused the light on the table. Karin's dead gaze met her eyes.

The girl was naked and laid out as if on display.

"Oh, you poor thing," Allyson whispered. A thought struck her. What if Dr. Testi had 'examined' the girl after she was dead and run his cold hands up and down the poor girl's cold thighs, as he had done to Allyson?

Her whole body shivered in disgust.

She needed to get out of here. But not before she had evidence. Allyson turned on the light in the room, raised her phone, and took several pictures of the girl, including one of just her face; it seemed wrong to shoot photos of a nude body, her nipples and pubic hair blatant and exposed.

Then she turned out the light and poked her head into the dark hallway outside.

It remained empty.

She didn't stick around to question it.

Allyson pulled the door shut and almost ran down the hall and back through the servants' wing. She stopped in the kitchen to catch her breath. She couldn't go back to bed now. She couldn't stay here either. There was only one thing to do.

She dialed Anthony.

CHAPTER FIFTY-FIVE

Berger Mansion, June 23, 4:47 a.m.

Martin did not like waking up at dawn. He'd planned to catch at least another three hours, maybe more. But he felt strangely wide awake. He hated those nights when you tossed and turned and couldn't get back to sleep. He didn't have insomnia often, but it really killed the day ahead when he did.

Luckily, he did know a cure. Often a tall glass of milk soothed the stomach and the brain, and within a half an hour he'd be snoring soundly once again. Ingrid had taught him that years ago. He decided not to wait to see if he could doze without help. If the sun came up, he'd never get back to sleep.

After visiting the bathroom, Martin padded down the stairs and through the foyer. But he slowed when he reached the dining room. Someone was talking just ahead. Urgent, frantic whispers, but loud enough that he could hear them.

He slipped up to the doorframe and stayed hidden against the wall. He could see Allyson in the dim light beyond, leaning against the counter on her elbows, the light of a phone shining against her cheek.

"He tried to make me believe I'd imagined it all," she was saying. "And then that creepy doctor came and shot me up with something that knocked me out. But I woke up a little while ago and, oh my God…Anthony…I found the body. Here, I'll show you."

She pulled the phone from her face and Martin saw the flash of a familiar face on the screen as she pulled up a picture of Karin.

"I wanted proof," she said. "But I can't stay here. Could you come and get me? Oh God, thank you. Yes. I'll wait out front."

She clicked the call off and Martin quickly moved into a corner and crouched to the floor. She wasn't going to be looking for anyone here; she would walk right past him as she made a beeline for the door.

Allyson proved him right. She didn't look around as she breezed through the dining room. He watched her hurry across the tile and up the steps to the front door. She let herself out and gently closed the door behind her.

Martin felt the rush of sure victory. There was only one person that she would have called. And he was going to greatly relish seeing Anthony again. But he needed to prepare.

Martin stood and hurried up the stairs to his room.

Allyson wasn't going anywhere.

CHAPTER FIFTY-SIX

Berger Mansion, June 23, 4:55 a.m.

Allyson paced back and forth in front of the oval section of the driveway, anxious to hop into Anthony's car as soon as he pulled up. He wouldn't even have to come to a complete stop.

The loose gravel poked right through the thin soles of her slippers; she supposed she should have gone upstairs to get her shoes, but she had been frightened to spend another second inside the house.

In the distance, the lights of a car flickered visibly between the trees and she sighed in relief. "Hurry," she whispered like a prayer.

"He won't be fast enough," a deep voice said just centimeters from her ear.

As her eyes sprang open wide, a hand wrapped across her mouth to silence her. At the same time, an arm slipped around her ribs.

"It's a little early to be going out, don't you think? Your uncle would never approve."

She looked up to see the piercing blue eyes of the man smiling down at her.

Ivan.

He saw the recognition in her face and nodded. "Yes, we've met before," he said. "I always liked your mom, so I tried to warn you at the Hofbräuhaus to stay out of things here, to leave. But you didn't listen. And now it is my job to bring you back. I work for your uncle, taking care of all those unpleasant things that crop up from time to time and threaten his career. Unfortunately, I'm afraid you have become one of them."

Allyson twisted in his grip, trying to escape, but he was strong and much bigger than her. His arm held her in place easily.

"I'm going to take my hand off your mouth now," he said quietly. "But I promise you, if you make a sound, it will be the last sound you make. Nod if you understand."

She nodded quickly.

"Good."

His hand withdrew, but a moment later, there was a metallic click next to her ear. And then his hand moved in front of her face so that she could see the glinting silver of the switchblade.

"It's quite sharp, I promise you," he said. "It will have no problem poking right through those tiny ribs of yours. Now we are going to walk back into the house. You are not going to try to escape or wake up the rest of the family. Either of those things will end with this blade in your heart, or your back. Whichever I reach first. Start walking."

He kept one arm around her chest, while the other kept the tip of the blade lightly pressed against her side. With each step away from the driveway, her heart sank further. Anthony was going to pull up just a little too late.

A moment later, they were through the front door, back inside the pitch-black mansion.

And then it *was* too late.

CHAPTER FIFTY-SEVEN

Berger Mansion, June 23, 5:01 a.m.

Anthony drove up the long driveway to Berger Mansion. There were no lights on yet in any of the windows, so that was good. Nobody would be there to stop Allyson's getaway. He cut the car's lights so he wouldn't wake anyone inside as he pulled into the curved area near the front of the house. He put the car in Park but left the engine running. Anthony stepped out of the car and scanned the house.

She'd said she'd be waiting out front, but he didn't see her anywhere.

Anthony took the walkway toward the house. The night was utterly still. The bushes and trees that decorated the front areas of the mansion looked like midnight sentinels, guarding the grounds from intruders. Like him.

"Allyson?" he called out in a loud whisper. "Are you out here?"

A branch snapped behind him.

"Allyson?" He turned.

"Not exactly."

Martin stood behind him. A black pistol perched in his hand, its muzzle pointed at Anthony's chest.

"Where is she?"

Martin shrugged. "Maybe she had a change of plans. Maybe she went back to bed. It is a little early for a date, isn't it?"

"What have you done with her?"

"Me? I haven't done a thing. I don't have any problem with her. But I do have one with you. And honestly, she should be angry at you about it as well."

"What are you talking about?"

"I know you used Allyson to get into our house so you could take back the USB drive."

Anthony laughed. "You didn't pay me what you said you would for the footage. So, I took it back. It occurs to me that I can probably make a lot more money for it on my own than I would ever get from you anyway."

Martin ran his tongue across the top of his teeth as he considered that statement. "I see. So, you would double-cross the guy who told you where to be and when to be there to make a few extra dollars."

"You didn't keep up your end of the bargain," Anthony said. "And I need cash for my own projects. I don't care who the bankroller is in the end."

"I got the money," Martin said. "I just didn't have it before. You need to learn a little patience and trust."

"I don't trust a guy who would blackmail his own father," Anthony said. If words could spit, his would have made Martin wet.

"No matter," Martin said. "As it turns out, I don't need Dad's kinky sex pictures anyway. I got something better."

"I've added a couple more to the collection since I gave you the USB," Anthony said. "Your father is an asshole."

"True," Martin said. "But I don't need them now. And since you took all the photos and videos back, I don't really have any reason to give you any more money either, do I? Actually, you should be paying me back the advance I gave you."

"You're fucking crazy," Anthony said.

"Maybe," Martin said. "But let's discuss that inside. It's chilly out here."

"What else do we have to discuss?" Anthony asked. "You hired me to photograph your father doing things that he absolutely would not want in the public domain. Then you didn't pay me the second installment that we agreed upon, and I took the evidence back until you did."

"Start walking," Martin said. "This gun is loaded and if you're dead, well, that would be one way to solve my problem."

Anthony started to move toward the front door of the mansion, but the cold mouth of the gun barrel poked him between the shoulder blades.

"Not that way. Go left. There's a door in the back of the house that won't wake anyone."

Martin pushed him forward, step by step, with nudges of the gun, as they walked past dark hedges and black windowpanes.

* * *

Neither of them noticed a shadowed figure keeping pace with them just a few yards back.

* * *

"Here," Martin said, after they'd turned around the farthest corner of the house. There was a white door there down a small brick path. When they reached it, Martin pressed a key into Anthony's hand. "Open it."

Anthony fumbled the key into the lock and then twisted the handle. It ground a bit from disuse, but ultimately turned. And then they were inside a dark hall in the closed-off part of the mansion.

"Just walk forward slowly," Martin directed. "No sudden moves."

"I can't fucking see anything," Anthony complained.

"All the more reason to move slowly."

* * *

Neither of them heard the outer door open and quietly click close again behind them.

* * *

"Where are we going?" Anthony asked.

Martin didn't answer. They just kept moving slowly through the empty back halls of the mansion until finally the gun barrel pushed hard into his back again.

"Left," Martin said.

They walked through a large open area and then came to a locked door.

"Use the key," Martin directed.

Anthony struggled to see the keyhole but, ultimately, after slipping the key across the door a couple times, it sunk in. He turned the key and then the door handle.

They stepped inside a long, wide room with a small mosaic glass lamp lit in the corner, providing just enough light to rescue a small bit of the room from shadows.

"Took you long enough," a feminine voice said.

"He's a talker," Martin answered.

Ingrid stepped out of the darkness, with a broad smile on her face.

"Good morning, Anthony."

★ ★ ★

Outside of the door, a long-fingered hand turned the knob, ever so slowly, and presently cracked it open just a centimeter, then two... just enough to peer unseen at the tawdry scene unraveling inside.

CHAPTER FIFTY-EIGHT

Berger Mansion, June 23, 5:16 a.m.

"You're in on this too?" Anthony stared at Ingrid incredulously. He wouldn't put anything past Martin, the silver-spoon spoiled brat, but Ingrid? She had always struck him as the uptight, old-school German chick who never did any wrong.

"You should probably have stuck to delivering groceries," she said.

"Sit down," Martin instructed, and pointed to a wooden chair. As soon as Anthony did, Ingrid knelt next to him. She raised a strand of rope and began to bind first his wrists tight to the armrests and then his ankles to the wooden legs of the chair. Ingrid looped and tied the knots while Martin held the gun.

Anthony didn't try to struggle. He didn't trust Martin's finger not to slip on the trigger and, honestly, he was frozen in shock – completely floored at this alliance. He looked at Ingrid as she finished her knots and began to say just that.

"I can't believe that you and Martin would both connive to—"

Martin moved closer to Ingrid and slipped his free hand around her waist as she stood up. She smiled and arched her back closer to him, twisting to kiss his cheek. Martin didn't allow her kiss to stay chaste; he moved his mouth to meet hers and sucked her lips tight to his. Their tongues met in an anxious, needy way that said this was not the first time they had kissed. Or even the fiftieth. Her hand massaged his chest as he kept the hand with the gun leveled at Anthony. Not that it mattered; the ropes were tight enough that he had no illusions of pulling free.

Instead, he looked away from the two as they lost themselves in their kiss. Apparently capturing and tying him up was a turn-on.

But in looking away from one weird scene, his eyes fell instantly on another.

Across the room from him was a small, old, beat-up wooden table. Right in the center rested a small human skull that had clearly belonged to a baby or small child. It connected to an equally tiny rib cage. But the child was limbless; no arms or legs were visible.

"Let me guess," he said, interrupting the makeout session. "Those are the bones that were originally in the casket that got unearthed in the storm a couple weeks ago?"

The kiss finally broke.

"Well done, Anthony," Martin said. His voice dripped with mock approval. "You're a regular Sherlock Holmes."

"Where are the arms and legs?"

Martin grinned and took his hands off Ingrid. "Won't your deductive skills take you that far? Allow me to show you."

Martin walked to the far side of the room and opened a cabinet. He withdrew a black leather bag and cracked it open. From within, he pulled a fistful of euros. He walked over to stand in front of Anthony again and riffled the bills in front of his face in a fan.

"The arms and legs are right here," he said, barely restraining a chuckle. "It turns out that baby bones buried in the backyard are quite valuable to certain people."

The meaning dawned on Anthony almost instantly. "And…this is why you don't need the pictures I took anymore."

"Precisely." Martin grinned. "If these bones turn up, and someone thinks to do a DNA test – which of course, they will – Daddy's career will be flushed down the sewer faster than you can cry 'rat'."

"But why?" Anthony asked. "I get it, the kid was your sister's, but…."

Martin made a frown of distaste. "The kid was my sister's – and my dad's. The masses may be more open-minded about sexual preferences these days, but they just aren't enlightened enough to swallow the tale of a man who screws his teenage daughter and then sends her to the insane asylum after she births his baby only to have him kill it."

Anthony's eyes widened. "So, when the storm unearthed the casket, he wanted to make sure the skeleton was put back in the closet."

Martin smiled. "Precisely. And I got to it before he did that night and made sure he couldn't bury the evidence a second time."

"So...you've been blackmailing him for the bones?"

Martin nodded. "One tibia at a time. This baby is my ticket out of here. My dad's going to pay for his crimes." He laughed. "Pay *me*. And when he ponies up to get that skull back, Ingrid and I are going to take the money and run far, far away from here. So...I'm afraid you and your pictures need to disappear until I've finished doling out these bones. I need my ransom before you go releasing anything to take him out of circulation completely."

Anthony realized then that Martin was likely not going to let him leave this house.

"Look," he said, "I don't give a shit what war you wage with your father. I just want to take Allyson and get out of here...really the same thing that you and Ingrid want. That's why I came here this morning. Let her go with me, we call it even, and I'll bury the pictures and let you run your play the way you want. Now...if you wanted to drop just one of those little wads of cash in my hand, I wouldn't say no." He made a hopeful face before continuing. "But all I really want is Allyson."

Martin shrugged. "I can't help you there, man. I don't have her. One of Dad's monkeys grabbed her."

"Help me find her?"

"Not part of the plan, my man." Martin looked at Ingrid. "Do you want to get out of here for a while?"

She stood still...but a smile ran across her face. "Let's keep him quiet, then."

Martin walked to the side of the room and came back with a t-shirt that had been stored in a box.

"Keep it quiet and you stay alive," he said, before wrapping the shirt around Anthony's head and tying a knot in the back until the fabric slipped into his mouth, gagging him.

And then Ingrid slid her arm around Martin's back and gave him a long, sensuous kiss, right in front of Anthony. Her tongue slid easily into his mouth as her hands held the sides of his head and her fingernails slipped beneath his hair.

"No more free show for you," Martin said, after breaking the kiss. He took Ingrid's hand and led her out of the room.

Anthony was left to stare at the empty room in the dark. His mouth was filled with cotton but he didn't care. He was only thinking of one thing.

Where was Allyson?

CHAPTER FIFTY-NINE

Berger Mansion, June 23, 5:35 a.m.

"I'm afraid you have been a very bad girl," Otto said.

Allyson did not reply.

Otto sat behind the big wooden desk in his office, elbows resting on the surface as his fingers entwined and released again and again. It was as if he were doing hand calisthenics. Ivan stood behind her, hands on her shoulders, constantly reminding her that he was right there.

"I believe you were told as soon as you arrived here that sections of the house were restricted," her uncle said. "And yet, you went there anyway."

"And I found the proof of what you did last night," Allyson said. "You denied it, but Karin's body is lying in a room back there. And I have pictures to prove it."

"I see." His hands continued to fidget as if on their own accord. "Tell me, do these pictures show me laying a finger on the poor girl?"

Allyson shook her head. "No, but I was there in the room when it happened. I saw you come in and throw her on the bed. I heard the things you said. The things you did."

"So, then, the only real connection between these photos of Karin and myself is you. Do you see my quandary here? You've become quite the liability, my dear niece."

At that moment, Dr. Testi appeared in the office doorway.

"Otto, I have some very interesting news that I think you'll want to hear right away."

"Indeed?" Otto said. He reached in his desk drawer and tossed a pair of silver handcuffs to Ivan. "Lock her up until we decide what we're doing with her." Then he turned back to Testi and nodded. "Let's hear it."

CHAPTER SIXTY

Berger Mansion, June 23, 5:44 a.m.

Somehow his dawn rescue and escape plan had turned into a death sentence. Anthony shook his head back and forth, trying to catch the knot of his gag against the edge of the wooden chair. If he could wedge it right, he might be able to slip it up enough that it would come loose. He couldn't stand the texture of the material against his tongue, never mind being silenced.

Ingrid had done a pretty good job on the knots all the way around. He tried again and again to pull his legs and arms from the chair, but they did not budge. He needed help. But the only one who was going to help him was himself. And the sand in the hourglass was running.

Martin was a skeezy little chickenshit who wouldn't stand up to his father. A blackmailing coward.

But was he so much of a coward that he wouldn't ultimately use that little pistol of his to get rid of the only one who knew his plan?

Anthony didn't intend to just sit here waiting to find out. He might not be able to get out of the chair...but he could *move* the thing. If he could scootch across the room and knock the lamp to the floor, he might be able to use a piece of glass from it to work at the rope on his wrist. The piece would have to be long enough to reach, which was a gamble. But there was nothing gained by not trying.

He tensed his whole body and then pushed with his feet, which did, in fact, jolt forward slightly.

This was going to take a while.

He gritted his teeth and tried to hop the chair forward again. This time he got it slightly farther off the ground.

Five more centimeters.

He really put his body into it the next time. But instead of slipping forward evenly, his force threw the chair off balance. And suddenly he was tipping forward. He pushed off with his left foot, trying at the last second to stop the fall, or at least stop from going down face-first onto the wooden floor. He liked having his teeth.

The push helped, but didn't save him. The chair fell to the right of center and the wooden arm caught the impact first.

There was a snap just before his right cheek slapped on the floor and for a second, he wasn't sure if it was the chair or his wrist. There was a lightning crack of pain that shot up his arm at the same time as a flush of fire spread across his face.

He opened his mouth to scream and curse but nothing got past the gag.

However, he realized that the old wood of the chair had cracked with the impact and his weight behind it. The support strut that held the arm to the body of the chair had snapped, which made the arm itself slightly loose.

Anthony ignored the throbbing in his wrist and threw his body to the left, trying to roll the chair away from leaning on that arm. He needed it free if he was going to work on the fracture.

It took three tries but then he was on his back, face to the ceiling. He pulled on his right arm and the chair arm moved slightly. He pushed and pulled; the wood shivered back and forth.

But not enough to set him free. The rope against his wrist was digging painfully into his flesh as he tried to brute-force break the arm with his muscles. Wasn't happening.

He needed another impact.

Anthony rolled the chair over again so that his feet were usable, and then he pushed it across the floor with his toes. He needed to use a wall to give him something to balance against. And then, after rocking himself so that the back of the chair hit the wall, he pushed with his feet and leaned so that his head and the back of the chair smashed into the plaster.

That hurt like hell.

But with a quick twist and push, he got the chair back on all four feet again.

And then he readied himself to possibly break an arm.

Whether the chair's or his own was uncertain.

Anthony threw himself forward and to the right.

Again, the chair arm took the brunt of the fall, followed quickly by his wrist and face.

"Fuck!" he screamed into the gag.

But the chair arm was now bent farther inward, his right hand pointing to his left.

Anthony smiled through the pain and rolled the chair so that he was on his back again.

This time, after he bent the wooden arm back and forth a few times, the support strut completely snapped. Slowly, he shifted the rope up the loose arm until his hand slipped off the wood. And then, despite a red-hot throbbing in his wrist, he fumbled at the knot on his left hand until it was free.

★ ★ ★

Five minutes later, Anthony emerged from the back room sans a gag but with a stack of euros in his pocket. Little bastard was not going to kill him *or* get away with not paying him what they'd agreed on.

He started toward the front of the house, listening for any sounds of Otto or his henchmen. When he finally reached the dividing door between the 'unused' mansion and slipped into the front half of the house, he saw a shaft of light stretching across the floor midway down the hall.

Somebody was awake down there.

Anthony hesitated. Should he duck back into the empty part of the house?

But if he was going to find Allyson, he needed to find Otto.

It occurred to him that this might very well be the hallway where Otto's office was. He crept along the wall slowly, ready to run like hell at any moment if he was challenged. As he got nearer the door he heard voices, and instantly he knew that his hunch was right. This was Otto's office, and the fat cat was inside right now. He was currently telling somebody, "Let's hear it."

Another voice, higher-pitched but masculine, began to speak.

"Well, Otto, it seems that there are circles within circles of intrigue here in this house. Little Allyson here is not your only liability. I'm afraid your son has been taking you for a ride. You should have told us you were being blackmailed."

"Blackmailed?" another voice said within. A man's voice that Anthony didn't recognize. It occurred to him that there were things being said… and possibly about to be said…that could be useful if he got out of this crazy house. He wished he had his camera with him, but his phone would have to do. Anthony pulled it out of his pocket and turned on the video recorder to capture the conversation in the room just beyond his left shoulder. And then he hunched down and slipped the phone camera just past the doorframe so that it could capture what was happening.

He saw the dark shoes of a man and the feet of the desk on the phone screen. When he tilted it slightly, he could see the profile of Otto behind the desk, and two men standing at the front and side. He recognized Dr. Testi instantly.

"Apparently, you've been paying someone to get back the bones of Catherine's baby, a little at a time. True?"

Otto nodded. "I thought we were making a simple trade…but the asshole decided to piecemeal it. I have the arms and legs, but still need the ribs and head."

"You're not going to like this," Testi said. "But the *asshole* is your son. Apparently with help from your housekeeper."

"You can't be serious!" Otto raged. "Martin would never…."

Testi shook his head. "I wouldn't have believed it either if I hadn't seen the two of them in the other end of the house, tying up your delivery boy and bragging about extorting the money from you so that the two of them could leave here rich, and never return."

"I can't believe this," Otto said. His fidgeting hands now cradled his balding brow for a moment before he looked up and asked, "They have Anthony tied up? Why?"

"Apparently Martin was going to blackmail you with videos of your, um, evening frivolities at first and so he hired the delivery boy to creep around the house with his camera. At least until the bones came popping out of the ground. Then he switched gears."

"Ingrid, Martin, Ella, Anthony? Is there anyone in this house that I can trust? All I have given them and this is the thanks...."

"The good news is, the rest of the bones are in the room with the money he's stolen from you. Along with the delivery boy, of course."

"We have some loose ends to tie up this morning," Otto said. "We need a plan."

CHAPTER SIXTY-ONE

Berger Mansion, June 23, 5:47 a.m.

Martin and Ingrid ran through the kitchen, lit now by the early light of dawn. He squeezed her hand as they reached her room unseen by anyone else in the house. He opened the door and pulled her inside, pressing the door closed behind them with one hand, before pushing her back against it and kissing her hard. She liked it when he was a little rough.

Ingrid ran her hands up and down his back, tracing all of his pleasure spots with knowing fingers. When they broke the kiss, breathless, she whispered, "It's all coming together."

Martin grinned and began to rip her shirt off. "And we're going to come together too."

Ingrid pushed him back with her hand. "What are we going to do with Anthony?"

Martin batted her hand away and tried to kiss her. "We can deal with him later, he's not going anywhere."

"I know that," she said, shifting out of his reach. "But now he knows everything. We can't just set him free. But you haven't gotten all of the money yet from Otto."

Martin nodded. "I know. We're going to have to make him disappear."

"Forever?"

"Maybe."

"Martin." Her voice trembled. "You dragged him into this. It's not his fault."

He slipped his arm back around her middle and pulled her close. "How about we talk about Anthony later? We'll figure it out. I've been waiting to be with you all night."

"Me too." Ingrid relaxed into his kiss. It was deep and warm and only made her hungrier for the feel of his body. She broke from his lips and pulled his shirt over his head.

"That's my kitten," Martin said. He let her undo his belt, and a moment later, kicked his jeans to the side. Her face grazed his briefs and he instantly grew thick. But before she could go further, he pulled her up so that he could strip her.

When she shrugged her bra off and let it slide down her arms, Martin instantly buried his face between her breasts, and moved from suckling first one nipple and then the other. He'd been sucking them as if she were his mother since his teens. Every time he returned there, his worries and fears all melted away. Ingrid made him feel like a man...and at the same time a nurtured, protected, very loved boy.

Ingrid moaned as his teeth teased, and then he sank to his knees and slipped his fingers beneath the pink silk of her panties. With a sudden yank, he pulled them down to her ankles. Ingrid shivered faintly and then Martin's mouth was buried in that rich, glossy black tuft between her legs. He yearned for her scent, and hungered to lap deep, taking the taste of her sex all over his lips and coating his tongue.

Ingrid and Martin groaned together in pleasure. It didn't take too much longer before his legs were pressing her soft bare thighs deep into her mattress.

★ ★ ★

The early morning light was now stretching through the bedroom window and creeping across the bed. Ingrid lay there on her back, letting the sun kiss her all over, as Martin had just done. She stretched like a cat and lay with her hands folded over her head, one leg bent at the knee, letting Martin see everything.

He stood by the bed, pulling up his briefs before stepping into his jeans.

"I think I have a plan, at least for today," he said.

"What are you thinking?"

"Dr. Testi always has a tranquilizer handy in his doctor travel bag. If I can get into his room, I can get a dose and knock Anthony out for a few hours while we decide what to do with him tonight."

Ingrid smiled at that. He knew she'd be happy to hear he wasn't going to simply put a bullet into her delivery boy's head. Though that might end up being the resolution in the end. It wasn't what he wanted to have to do though, if he was honest.

"Okay," she said. "Be careful. I need to shower and start breakfast."

"You already gave me breakfast."

She threw a pillow at him. "Get."

★ ★ ★

Ingrid lay on the bed for a few seconds after Martin left, still reveling in the lazy, warm feeling of postcoital bliss. As much as she tried to stay focused on the feelings that Martin had brought out in her, she couldn't help but keep thinking about Anthony. She hated it that he'd been dragged into this, and she wanted to think of a way to get him out of here without impacting Martin's plans.

Finally, she sat up and shook her head. She did a lot of things well while lying down, but thinking apparently wasn't one of them.

Ingrid yawned and forced herself to stand. Then she walked slowly over to the wardrobe. She could feel the dampness between her legs and ass as she moved, and it made her close her eyes for just a moment, enjoying the knowledge of what it was. Then she chastised herself. "Enough. Breakfast won't cook itself."

She pulled a robe down from its hanger and was just slipping it on when her door opened.

"Did you come back for one more muffin?" she joked.

But it wasn't Martin who stepped around the wardrobe.

"You!" she said, surprised. "Don't you knock?"

Ingrid pulled her robe tight, but she realized a second later that hiding her nakedness was the last thing she should be worrying about.

He didn't say a word, but the long, curved tip of the hunting knife that he held in his hand said plenty. Ingrid opened her mouth to scream, but his hand was over it before she got out a single squeal. His other hand thrust forward in a gut punch.

Only...it wasn't a fist that broke the soft flesh of her tummy.

There was a sudden stab of bitter cold in her middle, and then a white-hot pain that spread across her gut.

"You should think twice about biting the hand that feeds," the man said. "You might find you don't get fed anymore."

He yanked the knife out of her belly and raised it high in the air. Ingrid's eyes widened as she saw her blood dripping from the steel. Three spots of crimson appeared on the breast of her robe before the blade continued its arc and sliced hard across her throat.

Ingrid saw a fire of red stars before the actual pain hit her brain. She opened her mouth to scream but his hand was still there. She tried to kick but he fended her off easily and dragged her effortlessly to the bed. He tossed her body up onto the mattress and then held his hand over her mouth as her blood spilled from her neck across the pillow.

"I didn't want to have to do this," he told her, as her eyelids began to flutter. "But I promised myself it would be quick if I did. Good night, Ingrid."

★ ★ ★

When Ingrid's body stopped twitching, and her eyes gazed sightlessly at the ceiling, he wiped his knife off on her robe, and then, when he was satisfied it was clean, slipped it back in the leather scabbard at his side.

He stared at her still body for a moment, and then whispered, "I'll be right back."

The man exited the room but returned just a few minutes later.

"Dolls were made to be broken," he said, and cracked Ingrid's porcelain likeness into multiple shards over her bloodstained body.

CHAPTER SIXTY-TWO

Berger Mansion, June 23, 6:34 a.m.

Martin slipped down the servants' quarters hall and into the 'unused' side of the mansion. He felt good. The way you only can after a good bit of thigh slapping. Nobody made him feel like Ingrid. She'd been his first, but not his only. He'd tried other girls at school, but it was always the best with her. And somehow, for the past few years they'd managed to keep their relationship undercover. Dad would have had a freakin' cow if he knew that Martin had been banging 'one of the help' since he was old enough to…well…bang.

Unseemly. Beneath his station.

Well, guess who'll be having the last laugh when Martin and Ingrid walk out of here hand in hand with a bag full of Dad's money?

He made his way through the halls and arrived at Testi's door. The doctor kept a place in town, but spent a lot of time here. Martin hoped the good doctor was elsewhere this morning.

He put a hand on the knob and slowly twisted. When the lock clicked open, he gently pushed the door inward, just enough to try to spy inside.

The doctor's bed looked unslept in. He pushed the door all the way open, confirmed that Testi was not standing somewhere inside, and then closed it behind him. The doctor's medicine bag was sitting on the floor near a small desk. Martin opened it and sorted through the contents. He'd seen the doctor knock girls out enough over the years that he knew exactly what he was looking for.

His father had kinks.

What his father didn't know was that his son had peepholes.

He found the right vial, and a clean hypodermic needle, and closed the bag. Then he left the room as quickly as he could; it wouldn't do for the doctor to find him rooting about in here.

Martin slipped back into the servants' wing of the house and went straight to Ingrid's room. She'd feel better knowing that he'd gotten the stuff to put Anthony to sleep for a few hours. As long as the delivery boy remained quiet, he'd pose no problem for them in the short term.

He made sure nobody was in the hall and then opened the door to Ingrid's bedroom and ducked inside.

"Ingrid?" he said. He could see her bare feet on the edge of the bed. "I got it. We're all good with your delivery boy."

And then he stepped past the wardrobe and suddenly saw that they weren't all good at all.

The needle and vial dropped to the floor, and Martin dropped to his knees at the edge of Ingrid's bed.

"No, no, no!" he cried. The red gash on that perfect belly he'd kissed so many times had made the sheets beneath her body sodden with crimson. And the beautiful silken curve of her neck now hung broken, in ragged tatters. Blood formed a halo on the bed around her still face.

The broken shards of the doll that lay between her pale breasts were not lost on him. This was a Berger hit. And he'd been meant to see this.

Martin ran his fingers across her cheek; she was still warm. If he had come back just a couple minutes sooner, he might have stopped it and saved her. That thought hurt. Bad.

Who had his father instructed to do this? Ivan? Some less traceable thug? Martin vowed to kill whoever it was. Right after he killed the old, fat bastard.

All of his plans were now undone. What was the point of bilking his father for a dowry if he had no bride to run away with?

This also meant that his father *knew*. Why else would he have had Ingrid killed? Martin would be next. Would his father actually kill him? Oh yes. He had no doubt. But it would need to look like an accident. Otto Berger's son couldn't simply disappear the way so many wayward girls had who'd passed through this house. So his sentence might be delayed.

And that meant he had to strike first.

Martin pulled the revolver out of the drawer by Ingrid's bed, where he'd left it before they'd made love. He practiced aiming it, drawing back the trigger until it was almost ready to release. And then let it relax, unspent.

Not yet. That bullet would find a new home very, very soon.

With tears streaming down his cheeks, and hate burning bright in his heart, Martin walked away from Ingrid's naked corpse.

It was time to put an end to the things in this house that happened on the other side of the peephole.

CHAPTER SIXTY-THREE

Berger Mansion, June 23, 6:39 a.m.

"We have the opportunity here to take care of all the loose ends at once and make you a sympathetic victim at the same time." Ivan put his hands on Otto's desk and looked directly at his employer. "But we need to move this out of Berger Mansion now."

Otto nodded. "What are you thinking?"

"The delivery boy has compromising videos of you, and Martin has him tied up at the other end of the house. I suggest we grab Martin, and take him, Anthony, Allyson and Ingrid to Anthony's house. There we can retrieve the videos and set it up to look like a murder homicide. Anthony killed your family and housekeeper, and then took his own life."

"What about Ella?" Otto asked.

Ivan nodded. "Might as well. Maybe we can stuff her in his trunk to spread out the damage."

"No!" Allyson cried out. "Just let Anthony and me go. We'll disappear and not say anything about any of this."

The heads of Dr. Testi, Ivan and Otto all turned in her direction. They stared for a moment, as if considering. And then without a word, the three all looked back at each other.

"Not Martin," Otto said. "There has to be another way."

"Your son has already blackmailed you for 500,000 euros. Do you think he will stop there?"

"I hate to say it, but he's right, Otto," Dr. Testi said quietly. "A snake in the henhouse will always eat the eggs."

"We can take some dolls to Anthony's house and that way, when the police find the bodies, they'll connect him with the previous murders," Ivan suggested.

"I don't know why you insisted on leaving that trail of glass," Otto said.

Ivan shrugged. "You gave me the dolls to finger who to kill. I liked the symmetry of leaving them behind broken. Job done. And… now they can serve as the perfect deflection."

"Hmmm," Otto said. He looked at Allyson, who was quietly but desperately trying to free herself. "My late wife became obsessed with making dolls after she had Catherine. When he was a boy, Martin took in her footsteps, trying to make dolls as perfect and beautiful as she had. I'm sorry that he hasn't made one of you yet, but we'll make sure that a suitable doll is chosen from the collection to represent you."

Ivan shook his head. "Actually, Martin did make dolls for both her and Karin."

Otto's eyes raised. He looked at Allyson with a sad but strangely kind gaze. "Well then, you'll be honored just as the rest of the family have been." Then he nodded, as if this made perfect sense.

The man is mad.

The door to the office suddenly flew open.

Martin stepped inside, a gun held out in front of him. The barrel swerved back and forth between Ivan, Testi and Otto.

"There will be no more dolls, Dad," he said. "But it's time you paid for all of the ones you've ruined, including Mom and Catherine."

He turned the gun to aim at Otto's chest, but as he pulled the trigger back to shoot, Dr. Testi sidestepped and swung his arm around to lodge a hypodermic needle in Martin's back.

The gun went off, but the bullet went wild, catching Otto in the leg. The big man screamed.

An icy-cold stream took over Martin's body.

It was so fast. His muscles melted instantly, like hot taffy.

Martin collapsed to the ground and Testi stepped back, a grim smile on his face.

"Perhaps we buried the wrong baby all those years ago," he said.

Ivan pried the gun from Martin's limp hand and showed it to Testi before he dropped it in the inbox on Otto's desk. "In case you have any other unexpected visitors. See to his wound," he directed, pointing at Otto. "I'm going to get Anthony. Then we're all going to take a little drive."

CHAPTER SIXTY-FOUR

Berger Mansion, June 23, 6:44 a.m.

Anthony watched as Ivan stalked out of Otto's office and headed toward the empty half of the house. He'd ducked into the room across the hall when first Ivan and then Martin came marching toward Otto's office.

He heard Martin's threat, and the gunshot...but had the guy actually been able to take out Otto?

He had to know.

Anthony slunk across the hall to peer inside.

Martin lay on his side on the floor. That didn't bode well.

Behind the large wooden desk, Dr. Testi knelt on the floor next to Otto. He was doing something with the man's leg. Anthony saw a flash of crimson, and the ripping of cloth.

So, Martin had done *some* damage apparently. But maybe not enough.

Across the room was Allyson.

Her eyes widened when she saw him, and she vehemently shook her head, *No.*

But Anthony ignored the warning. Otto was down, Testi was occupied and Ivan was out looking for him. The hit man would quickly find that Anthony had escaped. There wasn't going to be a better time. He watched Testi's head carefully. When it seemed as if the doctor was looking in exactly the opposite direction, he made his move.

Anthony hunched over and tiptoed into the room, moving quickly around Martin and putting the desk between him and Testi. He paused there, listening. No sound of alarm came from the other side of the desk. Just the faint moans of Otto as Testi attended to his wound.

He crept on all fours across the remaining floor between him and Allyson. When he reached her, he squeezed her arm. But she just made a face at him and pointed at her right hand.

It was handcuffed to the chair arm.

Where is the key? he mouthed, making unlock motions with his hand.

Allyson pointed to the desk, but then shook her head and motioned for him to leave the room.

Ivan, her lips said.

He nodded. A louder groan erupted from the other side of the desk.

Anthony used the noise to mask his crawl to the desk. He raised his head until his eyes were just above the wood. He stared across the glossy surface, searching. Somewhere amid the papers and paperweights and pens was a key.

Then he saw it. Less than an arm's length away.

He slid his fingers over the top of the desk surface until they touched the silver ring. He slipped his index finger through the ring, and then lifted his hand to bring it back across the desk to him.

But as the key lifted, the metal shifted, making a faint clink on the polished wood of the desk top.

Anthony's eyes bulged and he yanked his hand back, the key squeezed in his palm.

He waited, fist clenched and ready to fight. If Testi rounded the side of the desk, he would take the guy out with his knuckles.

But Testi didn't appear. Instead, he heard the doctor murmur, "Now hold still, this may hurt a little."

Immediately after came an answering moan from Otto.

Anthony crawled back to Allyson and held up the key.

Her answering smile was a mix of hope and fear. She lifted her arm so that he could reach the cuffs lock, and Anthony slipped the key in. The metal clicked faintly as the cuffs released.

Allyson slowly pulled the metal off her wrist. She rose and set it on the chair seat. Now they just had to both slip through the gap between the desk and the door unnoticed.

Anthony kissed her soft on the lips, just for a second, but Allyson's eyes bloomed with the touch. Then he nodded, and they both turned to exit the room.

A voice interrupted them.

"There you are. I've been looking all over the house for you. Think you're going somewhere? Think again."

Ivan blocked the doorway.

CHAPTER SIXTY-FIVE

Berger Mansion, June 23, 6:44 a.m.

There were noises in the house.

Thumps.

Voices.

Ida had been lying in bed listening to them for at least half an hour now. She rarely slept past dawn anymore, but she tried to stay in bed until the rest of the family was up and about.

But when she heard the crack…she got up. It sounded like a muffled gunshot from downstairs.

Ida walked out into the upstairs hallway. All the doors were closed. She stood still and coughed, painfully this time. That cat was really starting to scratch out her lungs.

She moved to the stairwell and looked downstairs.

The foyer was empty. The dining room dark.

That meant Ingrid and the new girl were not up yet, starting breakfast.

She was close, so she knocked on Martin's door. Maybe the boy knew what was going on. He didn't answer. She tried the door, and it opened. His bed was made and empty. Had he gotten up early, or never gone to sleep?

Okay then.

She walked over to Allyson's door and knocked.

Again, no answer. And the bed inside was rumpled but empty.

Hmmm.

She tried Otto's room.

He had clearly been there at some point. His bed looked

like someone had staged a wrestling match there, but the room was unoccupied.

She closed the door and walked to the end of the hall. Ella hadn't been at breakfast yesterday, so she may not have stayed here last night either, but who knew? The minx was here catering to Otto's whims most of the time. She knocked on the door.

A second later, there was a thump from the inside.

"Ella?" Ida called through the door. "Are you in there?"

Again, something thumped faintly.

And then again.

"Ella?"

Three more thumps came then, more insistent. Louder.

What the heck?

Ida turned the knob and pushed the door open just a crack. She'd never barged in on Otto's secretary and felt unsure of doing so now, but…something was going on.

She saw the bed through the crack in the door, and almost pulled it shut when she saw Ella's body lying on it. My God, what if she was interrupting the woman lying there masturbating?

But just before she pulled it shut again, something else caught Ida's vision.

Instead of closing the door, she pushed it open another centimeter. And confirmed what she'd thought she saw.

There was a red rubber ball gag in Ella's mouth. The woman's wrists and ankles were tied with ropes and secured to the posts of the bed. She was dressed only in a provocative set of black silk bra and panties. One of her legs was covered in black hose; the other was bare.

Clearly she'd stumbled on one of her nephew-in-law's kinks that she really didn't need to see. She began to pull the door back shut. This wasn't her place.

But then the smell of urine from the room hit her, and Ella banged her bound fists wildly on the headboard again and again as she shook her head frantically.

Something was amiss here. This did not seem like a sex game in action suddenly.

Ida opened the door.

CHAPTER SIXTY-SIX

Berger Mansion, June 23, 6:46 a.m.

"You have a way of turning up in all the wrong places," Ivan said to Anthony.

"What's going on?" Otto called from behind the desk. His voice sounded weak.

"Our delivery boy thought he was going to fly away with your niece," Ivan said.

Testi stood and peered across the room over his spectacles at where Anthony and Allyson stood frozen by the chair.

"I never heard him come in," the doctor said. His hands were red with blood.

"Apparently, he's very quiet on his feet," Ivan answered. "I think it's time to make him quiet on his back. Bring your tranquilizer, Doctor."

Testi nodded and bent down to retrieve it. When he stood up, he held it out in front of him like a knife. "Just call me Doctor Sleep."

Then he and Ivan began to walk toward the cornered teens.

Anthony took Allyson's hand and squeezed. And then suddenly he pulled her after him.

They ran to the far side of the room, putting the large leather couch between them and their pursuers.

Ivan and Testi followed, meeting at the middle of the couch back and then separated, moving to the edges step by step. No matter which way Allyson and Anthony ran, they'd have to get through one of the men.

"There's only one way this can end," Ivan said. "Don't make it more painful than it has to be."

Anthony had to choose. The men were closing in. Once they both rounded the couch sides, he and Allyson were lost. He bet on Testi as the weakest link.

"There is *always* another way," Anthony said. He squeezed Allyson's hand again, and pulled her to run toward the doctor. As he plowed into the man's shoulder, he let go of Allyson's hand and yelled, "Keep going."

Testi had not expected the rush and staggered back. But the older man recovered fast. Allyson rounded the corner of the couch, but before Anthony could turn from his near-tackle, Testi brought the hand holding the hypodermic around like a tennis racket.

Anthony struck out with his right hand and blocked the needle, catching Testi right in the forearm. But Testi whirled. Instead of falling back, he threw his arms around Anthony, determined not to let him get past. Anthony's legs caught on the arm of the couch and he lost his balance, falling backward onto the leather.

Testi came right along with him, one bloody hand holding the needle like a knife. This time he was bringing it down straight at Anthony's heart.

Anthony grabbed Testi's arm with both hands. He twisted as the man's weight came down. And then the doctor lay on top of him, trapping him on the couch with his body. But the icy pinch of the needle did not connect with Anthony's chest.

"Ouch," the doctor bleated.

Anthony's fingers found the base of the hypodermic and pressed. He'd managed to turn it enough that it had stabbed itself deep in Testi's shoulder.

Meanwhile, behind them, Ivan had whirled from the side of the couch and moved straight for the door, intent on stopping any potential exit. But Allyson had not run for the door.

Her eye had been trained on one thing for the past two minutes.

Martin's gun.

It remained in the inbox.

She launched herself into the air and onto the desk in a desperate grab for the weapon. By the time Ivan realized what she was doing, her fingers had closed on the cold metal of the grip. But she'd miscalculated her force. Allyson's body swept papers and pens and the metal basket onto the floor as she slid out of control across the slick desktop.

She held on to the gun, but a second later she landed on something lumpy and warm on the other side. There was a grunt of surprise and pain, and then two gorilla arms wrapped around her like a vise.

Ivan appeared. He stepped around Otto's bloody leg.

"Time to go," he said, and began to bend down to grab her.

But Allyson still held the gun in the hand that was twisted behind her back. The muzzle pressed cold at the edge of her rib cage as Otto kept her locked in a bear hug.

"I will never go with you," she said.

With one desperate twist, she rolled her body to the right and prayed that she rolled enough.

Then she pulled the trigger.

CHAPTER SIXTY-SEVEN

Berger Mansion, June 23, 6:49 a.m.

"I have to go, now," Ella said, as she pulled her shoes on. She'd thanked Ida profusely, crying the whole time, once Ida had managed to release her gag and undo the knot at her wrists. Ella had untied her feet herself and then leapt out of bed. She'd yanked off the wet panties and hadn't even bothered to find another pair. She pulled on her jeans and a t-shirt.

"He's crazy," she said. "He'll kill me if he catches me in the house. I'm sorry, Ida, but I have to get out. I'll call you when I'm safe."

She grabbed her keys and ran out of the room.

Ida followed her, watching the girl disappear down the stairs. Ida walked slowly into her bedroom. Before she thought Ella could have made it to the front door, she heard a sharp report. Another gunshot.

She moved toward her phone and pulled the white business card out from beneath it.

Berger Mansion was undone.

With a shaking, wrinkled finger, Ida pulled the dial wheel of her treasured old rotary phone through the sequence of numbers on the card.

"Hello," she said when someone answered. "I need to speak with Inspector Wagner."

CHAPTER SIXTY-EIGHT

Berger Mansion, June 23, 6:49 a.m.

Ella had her hand on the front door when she heard the second gunshot.

It came from the hallway of Otto's office. It was followed by a tortured howl. And then the faintest cry.

Then silence.

Ella turned the knob and cracked the door open. The cool rush of morning air slipped into the foyer.

Could she really just leave?

Yes. Because to stay is to be killed.

Ella started out the door.

And then there was a scream. It sounded like Allyson.

"Help!"

"Oh shit," Ella said. She turned and looked down the long, dark hall. And began to follow the path she had walked every day for years.

This time, it felt like the path to her grave.

CHAPTER SIXTY-NINE

Berger Mansion, June 23, 6:49 a.m.

Ivan let out a surprised howl and fell to the floor next to Otto. "You little bitch!" he swore. "I am going to make your death *hurt!*"

He rolled to his side, holding his left shoulder with his right hand. Blood was seeping through his fingers.

But blood was also seeping across Allyson's shirt. The bullet hadn't fully cleared her body when she'd pulled the trigger from behind her back. It had grazed a burning trail along her rib cage before it buried its tip in Ivan's shoulder.

The assassin was not going to be stopped by a simple wound. If anything, his rage at being foolish enough to get shot made him more dangerous. He pulled himself off the floor and leaned over Otto's side to backhand her in the face as hard as he could.

Allyson screamed. He reached down between her back and Otto's belly to retrieve the trapped pistol.

"Help!" she cried.

An arm suddenly appeared around Ivan's throat. Anthony!

He yanked back hard, choking the man. Ivan tried to shrug him off as he wrestled for the gun in Allyson's grip. Anthony didn't let go, but instead punched as hard as he could at Ivan's wounded arm.

That did it.

The blue-eyed killer screamed in a mix of pain and anger and turned from Allyson to attack Anthony head-on. He threw himself at the younger man, using his weight to topple and pin him to the ground. Wounded arm or not, Ivan was used to fights. And outweighed Anthony by at least fifty pounds.

Otto yelled in anguish as the two rolled over his wounded leg. His grip on Allyson weakened and she didn't miss the opportunity. With a fast jab she elbowed him in the gut and jumped free of his bear hug.

She still held the gun. Otto struggled to sit up and grab her, but she dodged, landing on the other side of the desk closest to the door.

Ivan and Anthony wrestled on the floor, rolling back and forth as each man tried to get a stranglehold on the other. She aimed the gun but couldn't commit to a shot. Each time she thought she could hit Ivan, Anthony twisted and put an arm or leg in the way.

"Shoot him," a voice suddenly called from the door.

Ella.

"I'll hit Anthony!" she cried.

At that moment, Anthony screamed as Ivan twisted and pinned his arm behind him. Anthony was on top, but Ivan threatened to break his arm while using him as a shield.

Ella walked quickly behind Allyson to the desk. She picked up something and then started toward the fight.

"Drop the gun or I'll break his arm so bad he'll never hold a camera again," Ivan threatened.

Ella sank to her knees and pressed something silver to the inside of Ivan's exposed ear.

"Let go of the boy or I'll put this letter opener to the best use it's ever had."

"I don't think so," he said.

Ivan released Anthony and swatted her arm away. The letter opener clattered to the floor as Ella fell backward. Ivan took the opportunity and grabbed for the blade.

Anthony rolled forward but Ivan brought the letter opener up, aiming it at Anthony's back. For one second, Allyson had a clear shot at Ivan's face.

He understood his mistake a second too late and his ice-blue eyes flared open wide.

She pulled the trigger again.

CHAPTER SEVENTY

Berger Mansion, June 23, 6:59 a.m.

Allyson heard the sirens, but they didn't register. Blood was dripping down her face. It wasn't hers.

"What have you done?" Otto cried. He dragged himself out from behind the desk finally. He took one look at Ivan and his face turned brutal. "I will kill you myself, bitch," he breathed. He launched himself at Allyson's legs. But Ella rolled herself away from the wall and retrieved the letter opener. With a fast stab, she jabbed it right at the epicenter of the red mess that was Otto's left leg.

He screamed and Anthony pulled Allyson away from his grasp.

"That's for all the times you stuck it to me," Ella said. And for good measure, she lifted and brought the dull steel blade down again. Otto's voice rose high and cracked with pure agony.

"That's enough," a male voice called from the door. "Everyone, freeze."

Ella put her hands in the air.

"They attacked me!" Otto cried. "And when Ivan tried to help, they killed him in cold blood."

Officer Wagner stepped into the room with his pistol out. Four uniforms followed, each of them moving to cover one of the people in the room.

"I suspect there's a little more to the story than that," Wagner said in a cool voice.

From the doorway, a painful cat-scratch of a cough erupted. And then Ida said, "A lot more than that."

CHAPTER SEVENTY-ONE

Berger Mansion, June 23, 7:19 a.m.

The paramedics insisted on putting Allyson on a gurney once they'd bandaged her up. "We don't want you to get the bleeding going again," one explained when she tried to get up.

Ivan's body had been left where it fell in the office until the coroner could finish his investigation. Not that there was much to investigate. Ivan's face had been blown off by Allyson's gun at point-blank range. But they'd still want to do all of their photos and measurements and ballistics.

Allyson told them where to find Karin's body.

"I can show you the way," Ella volunteered.

Martin and Testi and Otto were all wheeled out of the mansion on gurneys, their wrists in handcuffs. When the sun hit his face, Martin began to stir.

"Ingrid," he moaned, blinking in blurred confusion.

When Wagner looked askance at Anthony and Allyson, they shook their heads in unison.

"In the servants' quarters off the kitchen," Ida said.

Wagner pointed and two uniforms went to find the body.

As they loaded him into the ambulance, Otto saw Anthony holding Allyson's hand on the gurney.

"I will see that you pay for this, delivery boy," he threatened, glaring at Anthony. "Both of you."

"They don't treat sexual predators kindly in prison, old man," Anthony said. "Especially perverts who force themselves on their daughters and then murder their babies."

The door closed and the ambulance began to pull away.

One of the paramedics tapped Allyson's shoulder. "Time to go," he said.

"Can I ride along with her?" Anthony asked.

The man looked at Wagner before answering. The cop nodded and waved them toward the waiting ambulance. "I think I'll come along too," Wagner said. "You can start trying to explain to me just exactly what happened here. And what do broken dolls have to do with it?"

From just behind them, Martin spoke.

"Dad broke every doll he ever touched."

EPILOGUE

Berger Mansion, June 26, 12 p.m.

"Here's your lunch, Ida. Nothing fancy, I'm afraid. Anthony owes us a shopping run."

Allyson set down a platter that held two ham and cheese sandwiches along with some pickles, a jar of mustard and a bowl of potato salad. She grimaced a little as she bent down to the terrace table. Her ribs were stiff and the bandages itched when she moved. Ida had been sitting outside the game room upstairs staring out at the gardens.

"Oh goodness, thank you, child," Ida said. She stifled a cough and then made a rueful face. "I should be making my own. You should be the one resting. Don't want that to get infected."

Allyson smiled. "I'm fine. Really. And it is such a perfect day, I thought I'd join you up here for lunch if that's okay."

She eased into a seat and the two of them prepared their plates.

"Did Ella say goodbye to you?" Ida asked.

Allyson nodded. "She moved the last of her stuff out this morning."

"I think we need to have the locks changed."

"Not a bad idea," Allyson said. "But I don't think Dr. Testi or Uncle Otto are going to be out on bail anytime soon."

"So how does it feel to suddenly be the mistress of the house?" Ida asked.

"I think that's you." Allyson laughed.

Ida shook her head. "I'm afraid I have no stake. But in a couple months, this place will legally be partly yours. And I think the other owner is going to be behind bars."

"Hmmm," Allyson said. "I hadn't really considered that."

"An old woman always considers where she'll be laying her head tonight and tomorrow."

"Well hopefully you'll be laying it here for many years to come."

Tires crunched on the drive below, and Allyson got up to look over the railing. Anthony had just pulled up to the front door. She waved as he got out.

"Come on up, the door's open!"

A minute later, Anthony walked through the game room and onto the terrace. He was smiling from ear to ear.

Allyson held her arms out and he walked right into them, spinning her around, carefully, in a hug. Then he kissed her before letting her go.

"I will let you two lovebirds alone," Ida said, beginning to rise.

"No, stay," Allyson said. "Enjoy your lunch."

She turned back to Anthony. "You certainly look happy today."

"I just got good news."

"You heard they suspended Dr. Testi's medical license this morning?"

He laughed. "Yeah, I heard that. But this is even better."

"Give."

"The Fenech Film Institute just approved a grant to underwrite my first feature!"

"Congratulations," Allyson said, grinning. "I'm so happy for you."

"And I want you to be in it."

She shook her head. "I told you before, I'm not an actress."

"Just do a screen test," he begged.

"You should do it," Ida said from behind them. "You have a face for the camera."

"Ida, you can go to your room now," Allyson said with a laugh.

"All right, if you won't do my art film, I have another idea for a film, and you would have the starring role. Picture, if you will, this young, beautiful British orphan, who comes to a strange, perverted castle in Germany, where her sadomasochistic uncle tries to—"

"Stop!" Allyson held up a hand. "I will do anything but that."

"You heard her, Ida," Anthony said. "She's doing my art film."

The old woman nodded. "That's what I heard."

Allyson rolled her eyes. "We'll see."

"Oh, hey, I had to stop by the police station to sign some paperwork and Inspector Wagner said he thought you might want to have this back. They found it in Ivan's knapsack."

"What is it?"

Anthony slipped off his backpack, unzipped it and reached inside. Then he held out something wrapped in a small hand towel.

She carefully pulled the towel away until something thin and cool remained in her hand.

The missing porcelain doll, perfectly fashioned with dark hair and bright eyes in the likeness of Allyson.

"Thanks, I think," she said.

"The inspector said to tell you to put that someplace very, very safe. Someplace where it can't ever get broken."

ACKNOWLEDGMENTS

This book wouldn't exist without Mario Bava, Dario Argento, Lucio Fulci, Sergio Martino, Umberto Lenzi, Luciano Ercoli, Ernesto Gastaldi and a host of other 1960s-70s Italian giallo film directors. What's a giallo, you ask? For those who don't know, the giallo was a murder-mystery-thriller type of movie that became hugely popular in Italy in the early '70s, thanks in large part to the directors I named above. There were dozens released in 1972 alone, and I personally own more than one hundred giallo titles on DVD and Blu-Ray. The films were known for their wild themes of madness, paranoia and often visually inventive and sexualized murders. They frequently featured a black-gloved killer and a female "outsider" character who gets caught up in the deadly intrigue, with the police "fumbling in the dark" as one such film was titled.

I've written largely supernatural horror in my thirty-year career, but a couple years ago, when I was looking for a new project, I decided to try something completely different – a non-supernatural horror novel 'love letter' to one of my favorite film types, the giallo. That book was *Five Deaths for Seven Songbirds*, and thanks to its reception, my editor, Don D'Auria, encouraged me to do another giallo-style novel. The result is in your hands, and plays, perhaps, more to the gothic style of Bava than the technicolor of Argento, and I hope you'll enjoy it. So, I have to thank Don and Flame Tree Press for encouraging me to indulge in my love of these films once more!

I also have to thank Stephanie Sack, a Chicago film event producer who has pulled me into several giallo-themed events since *Five Deaths* was released, including film showings with *Suspiria*'s Barbara Magnolfi and one of my favorite directors, Sergio Martino! I never thought when I named a character after him in *Five Deaths* that I'd end up meeting and talking to Sergio in the flesh. The heyday of the giallo may be forty years past, but its power lives on!

There are so many people I'd like to name for their support of my work over the past few years, but this would go on for a couple pages if I did! I do want to thank my best writing friends, Brian Pinkerton, W.D. Gagliani and David Benton, for always being my sounding board (and concert buddies). And my 'posse': Laura Johnson, Chrissy Papnick, Kay Ratliff, Mickey Thompson, Joseph Plochl, Tracie Mary, Jenn Summers, Coral Rose and Airen DeCarli, for coming out to so many of my appearances. Thanks to my Synapse pals, Jerry and Noa Chandler, Don May, Jr., Sean Provost, Carol LaBranche and Ryan Olson, for keeping me fed and hydrated at all the cons we do. And thanks to my friends at Ghoulish Mortals Monster & Horror Store in St. Charles, IL and Bucket O' Blood Books & Records in Chicago for hosting my events.

Special thanks to giallo film historian/commentator Troy Howarth and 'kings' of the giallo Sergio Martino and Ernesto Gastaldi for their kind words promoting *Five Deaths*, and Edward Lee, Tim Waggoner, Mike Rankin, Lionel Ray Green, Don Gillette, Luke Zehr, John Hinckley, Len Rokosz, Jonathan Tripp and Bob Meracle for all of their blurbs and review support the past few years.

Most importantly, to all of the readers who grab book after book, always supporting and looking forward to my new work – this is all for you. Thank you from the bottom of my bloodstained heart!

Dark Dreams!

John Everson
Naperville, IL
April 2024

ABOUT THE AUTHOR

John Everson is a former newspaper reporter, a staunch advocate for the culinary joys of the jalapeno and an unabashed fan of 1970s European horror, giallo and poliziotteschi cinema. He is also the Bram Stoker Award-winning author of fifteen novels, including the New Orleans occult thriller *Voodoo Heart*, and *The House by the Cemetery*, a novel that takes place at a real haunted cemetery – Bachelor's Grove – near where he grew up in the south suburbs of Chicago. His first novel, *Covenant*, was a winner of the prestigious Bram Stoker Award, and his sixth, *NightWhere*, was a finalist for the award. Both deal with demonic and erotic horror themes.

His novels have been translated into Polish, German, Czech, Turkish and French, and praised by *Booklist*, *Cemetery Dance* and *Hellnotes*; *Kirkus Reviews* called his work 'hard to put down', while author Edward Lee said, 'Everson is a MASTER of the hardcore; he's the rare kind of writer who's so good you can't proceed with your day until the book is finished.'

Over the past 30 years, Everson has also published four collections of horror fiction; his short stories have appeared in more than 75 magazines and anthologies. He has written licensed tie-in stories for *The Green Hornet* and *Kolchak: The Night Stalker* and novelettes for *The Vampire Diaries* and Jonathan Maberry's V-Wars universe. *V-Wars* was turned into a 10-episode Netflix series in 2019 that included two of Everson's characters, Danika and Mila Dubov. For more on his obsession with jalapenos and cult cinema, as well as on his fiction, art and music, visit johneverson.com.

FLAME TREE PRESS
FICTION WITHOUT FRONTIERS
Award-Winning Authors & Original Voices

Flame Tree Press is the trade fiction imprint of Flame Tree Publishing, focusing on excellent writing in horror and the supernatural, crime and mystery, science fiction and fantasy. Our aim is to explore beyond the boundaries of the everyday, with tales from both award-winning authors and original voices.

•

Also by John Everson:
Five Deaths for Seven Songbirds
The Devil's Equinox
The House by the Cemetery
Voodoo Heart

Other horror and suspense titles available include:
October by Gregory Bastianelli
Fellstones by Ramsey Campbell
The Lonely Lands by Ramsey Campbell
The Wise Friend by Ramsey Campbell
Somebody's Voice by Ramsey Campbell
The Haunting of Henderson Close by Catherine Cavendish
The Garden of Bewitchment by Catherine Cavendish
Hellrider by JG Faherty
The Toy Thief by D.W. Gillespie
One By One by D.W. Gillespie
Demon Dagger by Russell James
The Playing Card Killer by Russell James
The Sorrows by Jonathan Janz
We Are Monsters by Brian Kirk
The Dark Game by Jonathan Janz
Hearthstone Cottage by Frazer Lee
Those Who Came Before by J.H. Moncrieff
Stoker's Wilde by Steven Hopstaken & Melissa Prusi
August's Eyes by Glenn Rolfe
Ghost Mine by Hunter Shea
Slash by Hunter Shea
Lord of the Feast by Tim Waggoner

•

Join our mailing list for free short stories, new release details, news about our authors and special promotions:

flametreepress.com